---
★
---

Across the alley fifty feet from the explosion site a window in the second floor had shattered. I inched forward. The other side of my trusty, rusty Taurus was pockmarked where rocks had slammed into it. The paint was blackened and bubbled. My stomach flopped over sickeningly.

Above me the sky was a deep, brilliant blue. The pavement at my feet sunlit. Across from me, grapevines trailed over the ordinary wooden privacy fencing.

Normal, except someone had tried to kill me.

---
★
---

D0805301

# CURL UP AND DIE

## Christine T. Jorgensen

**W★RLDWIDE**®

TORONTO • NEW YORK • LONDON
AMSTERDAM • PARIS • SYDNEY • HAMBURG
STOCKHOLM • ATHENS • TOKYO • MILAN
MADRID • WARSAW • BUDAPEST • AUCKLAND

For Gaunt and Emma, Catherine, John and Denise, Vanessa and Paul, and to Kirsten, who sadly went before

**CURL UP AND DIE**

A Worldwide Mystery/March 1998

This edition published by arrangement with Walker and Company.

ISBN 0-373-26266-3

**Printed in U.S.A.**

## Acknowledgments

I wish to thank all those who contributed to this book, but my editor Michael Seidman informed me there would not be enough pages in the book.

So I will settle for a brief but heartfelt thank-you most especially to C C Gallo salon, Chuck Gallo, and Cheryl Aich for their humor and grace answering questions, and to Special Agent Nathan Galbreath, U.S. Air Force, Forensic Science Consultant, and Detective Mike Fiori of the Denver Police Department for their patience and assistance with grisly reality.

As always, I am in the debt of my writing buddies in the Rocky Mountain Fiction Writers.

# ONE

I⊤ WAS ONE of those late-October Sunday nights in Denver, warm on the inside, chilly on the outside, with a breeze that carried the scent of dead leaves and lurking winter. A harvest moon rode the eastern sky, smoky orange with a wisp of cloud across its middle, just right for a witch on a broomstick. It was nearly Halloween, usually one of my favorite holidays, but this year was different.

Lately, off and on, I had sensed someone watching me.

And it was giving me the creeps, right across the base of my neck. Every leaf crunch outside my window launched me into a state of hyperalertness, listening for footsteps. The neighbor's cat woke me at least five times a night. I'd even begun to get a thing about vans. I kept noticing them. And there must be at least seventeen thousand in Denver.

I figured my moods were a sort of autumnal SAD, Spooky Affective Disorder, so I hadn't told anyone. As a serious writer of an astrological column for the lovelorn, I have to watch my credibility. It's one thing to be Stella the Stargazer, quite another to be Stella the Space Cadet.

The trouble with change is that by the time I'd noticed it, it had already happened, so I couldn't say for sure when the creeps began, but once begun, it was hard to stop them. They're a kind of third cousin to outright paranoia. I had taken to wearing the brightest clothes I could find as a way of whistling past the cemetery. The psychosocial folks tout talking out fear, but frankly, I prefer denial. It's so much easier to be brave if you can ignore anything scary.

So when my best friend, Meredith Spenser, called to invite me for Sunday night pizza and a horoscope reading I was dead relieved. I wasn't exactly wishing disaster on Meredith, but what are best friends for if you can't focus on their troubles so you can avoid your own?

I wore a screaming red camisole and panties under a cherry-colored net sweater and orange silk trousers. Fluffy, my pet chameleon, wore drab, sulky brown and looked like a cigarillo with legs clinging to my shoulder. The only thing colorful about Fluffy was his yarn harness.

I found a parking space across the street from Meredith's third-floor attic apartment in Denver's Capitol Hill. Parking is at a premium there, the streets lined with mature trees and parked cars. In the spring the trees spit sap on the cars below; in the fall, leaves.

The sun had dropped behind the mountains, and the street-lights glowed in the heavy dusk. I locked my car and turned to cross the street. Meredith's windows were lit with a flickering light, probably a candle or two. That usually meant she was in a funk.

In the windows just below Meredith's I saw the plump silhouette of Mrs. Poland of the implacable curiosity, sitting with Bud, her parrot, behind her perennial lace curtains, checking the street for events. Any events. She waved at me. I waved back. She waved again.

I started across the street, crunching leaves underfoot, and waved back at her. She waved wildly, pointing. I followed her direction.

A van from hell. It was big, old, white, and racing toward me. Shocked, I couldn't move. I was fixed on the driver's shoulder-length light hair and his blue aviator sunglasses—sunglasses at dusk.

The van backfired, jolting me. I sprang out of its path, falling against a car. Leaves and dust swirled in the air as the van blew past without hesitation.

My knees wanted to collapse, and my head could barely organize. I squinted, trying to read the license plate, but all I got was the letter A. The rest was too smeared with mud to read. The van swept on down the street.

I staggered up to Meredith's apartment house and went inside.

"You're lucky to be alive!" Mrs. Poland greeted me at the top of the stairs on the second floor, her voice echoing off the oak woodwork. "You could have been killed. He was headed straight for you. Hold it while I adjust my aid." She did something to her hearing aid so my reply wouldn't deafen her, then patted a stray hair back into its springy, white nest. "I keep it turned up so I can hear what's happening, you know. You and Meredith going out for pizza tonight? You usually do on Sundays. Unless she has a date."

I stumbled around on my reply. "Well—"

"Good. She needs some cheering up. Do her good."

I escaped on up the stairs to Meredith's and knocked. As soon as she opened her door, I forgot all about the van.

I expected to see a candle or two; I was greeted by an inferno. One or two candles equals a bad mood; ten or fifteen makes for a depression. I couldn't even count how many she had burning. Her usual eclectic Victoriana decor was transformed. End tables, bookshelves, the top of the television, even the polished wood floor, all were lit by flocks of candles, flickering over her plush ivory furniture and her fluffy throw pillows in sage green, romantic rose, and lace. It looked like Frankenstein's rose garden.

I was instantly concerned. "You're in trouble, aren't you?"

Meredith laughed nervously. "Of course not. What gave you that idea?"

"The candles, the nervous look in your eyes, your high-pitched laugh, the tiny throb in my left temple." I was rooted to the threshold.

Meredith laughed again and pushed her thick chestnut hair back from her face, then absently smoothed her green velveteen lounge suit over her tall, slim frame. She pointed to the room. "Well?"

"It looks like a Lithuanian wake. I sort of expect to see a corpse propped upright in a casket in the corner."

"You're such a cynic. What do you really think?"

"I'm afraid you're in trouble and depressed. You're burning up two months' worth of your shop's profits as well as all the oxygen in the room. You'll suffocate. Or die of the heat. I thought we were going out for pizza."

"We are. I just thought it was cheery." She changed the subject. "I love your outfit."

Fluffy, who was harnessed to my shoulder, was trying to dig underneath my mesh sweater. "You'll have to snuff the candles. Flames terrify Fluffy."

"I've never seen him move that much before. He doesn't look very happy."

"He's not. He's been sulky for days. And he hates these colors—he can't match red."

She smiled too brightly and started snuffing candles. "He probably just needs a love life. Let's leave by the back stairs so Mrs. Poland doesn't stop us. She's a dear, but we're late for our table."

"Fluffy does not need a love life. Whoever heard of a love-lorn lizard?"

THE PIG N WHISTLE Pizza Palace is a favorite for many on Sunday night. We were too late for our favorite corner booth and had to settle for a brightly lit twosome table toward the front. It's my least favorite spot because it's in the path of the front door, and every time it opens the resulting gale chills the pizza. Tonight I was additionally worried because it felt so exposed.

I put in the order for the number-four Cholesterol Special Certain Death Combo pizza: five food groups—starch, fat, color additives, preservatives, and salt. I always order the food when Meredith and I have dinner together.

Meredith is just short of being a breathe-airian. Her idea of a pizza is a six-inch whole wheat crust topped with broccoli, cauliflower, and no more than four tomato rings. She can deliver a fifteen-minute lecturette on the evils of chocolate, cheese, salt, and sugar—my personal favorites—at any given moment.

On the other hand, I can date a Gummi Bear within moments of its creation and name the maker of almost any chocolate known to womankind. I'm not chubby, but I believe in sustenance.

We were waiting in companionable silence, the kind that heals emotional wounds without words, when Meredith suddenly looked at me speculatively, as if she was assessing me for a head transplant—never a good sign. "Stella, you should go for a makeover."

"Beauty's only sin deep."

"You've got looks, good regular features, great eyes—everything except...spiff."

"I need spiff?"

"And you wouldn't need much, just a little time, little effort, little makeup, and a really good haircut."

"Meredith—" It was tempting. I *was* tired of my plain straight, brown hair.

Meredith raised her eyebrows and grinned. "It's amazing how much difference your image can make. You could get your hair auburn, bring out the color in your eyes, shape your brows—"

"Disguise myself as glamorous? No one would recognize me."

"So?"

"The timing is wrong. My horoscope says to avoid sudden changes, and my bank account says to avoid sudden expenses." I hate it when Meredith tries to be subtle. I knew she was leading up to something. It probably tied in to the candles and her moods, and it was making me very suspicious.

"You'd be drop-dead gorgeous—"

At that very moment, in answer to my unspoken prayer, Mrs. Poland blew in the door of the restaurant. I waved surreptitiously to her.

Like an angel she fluttered over to our table. "I knew I'd

find you two here. I tried to catch up with you, but you were
too far ahead of me. I won't keep you, I'm just picking up
some takeout. Stella, I meant to ask about poor Ami, but I got
too flustered with the van.''

"Ami?"

"You know, your Venus in Aries friend—in your 'Stella
the Stargazer' column. I've been reading it every week.''

Meredith rolled her eyes and grinned behind Mrs. Poland's
back.

Mrs. Poland glanced at the counter to make sure her order
wasn't waiting, then thrust a folded *Denver Daily Orion* in
front of me. "I've been following that woman's problems
since she started writing to you. What happened to her? The
last I read, she left her husband and was going to contact you.
So did she?''

I've been writing an astrological column for the lovelorn in
a weekly paper called the *Denver Daily Orion* for nine months
now, and I still love it when people comment on it. I beamed
at Mrs. Poland. "I haven't heard from her yet, but I expect
there'll be something tomorrow, Tuesday at the latest.''

"Well, why don't you call her up?'' Mrs. Poland was a
case. I shook my head. "She never gave me her number, not
even her address.''

"Well, she better be very careful, if you ask me. Change is
a threat, you know. Her husband could get very nasty, you
know.'' She licked her lips in anticipation. "I thought you
were right to tell her to go slow and get counseling.'' Mrs.
Poland turned suddenly to Meredith in one of those it's-for-
your-own-good attitudes. "A little counseling could do any of
us good, you know. Helps to solve problems, if you know
what I mean.''

Meredith's lips stretched in a serenely phony smile. "Yes,
indeed. A great help.''

Much as I love it when people praise my writing, I was
growing uncomfortable. I don't like to talk about my clients'
horoscopes, especially not with people who are too curious. I

always get the feeling that they're not really interested in other people, only in other people's disasters.

Mrs. Poland leaned closer to Meredith. "Meredith, did you read her column this week? It was especially interesting."

"No."

"I'll read it to you." Mrs. Poland cleared her throat.

I was a little irritated that Meredith hadn't already read it. I had called her twice and told her to.

Mrs. Poland inhaled greatly and threw in as much drama as she could when she read.

Dear Stella,

When I first wrote you two months ago I was ready to kill myself because my husband wouldn't pay me any attention. You told me to value myself and get counseling. I did.

I also made myself over with the help of the most wonderful hairdresser. I'm transformed. And now—I'm ready for a sexual renaissance. It's good-bye to Big Dick.

All thanks to you.

      Ami, your Venus in Aries friend

Mrs. Poland leaned in close to Meredith again. "So, you see, Meredith. Counseling does it. Counseling solves problems." She slapped the paper on the table, vindicated.

Meredith jerked upright, reaching for the paper. "Big Dick? The scumbag who writes those vulgar letters to you?" Her brow furrowed as she thought. She lowered the paper abruptly. "When was your last sleazy letter from him?"

"First of last week."

Meredith dropped back against the chair, a dreamy expression playing across her face. "A sexual renaissance! I love it! Excitement. Beauty. Constantly changing moods. I see an aging, beautiful woman having her last glorious affair before she dies."

"Hope she buys some condoms."

"A sexual renaissance—"

"A figure of speech."

"A wild last fling. Imagine. Love springing wild and passionate from an aging bodice, ripped forth..." Meredith's voice trailed off.

That image didn't leave a pleasant aura for me. The front door of the restaurant burst open, a billow of cold night air enveloped me, raising goose bumps on my arms.

Meredith noticed. "You're sure on edge tonight."

I started to answer, but Mrs. Poland interrupted. "She's just upset because she was nearly run over in front of me. Right in the street, too. Oh!" She turned to the counter. "That's my order. I have to go. You girls have fun tonight. Bud and I are going to watch his favorite video, *Lakeside Murders*. The parrot's the detective. Bud watches every move the parrot makes."

Meredith smiled. "I'll bet he identifies."

I KNEW MEREDITH WAS very worried beneath all her pretense of gaiety, when she ate a whole piece of pizza without picking off any of the black olives. She usually eats only a naked salad and two bread sticks. Even for me the pizza seemed a little boggy. I think it was because I was worried about Meredith.

As soon as we got back to her place, Meredith buried herself in the couch, dying-opera-heroine style, her hair, with an unbelievable sheen, spread across the cushions. It even seemed a slightly different color lately.

I was just starting on her horoscope when Meredith leaned forward, put her elbows on her knees, and cradled her chin in her hands. "I know you think I asked you for a horoscope because I've got a romance problem."

I took a deep breath, not sure how to answer.

"Well, you're right. Stella, I've met a man."

I kept my face bland. "Meredith, you're thirty-five years old. You've met many men, hundreds of men. You've loved some, deranged a few, changed several, and left them all.''

"This one counts—for a lot of reasons." She ran a hand through her hair, dragging a long strand through her fingers. "He is so special."

I tried to keep my voice level. "They're all special, Meredith."

"I'm ready to do his laundry and look at him over the breakfast table. I'm ready to have his babies—"

"The problem—the M word?"

"Married? Oh no. Not that. Worse." She shook her head, sighing. "He says he loves me, but something is missing. I can't tell if it's commitment, or just the way he says it, or what."

"I don't know any men who haven't fallen in love with you once you focus on them."

"There've been a few—Jason Paul, your buddy at the *Daily Orion,* for one."

My pulse quickened. "I didn't know you were interested in Jason."

"I'm not, but I always check men out—so do you. Jason's just not interested in me, only you."

I was ready to change the subject. "Meredith, maybe this guy doesn't go for women."

"He does. That's the problem. Trust me, his wires are connected all right, but—" She paused and rearranged herself on the couch, a bewildered expression in her eyes.

I put aside the horoscope chart and eased into a chair. This was going to take some time. I felt the wicker knobby and solid against my shoulder blades. My gaze caught on a snapshot of a brooding dark-haired man with the look of an intense hero, propped on the end table, almost hidden behind two rose-shaped gold candles. I had a sinking feeling he was the object of all this. I knew if I asked she'd be launched on a flood tide of right-brained, emotional reaction, so I doggedly pursued a problem-oriented approach. "So what are you thinking you'll do to solve this problem?''

''I've done everything but show up on his porch wearing chocolate undies.''

It was a struggle to keep my face vanilla-pudding flat. I didn't want to offend her, and I wanted her to think carefully. ''Meredith, there have been other men, and you've been sure you're in love with them, too. At first.''

''I'm not sure. Stel—this is so different. This is one of the strangest things I've ever been in, and you *know* that's one hell of a lot of strangeness. I'm in love, that I can tell you. It's almost an obsession. I think about him constantly. One moment I'm flushing with lust, the next I'm almost nauseated from fear that he'll go for someone else. It's delicious and killing at the same time. It's like he's my existence.''

A puff of wind caught the snapshot, and it sailed to the floor. I retrieved it, still digging for something effective to say. ''Maybe you're exaggerating a bit?''

She stretched out her long legs, and I noticed a tiny chain around her ankle with a beautiful little gold letter *M* encrusted with diamond chips. She saw me looking at it and fondled it. ''He gave it to me, isn't it beautiful? I'm, like, totally caught in his web of love.''

*Web of love?* Gag me. ''Meredith, get a grip.''

She shuddered, her dreamy voice reappearing. ''I love the way he blows the hairs off my neck and touches my ears, the way he loves my jowls. He pulls my hair back just to look at them.''

She continued, her words a torrent. ''He's kind, he's gentle, he's unbelievably handsome and loving, and he has the nicest hands when he washes my hair. And he never really wants the money. Half the time he says, 'Never mind, it's free.'''

I peered more closely at the snapshot. ''Is this him? He's got great hair.''

''That's him. DeAngelo.''

''DeAngelo? Rhymes with gigolo. Meredith, I've heard of

fetishes for feet, gloves, whips, but washing hair? I mean, you've got great hair, but wet, it's just long and stringy.''

"DeAngelo is my hairdresser."

A shiver ran over my arms, and Fluffy dug into my shirt pocket. I didn't know what to say next. This obsessive streak in Meredith was something new and scary.

I WAS ON the floor, reworking Meredith's chart. It was unusually difficult for me tonight; it could have been the green pepper fighting a battle with the olives in my stomach, but it wasn't. It was the horoscope itself.

Meredith is a Pisces with Gemini rising, so she usually ruminates over anything negative until whoever is listening to her, usually me, is comatose. This one would have put us both over the edge.

Troubled, I rose, flexed my thirty-four-year-old knees, and limped across the hardwood floor to the broad front window. I raised it all the way to let in fresh air, hoping the extra oxygen would stimulate my mind. The hardest thing about writing my column is interpreting my readings in an honest, constructive way.

The smell of autumn poured in with the breeze, and I pressed my forehead against the screen, fascinated with the play of the breezes and the shadows on the leaves of the silver maple outside her window in the front yard. A puff of wind tossed the branches, casting nervous, flickering shadows. Leaves swirled to the ground, skittering into the street. A van rolled down the street, scattering the leaves, crunching them like so many tiny brittle bones.

I shivered.

The van rounded the corner and was out of sight before I could read its license plate. A sudden gust, and the leaves rattled again, louder. I thought I heard the scuff of shoes on pavement—the same kind of subtle footsteps I'd thought I'd heard in the night.

I had the creeps again, just like every night the last couple weeks. I lowered the window and flipped the safety latch, leaving only a two-inch crack.

Meredith stirred on the couch. "Stella, just tell me. What does my horoscope say?"

"Meredith, horoscopes don't predict the future, but the last time you had a horoscope like this one, murder went on a gambling trip with us."

# TWO

I LEFT MEREDITH'S sometime after eleven, Fluffy sound asleep on my shoulder. The breeze had picked up, tossing the leaves in little whirls around the street. When I was a child, my grandfather had maintained that spirits, elves, were chasing the leaves around. Whatever spirits were out that night, they did not feel like the friendly sprites of my childhood.

I was edgy and distracted. I hadn't managed to sidestep my nagging feeling of impending doom, and I hadn't persuaded Meredith to cool her passion for her hairdresser.

It was a complete leap of logic, but I also couldn't shake the uneasy feeling that it was a very ill omen that Ami had also connected with a hairdresser. I don't believe in coincidence. Usually.

I started the engine of my Taurus and eased down the empty street toward home. Every elongated shadow cast by the streetlights, each rattle of the leaves, seemed to call forth another thing I should have said to convince Meredith to get some distance from this obsession. I suppose I wasn't paying attention to my driving. It *was* an empty street.

The intersection of York and Fourteenth Avenue was a puddle of light and whirling leaves. The stoplight flicked to amber. I hesitated—to brake or accelerate through the intersection? I hate when I do that. I mashed the gas pedal.

Then I saw the ancient Chevy, barreling into the intersection.

I stood on the brakes. The front wheels hit a pothole, the steering wheel bucking under my sweat-slicked hands. My Taurus slewed to the side. Stopped with a jerk, at an angle. My engine died. The Chevy roared past, inches from my front bumper.

I turned the ignition key. Movement flashed in my rearview mirror. A big white vehicle loomed up behind me, swerving away from my right rear fender.

A horn blared a second before a jolt shook the car, throwing me against the steering wheel. Then I heard a hair-raising screech of metal on metal and saw a white van accelerating past. Light from the streetlamp flashed on the driver's middle finger, held high.

And then all was quiet. It happened too fast to get a license number, but it looked like the other near-miss van—big, white, and ugly.

The building on the near side of the street, a nursing home, was shuttered against the intrusion of the night. No one stood at the windows, looking out from behind the curtains. On the far side of the street the homes were buttoned down. No one flicked on a porch light to see what was happening.

I tried the ignition again. It caught. I had bought the Taurus because I figured if it was anything like its astrological namesake it would cling stubbornly to the road and to life. Qualities I like in a car.

I drove the Taurus over to the curb, cracked my window for air, and drew a few deep breaths. I laid my forehead against the steering wheel for a minute and told myself I was fine. Absolutely frigging fine. Fluffy scrabbled in the bottom of my shirt pocket. I stroked him and told him it was safe, but he didn't believe me. I could tell because he tried to burrow deeper in my breast pocket.

I scouted the streets for lurking shadows, unfriendly muggers, thugs, and rapists. Finding none of these, I stepped from the car and inspected the damage to my rear fender. The red taillight cover was in several pieces, and there was a nasty wrinkle on the side, with a long streak of light paint. Ugly, but quite drivable. The van's headlight had shattered.

The taillight pieces and the bigger shards of headlight glass from the hit-and-run van lay in the middle of the street. I picked them up, dumped them into an old grocery bag, and put them in the trunk of my car.

A gust of wind lifted my hair, chilled my neck, bent the branches of the locust trees, and sent a cloud of tiny gold leaves whirling down the street. All in all it was a hell of a Sunday night.

Every couple of hours that night I woke, drenched in bad-dream sweat, and heard a lewd cat chorus yowling among the branches of the lilac bush beneath my window. The long body pillow I wrapped myself around as a replacement for a long, lean, and lustful male body was little comfort. I finally opened the window and threw down an old tennis shoe, which moved the action to the alley.

By the time sunlight shimmered on the treetops Monday morning I had reviewed last night's events and Meredith's horoscope a hundred times, trying to feel better about them.

A feeling of dread connected to Meredith drove me from bed and into the shower. It didn't help, but at least I was awake and clean.

I still didn't understand my creeps, but they stirred in me the kind of primal fear that craves food. I went for my old-time favorite, strawberry jam on bread and butter, but I was out of jam and the bread had grown a green winter coat on the bottom of the loaf.

I am not a brave woman. I do not aspire to be a detective. I have no wish to mix with dangerous people. I pay my taxes gladly, such as they are, so that the police will take care of evil deeds.

But I do get curious at times. And I was very curious about this DeAngelo character.

I had met Detective Lee Stokowski of the Denver Police Department before, and while we weren't quite friends, I thought I could probably get him to help by looking up DeAngelo. At least I could find out if he had a record of any kind.

I put a call in to Stokowski, but I only reached his voice mail. I left a message to call as soon as he got in.

I padded around my apartment wearing my latest lingerie treat to myself, a crimson, Chinese style wraparound made by Cleota at the Little Nothings Lingerie Shop.

Lingerie is a passion of mine. I think it began in my late twenties as a revolt against the dull exterior clothing I wore as an accountant, but I'm a confirmed lingerie addict now. I'm more chaste than chased, but give me a bit of lace and silk or satin against my skin and I'll happily slither through the day, or night. But even that didn't settle me down this morning.

While I was dressing I ruminated over what Meredith actually told me, as opposed to all that I'd assumed between the lines. In the light of reasonable day, I decided the only facts were that Meredith had a capital passion for DeAngelo, and was planning their future and lusting after his body while he washed her hair. Just exactly how nonmutual this affair was remained unclear. With Meredith it pays to be very specific, and I hadn't been as thorough as I should have been.

And I never had read Meredith my reply to Ami's letter. I scanned it again while I brushed my hair.

Dear Ami,
Good for you! You need to stand up for yourself. You should hold out for a mutually respectful relationship. There are a lot worse things in life than being single, and one of those things is emotional slavery.

Self-esteem is crucial. Without it you end up with a partner who believes you are as worthless as you are willing to believe you are.

But remember, Aries can be too pushy at times. You need to tune in to the effect you have on others. Change can be scary—for you and for your partner. So take it easy.

Stella

I was quite proud of it. It was on the lengthy side, but I have a thing about the necessity for emotional independence and mutual respect in a relationship. It's left over from a former lust-slavery relationship, now thankfully in the past.

I replaced the letter in its file and discovered the snapshot of DeAngelo in it. It must have fallen in last night. Or maybe in some perverse way I'd stuck it in there, an unconscious attempt to remove DeAngelo from Meredith's life.

My fingers went cold and numb. The snapshot slipped to the floor. Then the file. I was suddenly too dizzy to reach for it. A roar echoed and re-echoed in my ears.

I was having one of those spells.

The taste of metal flooded the inside of my mouth, and the room grew dim. Chill washed down from my forehead to my cheeks, and down my neck to my back.

I gripped the counter in the bathroom, trying to diffuse the spell, but the sensation grew. My limbs were cold, heavy, the room spinning slowly, growing dimmer. I had to get to the floor before I fainted and hit my head. I couldn't feel my legs.

I could only dimly hear the ringing in my ears and see a growing fog in my head. I blinked to chase the gathering darkness. It didn't help. My cheeks were cold, my forehead damp and sweaty, my limbs paralyzed.

Out of the darkness a pinpoint of light grew, spreading, illuminating the room. My heart inside my chest was icy and barely beating. I felt suffocated; other pinpoints of light seemed to burst in the periphery of my vision. I labored to draw air in. Fear chilled me. I was trembling.

A shadow formed, daggerlike, long and thin, across what must have been a floor, black on dark gray, the absence of warmth and light. It slowly metamorphosed into a seated figure. I recognized the shadow. It was the shadow of death, and it was sitting with its feet in a box.

# THREE

THE SPELL LINGERED, neither becoming clearer nor fading. I tried to call out. I couldn't make a sound. My mouth was full of the metallic taste of blood.

The room gradually fell back into place. The dreadful taste left my tongue. I was still in the bathroom, clutching the counter. My hands ached from gripping it.

I've had these spells since childhood, although lately they've been far more vivid and, unfortunately, a whole lot less identifiable. As a child I simply knew, or would "see," something as I played in my room. Like Mrs. Klinefelter pocketing cans of cat food at the grocery store even though she didn't own a cat. Or Melville Baxter filching Evening in Paris perfume from Woolworth's, although his wife never wore it, because it made her sneeze. My latest spells were more sinister and murky.

For a long time I thought everyone had the same ability, especially my mother. Then as I grew older I realized I was different, but by then I was in junior high and would have died rather than let anyone know just how different I was.

Now, stiff to the point of creaking, I forced myself out of the bathroom to the telephone at my bedside. Carefully, I sat on the edge of the bed and dialed Meredith.

Meredith is the only one I've talked to about these spells. One of the things I like best about Meredith is her ability to keep her mouth shut. Discretion is a gift granted to only a few people on this earth, and when you find one, you treasure them forever.

Meredith's sleepy voice mumbled over the line. "It's only six-thirty."

"I couldn't sleep—"

"Told you those anchovies would make you nuts."

"Meredith, listen, I've got to talk to you." I told her about Ami's letter, the snapshot, and the spell.

She was shaken. "What's this box? Didn't the spell get more specific? I mean, some of your other spells have been clearer. This is pretty vague."

"I can't control them, Meredith. This is all I saw."

"Did you have this spell because of me?"

"Meredith, what haven't you told me?"

"Nothing. I told you, I get a little obsessive."

"You're holding back. All that stuff about DeAngelo—"

"What?"

"The *virginal relationship* crap—"

"Stop it! You've got the mind of a guttersnipe."

"Guttersnipe? *Guttersnipe?* What's with this antique language? Is DeAngelo some kind of sixteenth-century hangover?"

"He's not a hangover. And it's not antique language. I'm just...into this renaissance idea, that's all. Is this a diversion tactic—to make me talk about DeAngelo so I'll stop asking about the spell you just had? It was really bad, wasn't it?"

I couldn't tell Meredith exactly what the spell was about, because I didn't know. But I was convinced it was connected to Meredith, and that frightened me. "Maybe if we spent more time together, I'd figure it out. Let's do a little retail therapy after work."

"Ummm. Can't."

I plunged for the supreme sacrifice. "Then let's go exercise together tonight."

Meredith exercises to a degree I consider fanatical. At least four times a week. I heard her roll over in bed.

"Can't. I'm getting my hair done tonight."

"You just got it done."

"Stella, don't start. You could stand a little love in your life, it might make a difference. You don't even know De-Angelo. It's *my* future, you know." She hung up.

"It's your future I'm worried about," I shouted. But she couldn't hear a word. Since she wouldn't listen to me, and I couldn't reach Ami, I'd start with DeAngelo. "Suspicious" doesn't even come close to describing the feeling I had. The word "gigolo" flashed in neon pink at the front of my brain.

I fluffed my hair and caught sight of myself in the mirror. Blah-brown, shoulder-length hair. Slightly cynical gray eyes, not too close together. Lips that could stand a little more kissing. Hell, a lot more kissing. My love life was in the deficit column. Cold realization struck at my heart. Like Ami, I, too, wanted a good transformation. I *needed* a good transformation. How dangerous could a haircut be?

BY NINE O'CLOCK my doom hangover had lifted and I was feeling better, although a little edgy. If I could just get through the day without hassle, get an appointment with this De-Angelo, and avoid Jason, I'd be okay.

I watered Fluffy and turned on his full-spectrum lamp. He'd been drooping for the last month and a half. The people at the Colorado Seed and Pet Company had reminded me he was really a green anole and said a full-spectrum lamp was a total necessity. So last month I bought him one. It seemed to help, at first.

I put my hand into his terrarium and waited for him to jump on. He didn't move from his twig.

"Fluffy, wake up."

He blinked slowly, a sad, depressed blink.

I caught a fat fall fly and dropped it into the terrarium. The fly crawled up Fluffy's twig, then up his back and over his nose. Fluffy yawned, stalked to the glass wall, and closed his eyes.

"Fluffy, what's the trouble?" No answer. He pulled his tail up over his eyes and went to sleep. Fluffy is stoic, with a minimal range of expressions. I'm pretty good at understanding his various blinks, but this had me stumped. Something was definitely wrong.

I needed to take him into the Colorado Seed and Pet for a diagnostic workup. I wasn't sure what that would entail, but I hoped it would be less than twenty-five dollars.

He was upside down, clinging to the glass wall of his home, eyes closed, when I grabbed the mailing tape, pulled the door to my apartment shut, and locked it. It took only twenty minutes and a few yards of the world's stickiest mailing tape to reconstruct my taillight cover, but at least I wouldn't get a ticket.

The *Denver Daily Orion* building, with its dusty windows and storefront appearance, falls into the category of one of the buildings that still need restoration, but it has a charm of antiquity and snugness that fits into the block, almost.

I parked down the street and walked the half block to the *Daily Orion*. It's located south of Speer Boulevard on Pennsylvania in a section of the city characterized by a mix of two-story Denver squares and Victorians and little brick bungalows, sheltered by silver maples, Siberian elms, and the occasional catalpa tree.

In this area many of the homes were built prior to World War I, and while some have sagged into old age without the loving care of moneyed upkeep, others have been restored to a mellow content.

There's a certain sense of humor in the streets, maybe perpetuated by the large cement pig rooting in the front yard of one of the homes. And the Halloween decorations on the porches and in the yards.

I pushed open the door and stepped into the small reception area, which contains two vinyl-seated chairs, a small table stacked with out-of-date magazines, and our receptionist's desk. Sunlight streaked in, highlighting Zelda's blond hair, this morning pulled into a towering heap on the top of her head and secured by a red plastic rose.

It was the irony of the gods that I was surrounded by women with glorious hair.

Zelda looked up from her paperback, a pulse throbbing in

her neck, her eyes unfocused, blank, visualizing a passionate scene.

"Hey, Zelda. What's up?"

"There'd be no problem if something were up."

"Excuse me?"

Zelda flapped her book down on the desktop, her jaw working hard, cracking her chewing gum. "I've been working on Stokowski since the first day his tight thighs walked in here. I've tried everything from perfume to pot roast."

"I thought you two were…getting along."

"Do you see him hanging around me?"

"Maybe you're trying too hard."

"Maybe I just need to be more obvious. I think I'm too subtle for him."

"Oh, I doubt it. I'd guess he's just got his mind on other things. He's kind of a workaholic. Probably afraid to open himself up, get vulnerable. You know cops and relationships—it's a hard road."

"I wish it were hard. 'Hard' I can deal with. It's avoidance that's impossible." Her rounded shoulders drooped slightly. She pitched her gum into the wastebasket. "You and Stokowski have a lot in common, you know…with that avoidance stuff. I was reading about it in *Glamour Guz.* People who avoid are afraid of intimacy. And that's what my manicurist says too."

She reached into her top drawer and selected a nail file from among the array of nail implements. "And she also says that just a little sex counseling can help. You know, lessons. Maybe that's it. Have you ever thought about lessons?" She grinned wickedly and drew the file across her blood-red left index fingernail.

I scooped up my mail. "I'm doing just fine," I said, grabbing the pink telephone slips in my message slot. I marched to the back and the relative safety of my desk.

The back room of the office was crammed with six small desks of ancient yellowed oak, scarred by those who worked there in the 1970s, when the paper was at its zenith. It might have looked musty and old to the casual observer, but to me it was a haven.

The *Denver Daily Orion* covers people and all the news fit to read plus obituaries, according to Mr. Gerster, Editor. Which means happy news—depending on your point of view, obituaries can be happy news. The day I got a telephone all to myself, I knew I was there to stay.

My desk is in the far corner, next to Jason's, which has been making it a little hard to ignore him, but I can do it. Mind over emotion.

Jason Paul slouched in his chair, long legs stretched out, one broad shoulder holding telephone to ear, brows drawn, face intent. Lately he's been taking his job and himself very seriously. I like to think it's because of me.

When I first arrived, Jason was fresh on the scene himself and flopping around like a twenty-six-year-old retriever puppy with no particular focus or sense of his own potential. I, of course, being the mature person that I am, told him to get off his butt and shape up.

This morning he waved at me and rolled his intense brown eyes. He still looked like a golden retriever, but more like a sleek, muscular one than a puppy. I wasn't quite sure what had made the difference, but it was increasingly unsettling in an exciting way that could only mean trouble. I had decided to ignore him entirely. I'd show Meredith how it could be done.

The light over his desk shone extra bright, highlighting his somehow sharper cheekbones and his hair, which was surprisingly gold from the summer sun and made the roots at his crown seem even darker. It occurred to me that I might even color my hair. And that reminded me to call the salon and get an appointment.

The salon was called Masquerade, and DeAngelo was a very busy person. His receptionist chirped in my ear, trying to persuade me to take an appointment with David, pronounced "Dah-veed."

It took a bald-faced lie, but I got an appointment with DeAngelo for Thursday, three days away. By the time I put down the phone I was exhausted and committed to a total makeover, including seaweed wrap, at a cost slightly less than that of a total body transplant.

Jason was frowning. "A makeover? Why are you doing that?"

I frowned back at him. "Why are you listening in on my conversations?"

"You don't need to look different. There's nothing wrong with you. You don't need to change or hide anything."

I was surprised by his reaction, and aggravated. "It's none of your business."

"You're wasting money, which you don't have, to change yourself. You look just fine."

"Never mind. I'll look any way I want to. I think I'll color my hair red and remove my eyebrows and have a tattoo."

"Now you're being ridiculous."

"I think I'll get a tattoo of Fluffy on my left arm."

"Why not on your right bun?"

"Then you'd never get to see it," I shot back, glaring at him. He glared back, then slowly a crooked grin lit his face and the back of his melt-your-heart brown eyes.

"Wanna bet?"

There was no good answer to that one. So I ripped open one of my letters. My eyes traveled down the sheet even as I spoke. "Jason, if you spent as much time being a reporter as you spend being a child—"

He rose from his chair. "I'm the one who was here at eight. You strolled in at nine-thirty."

I held up a hand to shush him so I could read.

Tues.

Stella baby,

I keep waitin to hear from you. I been writin to you

for 4 months and still no answer. Your spose to answer.

I read your letters in the paper and I seen your picture. Your right for me. I got desires to slake and we could dance the sheets so good. So write.

Big Dick<br>Willing to Share Heh, heh

I slapped the letter facedown on my desk. These letters always made me want to wash my hands. This one seemed even more weird now that I knew that Ami and he were connected, and that she'd left him. I had figured I would never hear from Big Dick again. Maybe that's why I felt shaky inside.

"It's one of those Big Dick letters again, isn't it? Have you told Stokowski about these?"

I was annoyed at myself because the letter bothered me, and because Jason had read over my shoulder. I shook my head impatiently.

Jason draped a condescending arm over my shoulders. "What you need is a strong man around to protect you."

"Jason, take your arm off me, and don't patronize me like that again."

"Hey, it's a joke!"

"Joke, my ass. You'd like to think that a little testosterone will solve anything. You know, under every righteous banner lies a seething load of testosterone ready to start more trouble."

"Whoa! Stop! *Male* hormones aren't the problem. You're getting clear out of hand."

"Damn right I am. Right out of your hand."

"Hey, Stel, listen up. I'm not trying to start a fight. I'm just your friendly local guy, trying to help out."

I could feel angry tears prickling at the corners of my eyes, and it infuriated me. "Jason, dammit, you're messing up my life."

He raised his hands high. "Stella, I'm not messing up your life. I'm a friendly. Don't fire on me."

Some of the fury abated. "Then don't belittle me."

"I didn't mean to. I was just trying to use a little humor because these Big Dick letters bother me. I don't think they're funny at all. I worry about you." His glance flickered over my shoulder at a spot behind me, and his expression became guarded. I glanced quickly around.

Methuselah in suspenders stood behind me. Mr. Gerster, my editor, cleared his throat, his lips working preparatory to speech. "Ah, excuse me. I happened to overhear your conversation—while I was still in my office." He hitched his trousers, a useless gesture. His trousers hung from suspenders because he was built without hips. "What is this about your letters?"

"Nothing. Jason's exaggerating again."

"I haven't noticed that he exaggerates. Do you exaggerate, Jason?"

"No, sir. I just speak the truth, as I see it."

"He sees things that aren't there, Mr. Gerster. There's nothing to worry about at all."

"That's not what it sounded like."

"Mr. Gerster, Jason and I were just having a philosophical discussion about a hypothetical situation."

"It didn't sound hypothetical. May I see the letter?" His eyelids lowered in deep suspicion. He edged closer to the desk where the letter lay. "I've learned ever since you came here that there are a lot of people out there who are deranged by what they call love. I don't want you or any of my staff in trouble from unbalanced people. Now, may I see the letter?"

"No, sir. I don't show my mail to anyone."

"You publish it in my paper."

Sweat gathered on my forehead. "Well, that's different."

"I'm asking again. May I see the letter?"

It would have been so much easier if he'd been loud, or

obnoxious. The letter lay bigger than life, facedown on my desktop. "I'd prefer not."

"I need to see it. You're my responsibility, you know."

"I'm my own responsibility. I can make my own decisions and take care of myself. This is not a matter that endangers the paper."

"This newspaper is like a family. You work here, you are my responsibility—and my liability." He held his hand out. He could have reached the letter on my desk.

He was rail-thin, with a bow tie under a stubborn chin, no hips or butt, suspenders that actually held his trousers up, and a nervous habit of lifting his hands as if someone had an Uzi pointed at him, but on this issue he was as tough as an old barnyard rooster. And he was the man who hired me.

I gave him the letter.

He read it twice, slowly, then gave it back. "What do you think of it?"

The fact that he respected my opinion enough to ask for it ameliorated some of my anger. My cheeks cooled. "I believe he's actually a somewhat educated man trying to look stupid, because of the word 'slake' and because his other letters have had similar educated slips, and the language doesn't sound genuine. For example, he consistently drops the ending *g* in '-ing,' except for the last one. I think he's harmless. His wife left him recently, and I think he tries to talk sexy to bolster his ego. My guess is he's impotent."

The word "impotent" made his eyebrows twitch. "That's a guess."

"True."

"If Jason's right, he could be mean."

"Nonsense. That's merely a guess."

Mr. Gerster nodded slowly. "But an excellent one. Have you notified that Detective Stokowski with whom you're acquainted?"

"I've got a call in to him." It was the truth, as far as it went.

"You're being careful?"

"Trust me."

He looked like he'd need a century to reach that point. "He's written other letters, is that right? Do you get many of these letters?"

"Very few. This guy is the only one who repeats."

He pursed his mouth. He doesn't have much in the way of lips either. "I'll have to think about this. I never thought a lovelorn column would be dangerous; maybe we shouldn't have one."

Jason stirred himself and finally spoke up, tellingly late. "Her column boosted circulation by fifty percent, sir."

Mr. Gerster rubbed his chin as though that would start the problem-solving mechanism in his brain working. "I don't like to hear my employees arguing."

Jason sidled up to me, slipped his arm around my shoulders, and gave me a squeeze. "We wouldn't argue if we didn't care about each other. And she's really a pretty damn good reporter."

I felt like a flaming idiot. Jason, the guy I had taught to be a reporter, was now being all-knowing and superior, and worst of all, Gerster was paying attention to him, as though he was somebody. I was ready to deck Jason and tell Gerster to get out of my face.

Instead, I smiled like a vacuous Barbie doll and promised myself I'd get even. "It was nothing, sir. Trust me."

Gerster ran his thumbs under his suspenders, as if he had a thick chest they were pressing against. He thought. He looked first at Jason, then at me, dubiously, over the tops of his half-lens reading glasses. "There are times when trusting you is difficult. You have a way of getting into trouble, Stella." He turned on his heel and left the room.

Jason, sensing my rising temper, stepped warily away from me. "You sure are…edgy."

Use of the word "edgy" instead of "hormonal" probably saved his life.

STOKOWSKI CALLED ME back after lunch, apologized for the delay, and then listened silently while I explained. For a while he was so quiet, I knew he was there only because I could still hear him breathing over the phone line. When he finally spoke up, his voice was dry as the leaves in the streets. "Meredith can't look out for herself?"

"The only thing she can see right now are the hands on her biological clock."

"I can't tell you if he's got a rap sheet. You know it's confidential."

"Right. Only after someone's dead can you hint that their boyfriend wasn't a nice guy."

He was very quiet. I could picture his crispy, dark hair, his eyes icy, tired, probably gazing at the crack in the ceiling over his desk. He was a very decent man, and a very careful cop. I figured he was tapping his pen irritably on his desk. That's what he usually did when I was around. "Of course, you probably won't find anything on him, but it would make me feel a lot better to know he doesn't have a previous conviction for rape, mayhem, stalking, or assault."

He drew in a deep breath. "All right. I'll look him up. What's his name?"

"DeAngelo."

"None of these hairdressers use their real names, you know. What's his real name?"

"DeAngelo is all I know."

"Birth date?"

"I don't know his birth date."

"Two things we use to identify people are names and birthdates. Memorize that, Stella. It helps. I'm not likely to find a damn thing under this DeAngelo name. Hold."

The click of computer keys came over the phone, then the scrape of a chair against the floor. Office sounds, muffled conversations in bursts. Minutes dragged by. He'd been caught up in any number of more important things. Or he was making sure I was impressed with just how much trouble this was for him. Finally, I heard a solid body sitting down in the chair again.

"Didn't find a thing. You get me a full name and birth date, it might be different." He was quiet a minute. "Anything else?"

"Not unless you want to take a traffic report on a white van that took out the right taillight on my car last night."

"Did you stop suddenly or something?"

"I knew you'd be sympathetic."

"Did you get a license number?"

"It was dark."

He sighed, barely containing his irritation. "There are hundreds of vans in Denver, Stella. Be sure to report it; telling me doesn't count for insurance. Sure there isn't anything else?"

"Positive, thanks. Talk to you later." I started to hang up.

"Hold it." Stokowski cleared his throat. "I heard you got a threatening letter."

I pulled the receiver away from my face for a moment and shot a glance at Jason's desk, innocent and empty. "I call you when it's important. Jason calls when he doesn't have enough to do. He has no business butting in. Trust me, Lee, it's nothing. I don't even have Big Dick's full name, either. I don't seem to have anyone's full name."

He snorted, and I hung up.

I spent the rest of this less-than-stellar day reporting my accident to the authorities. Never let it be said that they have a sense of humor.

# FOUR

By Wednesday morning I had a minor nervous itch and decided to reconnoiter the salon. Maybe if I knew what it looked like, my anxiety level—currently topped out because the spell I'd had on Monday was still vivid when I closed my eyes—would drop.

I put Fluffy in his harness, pinned it to my shirt, and then drove by the salon. Fluffy poked his head out of the pocket, lifting a lazy eyelid, barely interested in his surroundings.

Before it was discovered, the Cherry Creek neighborhood, lying east of the manicured lawns and large rambling homes of the country club area, snoozed in middle-class comfort along narrow streets under tall trees. Then, before anyone woke up, the area was commercialized. The quainter of the homes were renovated to terminal Victoriana, and many of the brick box bungalows scraped off in a frenzy of townhomeitis.

Masquerade was a credit to creative renovation and boutique fever. One of the larger, older homes just off the main thoroughfare, it stood quaintly on two lots, behind an iron fence on a side street. It was painted brick with peaked roofs and multihued Victorian color on all the wooden fishscale detailing, in various shades of mouse brown, mauve, and purple with accents of pink—colors I would never have thought compatible but which worked very well. It reminded me of a gingerbread house.

In the back, the garage had the same peaked roof and attention to detail as the house. The yard was a tidy square of straggling grass and packed dirt. The back door, protected by grillwork and a gleaming lock, was propped open. It had an inside break bar. It wouldn't be an easy place to break into, but at least you could get out fast. I felt oddly relieved.

The garage windows, cutely curtained with lace, were blacked out and secured with wrought-iron grilles. The lock on the side door also gleamed like new. It seemed like a lot of attention for a garage.

A man in crusty overalls and work boots knelt, pounding stakes into the ground, forming four-foot squares to make a parking skirt. He wore an old gray shirt, the kind gas station attendants used to wear, with an oval patch on the breast pocket, "Virgil" embroidered on it. He must have sensed me. He glanced up and waved me off. "Hey! Watch where you're going there."

Fluffy buried himself at the bottom of my pocket, and I moved on down the alley, feeling a little silly to be so apprehensive about a simple beauty appointment. Across from the end of the alley lay the additional salon parking, a mix of elegant sedans, sleek sports models, and vans. Among them, though, one stood out—a little yellow Volkswagen convertible with ordinary numeral plates and a ridiculous row of pink flowers along the side of the car. Meredith's car.

My heart sank. Meredith had said she was getting her hair done *tonight.* I checked my watch—it was only nine, and she was already at the salon—one very long hairdo. At this time in the morning she should be at her shop, opening up. She never opened late.

I reviewed my options. I could ignore the whole thing. I could wait here for her—maybe for several hours. Or I could step into the shop and find her and try to talk sense into her.

"What do you think, Fluffy?" I peeked into my blouse pocket. He blinked. "Shall we go find her in the shop?" He closed his eyes.

A shadow fell on my face. A man of medium height and slim build with blond hair pulled into a ponytail, wearing a black leather bomber jacket, little round sunglasses, and a gold chain at his neck, stepped from a red Corvette sporting personalized license plates, DAVEED. He had chiseled, sullen lips. "Lose something?"

"Just checking on my fleas," I shot back. To his credit, he laughed.

MEREDITH'S VW WAS parked next to a shiny black, four-wheel-drive Jeep Cherokee with gold striping, personalized license plates that spelled UBETCHA, and a bumper sticker that proclaimed "Hairdressers Do It Permanently." "Please, God," I begged. "Don't let this be Meredith's guy." I decided on only a quick stop to look for Meredith. If nothing else, I could learn more about this hair-washing Lothario who loved Meredith's jowls. I stepped inside.

The hallway woodwork was painted glossy white, the walls dove gray, with matching carpeting in the foyer and hall. The staircase leading upstairs was lined with an elegant wallpaper in an abstract design accented with a silver thread. Everything had been done with attention to detail and appropriate scale.

A huge, glossy, healthy rubber tree occupied the corner. I stepped over to it and pinched it to make sure it was real. Since there was virtually no light there, I assumed someone took the plant out for daylight strolls. Or traded it in when the leaves began to droop.

The theme here was small, elite, and elegant. There was no indication from this vantage point of the functional use of this building. Not a single hair dryer buzzed, no snip of scissors could be heard, the smell of hair color lotion was faint, overlaid with expensive scent—aromatherapy, I assumed. Get ready to exercise your wallet.

A young woman with mahogany-colored hair moussed to a short spike on top was perched on a stool beside a draftsman's desk, slim white telephone to her ear. She had long, thick eyelashes and earrings that glistened like diamonds, although I suspected they were good CZ. She wore a pink smock, which in no way either disguised her full bustline or hid her stockinged knees. Her ankles were slim, and one sported a thin gold anklet with a tiny gold bangle paved with diamond chips in the shape of the letter L. She waved immaculate dark, slut-red fingernails at me and smiled, lifting her chin delicately to indicate she'd be right with me. I recognized her voice. She was the one with whom I'd spoken when I made my appointment.

"How can I help you?" she asked.

"I need to speak to Meredith Spenser. I understand she's here."

Her face froze. Her half-inch eyelashes lowered suspiciously. "I don't think so."

"But her car is in the lot..."

Dark red fingernails tapped lightly on the desktop as her glance dropped to the large diamond flashing on her ring finger. She made a production of opening the mauve book and scanning the page. "She's not listed."

"With DeAngelo?"

"DeAngelo isn't here."

"Would his car be the one with the UBETCHA license?"

She didn't answer, but she forgot to control her eyelids. I figured I was right. When she finally pried her lips open, the tone of her voice was arctic. "Would you like to leave a message?"

Hurried footsteps sounded behind me on the porch, accompanied by the rustle of fabric.

"Uhmmm—" I stalled.

A woman of perhaps forty, wearing skintight black patent leather pants and a leopardskin silk shirt, rushed in. A cloud of extremely sweet, very expensive perfume floated in with her and wrapped around me, filling my nose. The scent was familiar, but I couldn't identify it. Fluffy dug deeper in my pocket, trying to escape.

I had been crowded aside by a Barbie doll with sixty-year-old hands. My guess was, her true age was somewhere in between the appearance of her face and her hands, and thousands less than her plastic surgeon's bill.

"Lizette, dear, do forgive me. I hope DeAngelo isn't distressed. I'm so sorry to be late."

"Absolutely fine, Suzanne. DeAngelo will be a moment or two. He had an errand. You're actually a little early—maybe you'd like to go on up and put on a smock."

"Well, that's fine. I'll just slip my little feet into one of his wonderful footbaths." She laughed gaily, waved her hand to us, and tripped on up the staircase. An entitled woman.

"And help yourself to a refresher, Suzanne," Lizette called after her. She turned back to me and smiled, completely controlled now, except for a tiny tic in the outer corner of her left eye. I smiled back. We both knew that Suzanne would help herself to whatever she wanted.

"Did you wish to leave a message for DeAngelo?" she asked.

"You've got the most beautiful fingers." I pointed to her dark red, almond-shaped nails. "Are you a manicurist?"

She sighed. "Well, yes, I am, but these were done by Gerta, our newest manicurist. Would you like an appointment with her?"

"Oh, no. Thanks. I'm coming tomorrow, for a total renovation. That's enough for now."

"Well, I really need to get to work here, so if there's nothing else—" She looked down at her ring, centering it carefully on her finger, waiting for me to leave.

I pointed to the large emerald-cut diamond set in heavy gold on her ring finger. "I was noticing your ring. It's beautiful."

She met my gaze defiantly. "It's my wedding ring... DeAngelo..."

"You're..."

She nodded. "I'm Lizette DeAngelo, Tony's wife." Her lips barely moved when she spoke. "We keep it quiet."

I considered the size of the ring. "He must love you a great deal."

"Of course he does." I wondered if the tic in the corner of her eye meant she wasn't so sure.

MY ANXIETY LEVEL about my makeover appointment had dropped to nearly ground level at this point, but my concern for Meredith had grown in proportion to the size of Lizette's ring. All the way back to the car I thought about the reasons why they would keep their marriage "quiet." None of them were reassuring, and most smacked of scam artistry.

I knew from Meredith's blithe assurance that she believed DeAngelo wasn't married. One of her cardinal rules is, Never go out with a married man. I had to tell her. Then I remembered the spell. It might have been to tell me she would be terribly, terribly upset. Devastated. I'd need to tell her gently.

I also needed to get Fluffy to the pet company.

I drove past the parking lot where I'd seen Meredith's car intending to leave a note on her windshield to call me, but the VW was gone. I swung by her apartment and then past her candle and flower store near the zooey Soopers supermarket at Ninth and Corona, but her shop was closed and her car wasn't there either. Finally, I left a note under the front door asking her to call me that evening.

From the pay phone outside the Soopers, I called Stokowski and gave him the UBETCHA license and the name Tony DeAngelo. Then I called the newspaper, just to make sure that Meredith hadn't been trying to reach me. Jason answered.

"Where's Zelda?" I asked.

"She's busy. Where are you? Is this the day of your make-over?"

"I'm taking Fluffy in to the Seed and Pet shop for a consult. He's not acting right."

"How can you tell? I mean, what's wrong?"

"That's what I hope to find out."

"Is there a story in it?"

I struggled to keep the edge out of my voice. "I doubt it. Just tell Zelda I'll be in later."

"You don't sound like yourself. I mean, I'm sure you look great, like you always do, but you sound a little down."

"Jason, I liked it better when you didn't try to flatter me. Now tell Zelda for me. Good-bye."

After the pristine elegance of Masquerade, the Colorado Seed and Pet shop was a vast change. Here no one would ever notice a ketchup stain, nor care if they saw one. Elegance was confined entirely to the birds.

I set Fluffy on the counter and explained to the clerk. "He's a very intense soul, and he's trying to tell me something, but I don't understand what he's saying. He left the waxworms to pupate on the floor of his terrarium. He yawns at flies. Usually he'll jump clear across the terrarium for them." The clerk shook his head sympathetically and said the woman I wanted to talk to was showing a customer a macaw. Would I wait?

I picked Fluffy up tenderly and drifted through the jumble of birdcages to the south side of the room past the musty-smelling baby hairless mice, the red-painted tarantulas, and the iguanas to Sam, the true chameleon from Madagascar.

Fluffy clamped his mouth shut and tried to burrow into my shirt pocket.

I pulled him back out and stroked him under the chin to persuade him to look at Sam. He tried to scramble away. I glanced over to the woman discussing parrots. The bell over the front door jingled. Jason entered. I didn't want to deal with Jason now.

I slithered back beyond the aquariums full of tropical fish to the bird room, filled with parakeets, finches, and best of all, the parrots. Rebecca, the giant blue parrot, was strolling along the floor, calmly menacing a younger blue-and-red macaw. Fluffy took one swift look, scrambled from my hand, leaped to my shirt, and dived to the bottom of my pocket. He's never been fond of the giant macaws. He thinks they view him as fresh meat.

Jason was peering around the shop. I bent down to talk to Rebecca, conveniently out of Jason's line of sight. Rebecca climbed up my arm. "Hi there!" she squawked.

"Shhhh!"

"Hi there!" she squawked again.

Jason was in the doorway. "Hey," he said.

I stood up. "Hey, yourself. What're you doing here?"

"I thought I'd come along. I was worried about old Fluff here. Bring him over to the anoles' cage."

"He's visiting Rebecca."

"Yeah, from the bottom of your pocket. Rebecca can't wait to chew him."

Rebecca stepped up to my shoulder. "Feed me!"

"Fluffy doesn't mix with the other lizards."

"Yes, he will."

"No, he won't." I put Rebecca on her perch and followed Jason to the anoles' terrarium. "See?" I looked down at my pocket. Fluffy had poked his head out and was peering around with more interest than he'd shown in days. He craned his neck and stared into the anole terrarium.

Jason grinned. "He's just lonely, Stella. He wants company."

"He's not lonely. He has me."

"Now, that's a lot of company for a red-blooded lizard."

"You don't know a thing about it."

"I know a lot about red-blooded loneliness, and I'll bet you do too."

I started to turn to him, but Fluffy leaped the full extent of his leash onto the screen top of the terrarium and started doing push-ups.

Jason cleared his throat, trying to keep a grin off his face. "Stella, that's a sign of lizard love, and you know it."

"There isn't room for another lizard personality—"

"Stella, Fluffy's personality isn't that big. You can do it. Look how happy he is."

The Seed and Pet people agreed.

Part of me wanted to cheer, I was so glad I'd found the cause of Fluffy's lethargy, and another part of me wanted to cry for the loss of his sole affection. But most of all I wanted to slug Jason for being there and being right. Instead of slugging him, I laid my head against his chest. "Give me a week. I have to get used to the idea."

# FIVE

THURSDAY MORNING ARRIVED, clear, crispy, and autumnal.

I was still bothered by the memory of Monday's spell, so I called Meredith to inquire about DeAngelo's real name and more about him, and she became suddenly vexed, with a capital *V*. I've known Meredith since we were kids, and she always has gone overboard on romance, but this extreme defensiveness was new. And it kept me from finding a way to tell her that DeAngelo was married.

"Look," she said. "If you want to meet him, get a hair appointment."

"I did, but do you think he'd like to come over this weekend? Dinner, maybe?"

She hesitated that moment too long.

"Meredith, is there something wrong? You never called me back."

"No. Nothing. We were just out—you can't imagine—Stella, let me get back to you."

"Meredith, I need to talk to you about him. Are you sure he isn't involved with someone…?"

"God, you're suspicious! Look, I've got to go."

"Meredith, be careful. Your horoscope is downright negative right now. You might want to stick close to home."

"Don't worry." She hung up.

After that conversation I felt even worse. It was as if there was a wedge named DeAngelo between me and my best friend. I had worked out Meredith's horoscope again, several times. Meredith's horoscope was scary.

It had helped some to see the salon and talk to Lizette, at least until she said she was married to DeAngelo the gigolo, as I had begun to think of him. Action of any kind gives me the illusion of control, so this appointment helped. I would get to see DeAngelo and form an opinion of him myself, based on how he treated people and what he did rather than through Meredith's admittedly biased view. Maybe then I'd feel better.

God knows, it was going to cost enough—I should look and feel like a million.

Fluffy had retreated into sullen lethargy since the visit to the Seed and Pet Company and was absolutely no help at all. When I left for work he was a moody mottled green and brown, hanging upside down at the top of his cage with his eyes closed.

I arrived at the office early and found Zelda buffing her nails. She held up one frosty pink-tipped hand for scrutiny. I scooped up my mail, choosing not to comment.

"So, Stella, what color are you going to get your nails done?"

I looked at my cropped fingernails. "I don't know. Maybe black. I could be a PIB. Person In Black."

She made a face at her index nail and attacked it with the buffer. "You can sneer, but you need to think about these things before you get there. Have you decided what you want done with your hair?"

"No. I thought I'd let him decide. He's the artist."

The front door opened, and Jason breezed in. The sun glanced off his hair and bronzed his cheek and brow. I wondered if he would look as good in blah-brown hair.

Zelda waved at him and continued. "You might get highlights. You could look like Jason, a blond, without having to bleach it."

"I was thinking of a red rinse, maybe. I could be an entirely different person—and hide out in plain sight."

Zelda grinned. "Jason, what color do you think Stella should do her hair?"

He stopped at the mail slot, irritably pulling out envelopes with his right hand and slapping them into his left. "This isn't as hilarious as you both think. There's no reason why Stella needs to change a thing. Trying to be someone different is the mistake of a lifetime, believe me. It's just asking for trouble.''

''Heavvvvy! The fleas are sure biting his hmmm-hmmm,'' Zelda said, dropping her nail buffer into the drawer.

THE SALON WAS exactly as yesterday, an oasis of gray-and-silver elegance, a mystic inner sanctum of beauty and sophistication where I would be anointed with the frankincense and myrrh of beauty that would change me from a caterpillar to a beautiful butterfly. Or a cabbage moth, whatever.

David, the young blond man I'd seen in the parking lot yesterday, was bent over a wet, stringy head, snipping at a client's neck hairs.

Lizette was even more porcelain-perfect than before. Her red fingernails ran down the page of the appointment book, verifying my admission to the sanctum sanctorum, then she murmured into a darling little telephone, replaced the receiver, and slid from the stool to lead me upstairs.

An entire room was devoted to changing into a gown so one's precious wardrobe wouldn't be stained in any way. I put my precious clothes into a pink locker and pinned the key to my gown. I had trouble fastening the pin, and I realized I was actually apprehensive about meeting DeAngelo.

Lizette directed me to a pale, creamy, elegant room lit by skylights, no harsh glaring lights. The room had been designed to flatter. Even the mirrored walls reflected just a hair taller and thinner, assisting in the ''experience of a new you.''

DeAngelo was finishing a head of hair. He was far, far better looking in real life than he had been in the snapshot in Meredith's living room.

He was tall and lean, with dark, intense eyes, a mop of dark hair that fell becomingly over his forehead, and the kind of eyelashes women pray for. I caught my breath. He was exactly the kind of man to whom Meredith would fall victim.

DeAngelo finished the hair in the next chair, trailing his

fingers along the client's cheek and over her ear, causing a
visible shiver of electricity through her. She looked wonderful,
spectacular. There was no doubt that he was an artist.

After the hair in the next chair left, DeAngelo turned his
intense gaze on me. To Meredith it would be thrilling, but to
me the gleam in his eye was his simultaneous calculation of
my net worth and my glamour potential. But it was the pager
on his hip that made me think, "Uh-oh, Mommy, trouble."

He swished my hair here, then there, then stepped back and
announced, "I know exactly what to do. You will be gorgeous. Unbelievable." He put his hands alongside my jaw.
"You have marvelous jowls. Absolutely phenomenal. We
have to show them off."

He had adored Meredith's jowls, too. "I'll bet you tell
everyone that."

"How could I? Most women have no jowls, no strength,
no magnetism, but you——" He shook his head dramatically
from side to side.

"Meredith seems to think you liked her jowls quite a lot."

His hands dropped from my jaw. "Meredith? Ah yes, Meredith. A remarkable woman. A true beauty there. You must
be sisters."

I wanted to make him squirm, so I pushed it further. "I had
the impression that the two of you were very, especially, close.
Like—a relationship going there."

DeAngelo's eyelids lowered a fraction. "Meredith is special, a very good customer and a friend. Now. I think we'll
do just a hint of red here. Lizette, what do you think? Auburn,
for her?"

I had entirely forgotten spiky-haired Lizette, standing to the
side. I dragged my gaze from the reflection of DeAngelo to
Lizette. Her shoulders were rigid, her brow drawn into a deep
frown, but not one of concentration on hair color. She stared
at his shoulder, her jaw muscles working.

"Come with me," she said. Her voice was quiet, but steely
hard. When he turned to follow her I saw a bright red lipstick

smudge on the shoulder of his shirt. It didn't match Lizette's dark red lips.

God knows I tried not to listen in, but I've got incredibly good hearing.

"You told me you were finished with her."

"Ow! Lizette, cut it out. You know better."

"You don't have another chance, DeAngelo."

"It's over with her, Lizette. I told you."

"It better be. Or you're roadkill."

When Lizette left, her heels clicked so loud it was a wonder they didn't poke through the floor.

DeAngelo returned, moving slowly with a slight limp, smiling through his teeth and flexing his fingers, like he'd just as soon cut my throat as cut my hair. I hoped he had really good temper control.

His voice was strained when he spoke. "What I'm thinking of is a shorter, swingy blunt cut, shaped a little, tinted with auburn. Days, you wear it down, evenings we have enough left to wisp out and up. You'll be fantastic."

His tone of voice was warm, to the point of wrapping itself around me, as if we were bosom friends, yet I'd just challenged him, embarrassed him, and caused a fight between him and Lizette, his supposed wife. His control was scarier than anger would have been.

He moved to the side, flipped my hair behind my ear, and studied the effect. "You have fantastic ears. If we pull your hair just back like this, do it deep auburn, your eyes will be gray velvet, your cheekbones will glow, and your ears—sensual pink shells. Makeup, shape the eyebrows, you'll be irresistible. The *real* you is auburn with ears showing."

"The *real* me just wants to look good."

"*Good* you can have any day. *Fantastic* is what you get with me."

It might have worked wonders on a vulnerable woman.

His pager buzzed. He excused himself. The reflection of his lean body in the mirror limped to the closet. He picked up a cellular phone, punched in numbers, then pinned it to his shoulder with his chin. While he talked, he reached for plastic bottles from the cupboard.

I couldn't quite hear what he said, so I stood up, stretched obviously as though I was preoccupied and stiff, then strolled over to the magazine stand, where I pawed through the selection, conveniently close enough to hear.

"No, that won't work for me. I absolutely cannot miss my three-forty-five soak."

Again, by glancing into the mirrored wall I could see him. He, of course, did the same thing, saw me, and lowered his voice—fortunately, not enough. "Let's stick to the time we had set. We'll have a late one." I wondered if a late one was anything like a nooner.

I took two magazines and drifted back toward my chair, but not so far I couldn't hear.

"All right! In fifteen minutes. You know where."

I checked my watch and slipped back into the chair. It was five minutes to three.

DeAngelo emerged from the closet, stirring a bowl of thick purplish gray stuff that he thrust into my hands. His magnetism seemed to be turned off. He dabbed into the bowl and began brushing the stuff along the part of my hair. I hoped he wasn't so angry he'd bleach my hair orange. "Like, how red is my hair going to be?"

He smiled into the mirror at me. He was a human chameleon. But where Fluffy turned on colors, DeAngelo turned on charm. He didn't seem the least aware of his transparency, and only vaguely aware that the charm wasn't working on me. "Fantastic dark auburn."

He brushed the color through my hair, working rapidly. Twice he checked his watch. He was nearly finished when movement in the mirror caught my eye. I blinked. Long, velveteen-clad legs silently ascended the attic stairs.

DeAngelo was busily brushing goo into my hair, totally

absorbed. Was it my imagination, or was there a slight flush rising on his neck?

When he finished, he swirled the whole gooey mess up on top of my head and whipped off his latex gloves, a surgeon finishing a transplant. He picked up a three-by-five-inch index card, made a note, and turned to me.

"You'll be here for about twenty minutes while your hair is transformed and Gerta shapes those phenomenal eyebrows and your fingernails—" He pointed to Gerta's reflection in the mirror, left the room, favoring his right foot, and hurried up the stairs to the attic.

I hadn't seen Gerta when she entered. She was petite, with dark hair and a pixie face, startlingly blue eyes, and pointy turned-up lips. She wore the pink smock of the establishment, sashed at the waist with a bit of chiffon. I checked her eyebrows. They were perfect dark little wings.

"Gerta, where are all the big people in this place?"

"What?"

"Never mind. What happens after my glorious eyebrows emerge?"

Her voice was unnaturally flutey. "Then I rinse and feed your hair, fatten up those shafts and give them energy, while your whole body renews and re-forms and sloughs those noxious fat cells with the seaweed wrap—"

"What if it takes too long? Will my hair burn off and fall out?"

"No. It's all fine. Your hair isn't going to burn up, even if we wait an extra half hour. I assure you, we take the greatest care—"

"So when does he cut it?"

She smiled impishly. "After all that, DeAngelo does his special relaxing neck massage, then he'll cut and style. After that, I'll come back and do your makeup. By five this evening you will be transformed, and your beautiful inner self will have emerged. I hope you have a wonderful evening lined up, someone special to show off to."

I thought of Fluffy. "Sure."

She knew, the way women do, that I didn't. Her voice dropped to a more authentic tone. "You really will look great. You've got all the right features, all you need is to make something of them."

Liking this Gerta with the real voice much better, I settled into the chair. "So what's DeAngelo like to work for?"

She lowered the back of the chair before she answered. "Wonderful and horrible. Wonderful because he's such an artist. And horrible because he can be so exacting. You really get to know people. You wouldn't believe what people tell you while you're doing nails. I think it's the hand massage that starts people talking. I mean, after a massage, what's left to hide?" She had changed the subject masterfully.

"I noticed DeAngelo's limping."

She plucked gently at my brows. "Really? I didn't notice. Now, I'm going to put this over your eyes to relax them." She laid a scented cloth over my smarting brows. "Give me your hands."

Gerta carried the conversation throughout the manicure, and by the time she did the hand massage I was all but snoring.

Nails done, Gerta led me to a room with a stark white walk-in shower big enough for a group. There, she rinsed the hair coloring out and replaced it with apricot-smelling bright pink stuff she called follicle replenisher.

"Okay, now it's time to feed those little skin cells. Thin muscles, fat skin, make a luscious body. Drop your robe." She looked at me with approval. "Now, those are gorgeous underthings. I've seldom seen such, but you'll need to take off your lacies, too, hon. This stuff will leave oil stains."

She slathered vivid green and turquoise paint over my entire body, up my neck, and around my face, leaving only eye and mouth holes. I knew exactly where they got the inspiration for the Creature from the Black Lagoon.

She wrapped me in a warm sheet, and I slimed my way in baby steps to the solarium, a fragrant, peach-colored room with two chaise longues, diffuse lighting from an overhead skylight, and breezes from unseen sources wafting scent and gauze curtains like some Shangri-la idyll.

She put me on a peach-colored chaise that would have been called a gurney in a hospital emergency room and covered me with scented towels until I was in a hot, steamy cocoon, with only a small hole around my nose open to breathe. I thought of the waxworm pupae on the floor of Fluffy's cage. Not a pretty comparison.

The chaise began to undulate. "That's the massage feature," she said. "Just relax while your cells revive and purify." I heard a faint rattle of curtain hooks. "I'm pulling the gauze privacy curtain," she explained.

"It's too stuffy. I can't breathe." My words were muffled by the towels, but she understood.

"Relax. This is all part of the treatment. I'm just going to put a little strap across here so you won't fall off if you go to sleep."

Suffocation. It makes breathing seem so rewarding.

She adjusted the towels, and I breathed more easily. "I'm putting earphones on you. You'll have relaxing music. It's a quarter to four now. A half hour, then I'll come get you for DeAngelo and your hairstyling." She left.

This was not the fun and relaxation it was supposed to be. With the hot towels on my face covering my mouth and eyes, the rocking motion of the chaise, and the slime on my body, I knew with an awful certainty what it must be like to be buried alive in an earthquake. I tried to like it. Tried to concentrate on the classical guitar music and relax. Instead, I grew increasingly restive.

I tried to get up, but I couldn't. The "little strap" held me fast. I shouted, but the towels muffled my voice. The music grated on my nerves. I tried to wiggle out of the strap. It was hard to breathe.

My head grew light, and stars burst behind my eyelids. I

was suffocating. I stopped struggling to conserve oxygen. Then I realized what it was. Another spell.

I drew in breath regularly and blinked my already closed eyes, trying to organize my senses without success. I couldn't move my arms or legs, nor could I sit upright.

The music seemed to fade, and the pounding of my heartbeat grew in my ears. The metallic taste of blood filled my mouth, and the sides of my face grew icy. The sounds intruded into the spell, at first faint and far away, dimly heard through the wrap, then quicker, louder ones. I couldn't tell whether they were footsteps or heartbeats.

A figure formed slowly before my eyes, tall, narrow, reaching toward me. Then it flashed, blindingly bright. I flinched, but my limbs were leaden, my body weighed down, held tight, hot.

Like fireworks in the night sky, the form held its shape, a human ember, slowly snuffing, dying. I tried to see more detail, but it faded. The spell lifted with the suddenness of an elevator arriving at the ground floor.

There was a yelp from the next room. I gasped for air, certain something terrible had happened.

I jerked upward against the weight of the sodden towels on my limbs, my head spinning. I had to get up. Get out of there.

There was a momentary tightening of the bondage, then a ripping sound as I loosened the straps and wrenched my arms free of the cocoon. The earphones flipped off my head and spun to the floor with a clatter.

I yanked the towels from my face, panting, and glanced quickly around, expecting some sign of violence. My hands shook as I pulled apart the Velcro straps over my thighs, and sat up.

The room was bathed in a murky, diffuse glow from the skylight. The gauze privacy curtain was pulled across the other half of the room. It hung ghostly in the diminished light, barely moving. The overhead fans no longer circled. The power was off.

An eerie, feminine whine from somewhere down the hall thrust me unsteadily from the chaise. The blanket and towels fell to the floor, swaddling my feet. The room spun briefly, then settled down. Conscious of my seaweed-smeared body, I grabbed first at the towels surrounding my feet, then at a robe on a wall hook.

Slipping on the robe, I belted it close and staggered to the door, grasping at the wall for support. The tile floor was cold and gritty under my feet, and my hair rose eerily as I hustled toward the sound.

Light seeped into the hall from downstairs. Apparently only this section of the building was affected. I was halfway down the hall when Lizette's slight form rushed up. At first sight of me, she gasped before she could stop herself. Then she collected herself. "Stella, nothing to worry about. It's only a little power outage, that's all. I'll be right with you, as soon as I take care of Suzanne."

I thought of the figure in my spell. "Wait. Don't go in there."

"I have to," she said, but she halted.

I stepped forward. "I'll come with you."

"Not necessary," she said, but she looked relieved to have the company and grasped my seaweed-covered arm in a vise-like grip I hadn't expected in such a wisp of a woman. We stopped at the doorway of the room, Lizette pushing me in first.

The room was quite dark as the skylight was covered. I could barely make out the form of a woman wound in a sheet, sitting on the edge of a chaise, her face buried in her hands.

The noise stopped, leaving a deafening silence, except for the thump of my heartbeat. Suzanne raised her face from her hands, a ghostlike movement in the near dark of the room. "Oh my God, a monster!" She sagged back onto the couch.

Lizette and I rushed to her. "It's all right, Suzanne," Lizette crooned.

"There was a...a—" She looked at me, her eyes wide with

terror. Her finger shook as it pointed at me. "Get away, you devil."

I stepped back. Lizette finally seemed to come to life. "It's all right, Suzanne," she said. "It's only a client in the seaweed wrap. See, I'll pull the skylight."

From somewhere on the wall, Lizette pulled the skylight shade back an inch, and my eyes stung from the sudden flood of diffuse light.

Suzanne, the woman who had whirled into the salon yesterday, was huddled on the edge of a padded chaise longue, her makeup gone and towels strewn below her on the floor. She and I looked at each other awestruck. I haven't a single doubt that she was thinking the same thing I was. A kind of mutual horror.

Modern cosmetics can perform miracles, but they had a lot of work to do on Suzanne. She dropped her gaze first. "I hurt my foot," she whimpered. "I think it's bleeding."

"That's what you were howling about?" I asked. I realized I was standing in a puddle of water.

"It hurts."

I looked down at my feet. Water was everywhere. Lizette gingerly stepped around me and went back to her. "You spilled your footbath, Suzanne." She bent to inspect Suzanne's foot, her knee just above an oblong, turquoise-colored plastic tub.

"I could have been killed. Electrocuted in the water."

"No, you couldn't," Lizette said. Was there a brief note of regret in her voice? "These footbaths are brand-new. There's a safety switch on them. See, right here." She held up the electric cord with a plastic box on it. "Turns it off right away. You couldn't electrocute a toad with one of these."

"Well, something went wrong. I was just turning on the whirling thing, and the lights went off."

"Well, it's nothing. Virgil's fixing it right now."

Lizette had adopted a mothering voice, like my mother used

when I was five years old and she put an extra bandage on my scraped knee.

"I don't think Virgil even knows what he's doing." Suzanne pouted.

Lizette straightened. "Your foot will be fine. No bleeding." She turned to me. "Gerta will be up in a minute. She's just finishing up downstairs. You might as well go back to the solarium."

"Any way to open the skylight farther?" I asked.

She shook her head. "It's electric. Virgil will fix it. Virgil knows what he's doing. Believe me."

I moved back to the chaise longue and sat. The idea of lying down, vulnerable, with towels strewn over me while my cells purified held no charm. The seaweed was beginning to dry and peel off in places. I had the mottled look of a molting lizard. That doesn't even look cute on Fluffy.

The lights flickered on in the hall, then flickered off again. The privacy curtain billowed. I looked up at the overhead fan. It was still, but the curtain rippled lightly.

"Hello?" No answer. My voice was hoarse, hardly recognizable. I tugged on the curtain, then wrenched it back, the metal curtain hooks rattling along the slide.

DeAngelo, head lolling on his chest, slept soundly in the padded chair, his long fingers wrapped around the arms of the chair, his feet, long, skinny, and white, immersed in a blue plastic footbath. Like the spell.

"DeAngelo?" I glanced at my wrist before I remembered I didn't have on my watch. The clock on the wall was stopped at four-fifteen. I stepped forward and reached for his arm. It seemed odd he would sleep through all this. "DeAngelo?"

I sensed someone behind the curtain in the corner before I saw her. My skin crawled. I scanned the room, looking for something to use as a weapon for protection, saw an empty footbath, and snatched it up. I wished I had on something more than seaweed and a little cotton robe. "Who's there?"

The curtain bulged, rolled. I raised the footbath, ready to bring it down. Meredith stepped forward.

# SIX

I DON'T KNOW who was more stunned. I was shivering, and
Meredith was staring. At me briefly; then her gaze was glued
to DeAngelo's sagging face, the electric cord to his footbath
in her hand, forgotten. "I can't wake him," she whispered.
"I think he's had a heart attack."

I don't remember getting to his side, I was simply there. He
looked totally natural, but there was no discernible movement
of his chest. His marvelous cologne filled my nose.

I reached for his wrist. "I feel a flutter."

I grabbed a handful of his wonderful hair, pulling his head
back to feel for a carotid pulse. I didn't find anything. Meredith's face was dry, white, and frozen. She was so shocked
she stared stupidly at the footbath, her mouth drooping open.

"Meredith, get this damn tub and those cords out of the
way. We've got to get him to the floor and do CPR." Then I
yelled for Lizette.

Meredith crooned a mantra: "Please don't die. You can't
die." She shoved his footbath across the tile next to the wall.

Suzanne appeared at the doorway, wearing a shapeless pink
robe. Her mouth opened in a tiny "o" of shock. Again, I
assumed it was because of DeAngelo, although it could have
been my appearance again.

"Call 911. NOW!" I ordered. Suzanne squeaked and fled.
I vaguely heard her call for Lizette.

DeAngelo was totally limp, and heavier than I had imag-
ined. With a combination of our prying him up and his dead
weight sliding forward, we eased him to the floor. My robe
barely concealed my butt, but there was no time to look for
cover. "You do the mouth-to-mouth, I'll do the chest pump.
Hurry!"

I pressed against his chest, my hand against his firm but too relaxed muscles, counting the one, one thousand rhythm, willing his heart to beat. Was it my imagination, or was he slightly too cool?

Meredith's eyes were brimming with tears. "He'll be all right, won't he?"

I didn't think so, but I wasn't about to tell her. "Keep working. We can't give up on him. He's too strong and vibrant to collapse and die in a moment, unless—" I looked at him. "Did he use cocaine?"

"NO! He didn't use any drugs," she protested. Her eyes were full of tears.

"Yes, he did," Lizette's voice sliced through the room.

I glanced at Meredith, whose eyes were narrow slits of hostility, then at the doorway where Lizette stood motionless, her pink smock spotless, her face composed, her makeup coloring her cheeks so that I couldn't tell if she was pale. The only sign of her distress was her speech. She talked like a machine with the hiccups. "Not as much as he used to. Coke once in a while. Just to keep going."

Coke overdoses are notorious for cardiac arrest. "Did he use any coke today?"

Lizette shrugged, shaking her head vaguely, her gaze glued to DeAngelo's face. She didn't volunteer to help, nor did she leave. She was immobilized, seemingly unable to comprehend what was happening. "He liked to do coke and the footbath at the same time. Said it got him revved."

I looked at DeAngelo and wondered why, with everything he had going for him, he'd need to be revved.

It felt like hours that Meredith was huffing into his mouth and I was compressing his chest. My back, arms, shoulders, and thighs ached, and my knees felt permanently scarred from the grit on the floor, but it could only have been ten minutes before the ambulance crew and a uniformed officer in a squad car arrived. I heard a faint, murmured "Oh, my God!" Unfortunately, when I looked up, I found the officer was gaping at me and my seaweed, not at poor DeAngelo.

The emergency medical techs were more poised. Only momentarily taken aback by my seaweed coating, they quickly took over.

They weren't getting any response but kept the effort going. After radio contact with the doctor at Denver Health and Hospitals Emergency Department, they prepped him for the trip in and took him down the back stairs to avoid the rest of the customers under dryers in the section of the salon unaffected by the outage, who were completely unaware of what was happening. Virgil must have moved the barriers, because the ambulance had backed up right to the back door, flattening his cement frames.

They loaded DeAngelo into the ambulance. Meredith started to get in to go with him, but Lizette grasped her arm and pulled her away.

"Get away," she said. "He's mine." Lizette climbed in, incongruous in her pink smock and sensuous legs.

"NO! He's—" Meredith started to protest. I put my arm around her, seaweed and all.

"He's my *husband*," Lizette snarled, withdrawing into the ambulance.

A quiver of pain ran through Meredith, almost seeming to scorch me. The tears that she had barely held back coursed down her cheeks in a stream of salty sorrow. I tightened my arm around her and wished I'd been able to tell her before, so this wouldn't have been such a jolt.

The ambulance was pulling away into the alley, the police car trailing it, when Gerta burst out of the salon, followed immediately by the tall, blond fellow I'd seen beside the Corvette in the parking lot the day before—"Dah-veed," the other principal stylist at the salon.

He blinked heavily at the sight of me, then looked at Meredith as if she was an unwanted complication and frowned. Finally he spoke. "You better come in," he said and held the door. The only sign of any emotional reaction was his shaking hands.

I followed Gerta back into the kitchenette of the salon, where she took charge. She pulled folding chairs up to the tiny table, poured coffee, and thrust a cup into Meredith's hands. Meredith held the steaming cup for a minute, then put it on the table and laid her head on her arms, silently leaking tears onto the tabletop. Gerta moved a chair for me to sit next to Meredith.

Gerta meant well, but there was no way I was going to sit around in my slime, however much it refreshed my skin cells. When David motioned to Gerta, who followed him out the door toward the clients, I told Meredith I'd be right back and went after them.

"I'm going upstairs to clean this stuff off. Gerta, would you come and help me?" I said, and headed straight back upstairs.

She caught up with me before we entered the solarium. "Gerta, did you see DeAngelo eat or drink anything before he came in for his footbath?"

"No, why?"

"Did he say anything to you about using coke?"

"Do you honestly think he would?"

"Were you with him when he came in here?"

"I put you down, then went to start Suzanne's facial, then to the kitchen for cocoa. He was at his station then."

"Did you actually see him in the room where he cuts hair?"

She rolled her eyes from me to the ceiling. "No! But I'm sure he was there."

"Was anyone else there with him?"

"I don't think so."

"But you couldn't see in the little closet unless you came into the room and peered in." The expression on her face underwent a sly change that I couldn't quite identify.

"Right. But I'm almost positive he was there."

"Not in the attic? With someone?"

"Well, I wouldn't know, since he wasn't with me." Her

tone of voice made me wonder if she wished she had been with him. She continued. "Every afternoon at four he soaks. Like a ritual. We all have them. For him it's footbaths. For David, it's—" She didn't finish the thought. "For me, it's cocoa. Like clockwork. Why are you asking me all these questions? What kind of a ghoul are you, anyway?"

It was a good question. I wished I had a snappy answer. Instead, I felt like a slime slug, complete with seaweed slime. I stepped into the solarium. The pile of towels was gone, the chaise longue was sparkling clean. I stepped around the gauze curtain. Virgil was holding the towels and had an arm out to pick up the footbath by the chair.

"What are you doing?" I asked.

He startled. "Whaaa?" His face went blotchy, patches of red against bleached pale skin. He backed away from the foot-bath, as though it might bite him. "I was just gonna clean it up. He likes me to do things up right away." His hands were shaking; the load of towels looked precarious.

"I thought you were supposed to be fixing the lights."

His face settled into sullen lines. "They're fixed."

I flicked on the light switch. The room flooded with light. "Did you touch anything in here?"

He looked at me like I was an idiot. "I just picked up towels. Like I'm s'posed to. You're not my boss. He is."

"Virgil, DeAngelo is very sick—"

"Don't talk to me like I'm stupid."

Gerta appeared at my side. "He's just upset, Ms. Stargazer. We all are. Now, come along. Time to shower."

I'm sure he muttered a vulgar word when he passed me and went down the back stairs.

"Just leave the towels in the laundry for me, Virg," Gerta called after him. "Come on," she said to me and marched down the corridor. Gerta pointed me to the shower and handed me two thick pink towels and a fresh gown.

"Whoa, there!" It was the officer who stared so rudely at

me when the medical technicians came. He was still staring. "I need you all downstairs."

"I'm just going to shower."

"Well, that can wait." I swear he was enjoying this. There was a little crease at the corner of his eyes that tightened.

"Well, it can't wait. I'm beginning to itch." I backed toward the showers.

He tromped toward me. "Now you just come along, miss, or I'll have to move you." Without turning away from me, he addressed Gerta. "Please lock that room. We're going downstairs and I don't want anyone else up here."

"On what basis, Officer?" I asked. Still inching toward the showers.

"On the basis that a crime may have been committed here."

"But you don't know it has."

"Come along, miss." He grabbed my seaweed-slicked arm. He hadn't anticipated just how slippery it would be, and his fingers slid off my skin with a snap.

I smothered a grin. "You see? It needs to come off."

The humor went right out of his eyes and he clamped down on me, his thumb and forefinger circling my wrist.

Gerta pulled a ring of keys magically from her pocket and locked the door. She was closing the door when I asked about David.

"He's handling the clients. I'm keeping him informed."

"He didn't seem very upset or surprised. I thought the two were friends."

An expression swept across her face so fast I wasn't quite sure I'd really seen it. When she spoke, her voice was low and her words measured. "David is terribly worried. But the clients mustn't be disappointed—or alarmed."

"The show must go on?"

"Something like that." She dropped the keys in her pocket, and the three of us clumped down the back stairs to the kitchen.

It was five o'clock. I checked my watch on the way down,

more out of habit than anything else. I think that's when the emotional impact finally hit me. I'd been in overdrive through the whole afternoon, handling DeAngelo's collapse as though that sort of thing occurred every day. I'd even begun to organize questions and facts. Now, in the aftermath, hearing the ponderous tones of the officer's voice, the adrenaline evaporated from my system and my emotions cut loose.

My knees began to shake, my hands were suddenly clammy, and my chest had become tight and painful. I drew in deep gulps of air through my mouth while I blinked back stinging tears. The image in my spell had come to pass. I hoped DeAngelo was all right, but it was hope against hope; I knew in the depths of my soul that he was gone. His sore feet were never going to feel the pinch of shoes again. The police wouldn't return unless it was a fatality.

I'd like to say that the tears that appeared on my cheeks were totally unselfish, but I have to admit that at that moment I also realized I would never get my DeAngelo haircut. Any renaissance, sexual or just cosmetic, was gone with him. And so was the sheer fun of a makeover. Evil had stomped it out.

The door at the bottom of the back stairs was pushed to, with only an inch or so open. I could see into a thin strip of kitchen where the door was ajar. The room was closed to the front of the house so that the customers wouldn't be confronted with the sight of Denver's finest in the blues and guns. It never enhances a beauty-business image to have uniforms hanging out in the back rooms.

The officer sat at the table, facing me, and studiously began to pencil in names on a clipboard. His hat lay on the corner of the table; his light brown hair, already sparse on top, had a hat dent around his head. He chewed on a corner of his well-trimmed mustache as he wrote. Because of the position of his arms, I couldn't make out his name, but the stripes on his arm declared him a step above beginner. His voice was a carefully disinterested monotone, questioning neutrally about DeAngelo.

First Suzanne's voice, then Meredith's lower one answered. Finally, Suzanne's grating high voice cut through my reverie. "I don't see why you're here. I mean, it's nice to have officers come when someone's hurt or gets sick, but shouldn't you be out doing something? I mean, there are criminals. Out there. I mean, it's been nice, but you don't have to stay for me. I'll be fine. And I'm sure DeAngelo will be too, soon. So, thanks—"

The officer cleared his throat, uncomfortably.

I spoke up. "I was wondering if you've heard from the hospital about Mr. DeAngelo?"

Meredith's head came up, her gaze fastened on me. The officer glanced at me while his fingers fiddled with his black automatic pencil. He had large hands and long fingers with neat, square-cut fingernails. I was still into observing fingernails, since I'd had mine done in wonderful slut-red.

"Have you heard from the hospital?" I asked again.

The officer cleared his throat. "We'll hear soon, I guess. Now, what is your name?"

"It's Jane Smith. But I call myself Stella."

He wrote it on the clipboard in block letters. Footsteps sounded on the back stoop. The door opened, and the familiar figure of Detective Lee Stokowski, Denver Police Department, Homicide Division, entered the room.

Stokowski's brown tweed sports jacket was a little tight through the shoulders, and sprung at the elbows. He wore a dark red tie with navy-and-gold stripes, beige shirt, and camel-colored slacks. His five o'clock shadow strengthened his stubborn jaw, and his dark crispy hair was curling tightly at attention. It didn't take any sixth sense to know he was not happy to see me.

He scanned the room, his gaze halting first on Meredith, then on Suzanne, and finally resting on me. His dark brow curled into a frown, then he sighed. "Good God, Stella, what happened to you? You look like you stepped out of a lagoon."

# SEVEN

"DEANGELO IS DEAD, isn't he, Stokowski?"

Stokowski glanced around again, checking each of us for our facial expression. "I'm sorry. We got a call from the emergency room. Mr. DeAngelo couldn't be revived."

His words fell like pebbles on my numb brain, leaving little dents of pain. He wasn't very good at condolences. But why had he come?

"Oh, my God," Suzanne moaned. She covered her face with her hands, two heavy diamond rings sparkling coldly in the overhead light. Meredith sat like a stone—no sound, not a tear. Her hands were folded together prayerfully. I wondered if she'd heard what he said, but when I looked into her eyes, I knew she had.

I waited until Suzanne's sobs had subsided a little before I continued. Meredith's expression didn't change. The numbness in my head was wearing off, and silent alarms were whispering, Stokowski is with *homicide*. "So, why are you here?" I asked.

He answered indirectly. "Were you here when he died?"

"I found him in a state of collapse. I think he was still alive then."

He looked around, as though the room had grown too small. "Is there somewhere we can talk in private?"

He told the officer to remain with Suzanne and Meredith, asked them to wait for him, then followed me. Virgil was in the hall, pushing a broom. He stooped, picked up something from the floor, then stepped aside to let us pass.

"Good-luck penny?" I asked, hoping to make peace with him.

Virgil smiled crookedly. "Hope so." He glanced worriedly at Stokowski. I didn't blame him. Stokowski was a grim-looking man.

Stokowski wanted to go upstairs to DeAngelo's room. He looked around carefully, suspiciously, noting the details, then lowered himself heavily into a side chair. He pointed to one, indicating I was also to sit, warning me not to finger things.

It was strange sitting in this room with this solidly built, heavy-footed policeman whose whole bearing, style, and perspective on life was so different, so alien, to DeAngelo's. And mine, for that matter. Even stranger to think that DeAngelo wouldn't charm his way back to life. I wondered if we were trespassing. And then, because I had a sudden chill as though another presence filled the room, I wondered if DeAngelo's spirit was lingering in the room.

Stokowski did not appear to notice. He pulled out the little spiral notepad and ballpoint pen he carries in the breast pocket of his jacket and formed a desk by putting his left ankle on his right knee. It occurred to me that such casual but methodical little things send a subliminal message. *I can outlast you. I'll persevere. I'm prepared.* "All right," he said, voice cold and calm. "Explain why you're here."

I shivered a second time. This time I knew where the chill came from: his tone of voice. "I was having my hair done."

There was the tiniest glimmer of humor in his icy blue eyes. "Is it done?"

I wasn't up to humor. "No. DeAngelo collapsed in his chair while I was having my seaweed wrap. He hadn't cut and styled my hair yet. Gerta says David will finish it up later. So, why are you here about a coronary, Stokowski? And how'd you get here so fast? It wasn't because of my call to you last Monday, was it?"

He looked me in the eyes steadily, calculating the advantages and disadvantages of answering. "The uniform called from the emergency room. He was uncomfortable about the scene."

My heart rate skyrocketed. "Uncomfortable about the scene?"

Stokowski scratched his chin, loud in the uncomfortable stillness of the room. "He thought you looked suspicious. So, what do you know about all this?"

"DeAngelo was...murdered? Do you know I was there the whole time? I didn't hear..." Bile burned in my throat.

What had I heard? I'd had earphones on my head for the whole time. Gerta had stuck them on, turned high enough to blot out most intrusions, and I'd lain there in a pupa case, semicomatose. And I'd had one of my spells. I wasn't sure what was real and what was...surreal.

Some inner voice told me to slow down and think before I answered. I'd found Meredith standing over DeAngelo, in shock, but how would a well-trained homicide detective see it? What I said could make the difference between Meredith being a minor suspect and a major one.

Detective Stokowski is a relatively impartial, objective man. Like the rest of us, though, he filters things through his life experience. A policeman's life experience isn't your average happy, flappy life. It's filled with liars, cheats, murderers, rapists, and a variety of your workaday burglars. A filter like that leaves you with an overlay of suspicion. I felt like I needed to tread very, very carefully, or Meredith and I would be sleeping over in the city cell motel.

I took a deep breath, hoping the extra oxygen would pep up my brain cells and keep the details straight, then launched into a description of waking, finding the lights were out, Suzanne howling, and Lizette and I going into her room. "Suzanne's room was practically pitch-dark, and for some reason she kept saying she was afraid of a fire. Anyway, as soon as we knew she was all right I went back to the solarium.

"By that time I was chilly from the seaweed slime and too restless to lie down, so I peeked around the curtain, and that's when I saw DeAngelo sleeping in the chair. At least, I thought he was sleeping."

"You didn't think anything was odd?"

"I think it's flaming strange that DeAngelo would sit down and have a footbath in the same room where I'm wrapped up in a seaweed cocoon. That kind of gave me the willies. On the other hand, he apparently does it regularly. The footbath, I mean. Only usually, there's no one in there. I really pressured to get this appointment, so they made an exception. I s'pose that's why it happened that way."

Stokowski's right eyebrow lifted skeptically. "Oh? How's that?"

It is so hard to confess to lies. "I told them I was a reporter doing a piece on avant-garde beauty salons and I had a deadline to make."

"Why was it so important to you to get in here?"

"I needed a haircut."

He looked at me disbelievingly. "And a seaweed wrap?"

"I had to—I lied about a spa story, so I had to do the spa. Otherwise they'd think I was lying."

"God forbid."

He made some cryptic notes, then absently flipped his pen against the pad, the wheels of his reasoning turning. He finally roused. "DeAngelo didn't look sick?"

"He looked fine. Asleep. There was absolutely nothing different about him, except he wouldn't wake up."

"Drugs?"

"Lizette, the receptionist, who went to the hospital with him, said he used coke on occasion. Apparently he liked to take coke with his whirly footbath."

Stokowski rubbed his chin with the fingers of his left hand while he read through his notes again. "Some kind of new high?"

I shrugged. "The heat would rev up his heart. Could've enhanced his coke high."

"Did you try to talk to him?"

"He didn't respond. When Meredith said she couldn't wake him up, I thought he'd had a heart attack. We discovered he wasn't breathing, so we got him out of the chair and started CPR while Suzanne called 911.''

Stokowski shifted uncomfortably in his chair, looked at his watch, and then looked back at me. "Let's go back to Meredith."

I tried hard to keep my affect flat and my breathing regular. I'm not sure I was successful. Stokowski was staring hard at me.

"When did she come in?" His eyelids lowered speculatively, as though he were measuring me for an orange jail jumpsuit. "She was having a seaweed wrap?"

"I don't know what she was having, exactly."

"Well, approximately, then."

The muscles in my chest tightened. "I was actually surprised to see her there. She hadn't told me she was coming. She must have been there for a consultation. About hair, probably." Pubic hair, but I didn't mention that.

"On Monday you called and asked me to look up DeAngelo. You thought Meredith was interested in him. Three days later you're here getting yourself spa'd, and this very same DeAngelo turns up dead. Now, you explain. I've got all night."

I smiled warmly back at him. "Zelda was hoping to see more of you, Lee. She talks about you all the time. I think she's interested in you."

"You know I'll just have to keep asking questions, even if it takes all night."

"Only as long as I choose to answer them, unless you're charging me with something."

He rubbed his chin some more, flexing his whisker stubble. "You were worried about Meredith being scammed by him."

Something in his expression suddenly told me an information swap might be in the making. "You never told me what you found out about him."

"Clean. No record. Known to the motor vehicle department

only for some parking tickets. Pretty extended financially. Sounds like half the world. So is this guy gay?''

''Not in the least. What did they say killed him?''

''Don't know for sure yet. The doc in the ER said it looked like his heart just stopped. No reason. They ran tox screens, and the preliminary report shows coke. It's a coroner's case, and there will be an autopsy. Maybe he just flew too high. Doesn't look like there's anything to investigate here. Little heat, coke, you got cardiac arrest. Simple.'' He shrugged, but his eyes were sly, and too watchful. ''The only trouble is, you're here and very nervous, and the whole thing doesn't smell right. You inquired about him before. You didn't like him, did you?''

''Look, Stokowski, I didn't know him. I was just worried because Meredith was so taken with him.''

''And nothing else?''

''Nothing.''

''Show me the place.''

I had such mixed feelings about seeing that room again that I actually tripped over nothing as I led the way down the hall. There was still the faintest hint of DeAngelo's floral cologne floating in the air. Stokowski halted on the doorsill and, laying a restraining hand on my shoulder, turned me to him. His face was so close to mine that I could see the black flecks in the irises of his blue eyes. ''Need to stop here.''

''Only if it's a crime scene.''

He shrugged, but he kept his hand on my shoulder.

I glanced quickly around the room, feeling a little giddy. The pale pink sheet on the chaise longue was pristine, unwrinkled. The curtain dividing the room was pushed back against the wall, and the footbath was sedately resting nearly behind the chair next to the wall.

Stokowski leaned a shoulder against the doorjamb. ''Describe it, from here.''

I told him, right down to the number of towels that had

been piled on me. It steadied me to focus on the specifics of description, made it seem more clinical and less real.

"Who was in here? Where are the towels and stuff now?"

"Virgil picked up the towels. Gerta and I stood about where you and I are now and told him to leave. He left, dumped the towels in the laundry, and Gerta and I were escorted downstairs by the officer after she locked the room."

"Where was DeAngelo's chair?"

"Right there, in the corner, but pulled out, with the footbath in front—" I stopped, thinking about the footbath, trying to remember the room as it had been when I'd first come in and seen Meredith.

My face suddenly felt cold, and the background sounds of the salon slid off-key. DeAngelo seemed to materialize before me, slumped in his chair, head lolling on his chest, his feet in the footbath, surrounded by...

"Stella? Are you with me?" Stokowski's hand on my shoulder intruded, warm and earthy. The image of DeAngelo faded. The chair was there, but empty. Stokowski shook me again, lightly. "Hello, Stella. What is it?"

I looked into his eyes; his irises constricted minutely. "I thought I remembered something, but I can't identify it. He was murdered, wasn't he?"

He didn't answer.

Stokowski's most endearing quality is that he doesn't immediately scoff at anything I say. He does tend to arrest me, which is unpleasant as hell, but at least he doesn't discount me entirely. I think he's troubled by the fact that he finds me attractive. Actually, neither of us likes to think about it.

The skin over his cheekbones at the corner of his eyes wrinkled in concentration. His gaze was intense, as if waiting for me to say some particular thing, but I didn't know what. I couldn't tell by the expression on his face what he was thinking. But the vertical blinds on the windows were looking more and more like jail-cell bars.

There were footsteps on the stairs—heavy, official sounding. The technical crew straggled into the hallway, carrying black cases with their peculiarly arcane wares. At least one of them smoked, bringing a wreath of cigarette smell with him. Stokowski stepped over to talk to them in a lowered voice, so I could hear only occasional words.

He was occupied with the forensic crew. Maybe I could recapture the feeling. I tiptoed over to the chair, reached out to touch it.

"Hey!" Stokowski dragged me out of the room, frowning. "Let's go."

His fingers tightened on my arm. I pulled away from him, shaking myself indignantly. "You don't need to treat me like the prime suspect, unless I am."

"Maybe you are." He stopped in the narrow hallway, facing me, closer than I was comfortable with, close enough to intrude on my space and make me feel vulnerable. He glared at me. "You don't seem to get it, Stella. You were there. Now either you—"

"Look, Stokowski, I was asleep. And I had towels over my face and earphones on my head, and I couldn't move. You can verify all of that with Gerta. She's the one who locked me in. Maybe just so I wouldn't see DeAngelo soaking." I drew in a deep breath, remembering the suffocating sensation of the seaweed wrap and the terrible feeling when I discovered I'd been caught in the strap.

I'd been tied down, unable to move, unable to hear because of the earphones and music, unable to see because of the towels, but there. So convenient. If I was a witness, I was also a damn good suspect.

Stokowski turned to the forensic crew. "Treat the whole room as a crime scene." He waved to the crew. "Better tape off the place. I'm going to close it down."

"Lee, I have got to shower."

He turned to me. "What, have your cells replenished already?"

# EIGHT

IT TOOK MAYBE fifteen minutes to scrub clean of the seaweed and apricot hair follicle rejuvenator and don my clothes. I emerged from the changing room and tiptoed to the solarium doorway to peek in. The officer's back was to me. He appeared to be memorizing the room and making notes on a little pad. I glanced around him. The room was in perfect order. Chair in the corner, footbath shoved back against the wall, towels folded on the shelves. What had I nearly remembered? I withdrew and headed for the back stairs.

Why had the police returned? Homicide doesn't just show up on a whim. It needed something much more specific to bring Stokowski to the salon, some suspicion or accusation that must have come long before I told him that I thought DeAngelo had been murdered.

Lizette had gone with DeAngelo in the ambulance to the hospital. I remembered the look she'd had on her face when I inquired about Meredith yesterday. Could Lizette have accused Meredith? Yes, indeed. She sure could. She could easily implicate Meredith in a classic love triangle with enough motive to curl DeAngelo's hair permanently.

Stokowski would very soon learn that Meredith was there with DeAngelo when I found him. Then she would join me on the suspect list. I had to talk to her before Stokowski did. I needed basic information from her. Like, why was she there, and what the hell had she been doing with that electric cord in her hand when I walked in?

Stokowski took Suzanne for questioning next, with a nod to the officer that was cop-talk for "Listen to whatever they say." The officer self-consciously wrote meticulous microscopic notes in his black three-by-five loose-leaf notebook while Meredith and I sat like garden gnomes after a storm, mute and forlorn. Meredith's eyes were kind of glazed over. I kicked her under the table.

"MMMhhg," she grunted.

I kicked her again and glared at her, willing her to pay attention to me. She finally rolled her eyes in my direction. I moved my finger, signaling her to follow me. She frowned. I grimaced, pretending to be ill. Then I moaned. Then I slumped forward, put my forehead into my hands, and moaned again.

The officer looked over at me.

"It's nothing," I said, pathetically. I gripped my belly and grimaced again, moaning softly. "I don't want to bother you."

That was supposed to be a cue for Meredith to insist that I was ill. She didn't get it. The officer, though, looked vaguely concerned. There are few things worse than someone puking their guts out on the floor in front of you. I gripped my stomach harder, aimed my face to the floor in front of him, and panted lightly; I'd seen a friend practicing Lamaze for delivery. "Oh, dear. I'm...I'm going to throw up."

The officer rose from his chair, alarmed, pointing at the kitchen corner. "Get to the sink." I'd forgotten there was a sink in the room.

"I need a bathroom." I gagged and retched horribly. I'm good at it. When I was a kid I used to practice at night before I went to sleep. It always worked on my sister.

The officer headed for the door. "I'll find one."

As soon as he left the room, I started on Meredith. "You've been logging some serious time with DeAngelo. What were you doing here?"

She didn't answer directly. "I came to see him. I had to. Stella, he lied to me."

I wondered exactly how much she knew. "And—?"

"It was awful." She looked at me, her breath coming rapidly in shallow pants. "I was mad, Stella. I've never been so angry. I told him I wished he was dead. And—and I struck him. Stella, I've never hit anyone before."

"How hard did you hit him?"

"It doesn't matter—it's the fact that I hit him."

"It might matter. How hard? Did you leave a mark?"

"I think so."

I closed my eyes. God only knew how much trouble Meredith was in. "Where were you when this happened?"

"Upstairs. In his...office."

"Think carefully. Was anyone else around there? Anyone outside listening?"

Her eyelids fluttered as she thought, her forehead wrinkled with the effort. "Anyone could have been outside the office door, I guess. I just don't know!"

"Did anyone hear you?"

She shook her head. "No, I don't think so. I don't know. Maybe. I don't know."

"Could Lizette have been there?"

She shook her head numbly. "God, I don't know. Maybe the whole frigging place heard us. Hope not."

"Then what happened after you hit him? Did he hit you back?"

"Oh, no. He'd never do that. I'm the one who lost it. Stella, it's like *I* did it. I wished him dead. Right there, out loud. I hit him in the face. Now he's dead. It's like I killed him!"

She had to get a grip on herself before she saw Stokowski, or she'd put herself in jail. "Cut it out, Meredith. You didn't kill him. You just hit him. Now, what happened next?"

She answered in a choked whisper, "He was angry. He stormed out and came down here for his footbath."

"What is he, a frog, he takes footbaths when he's angry?"

"He always does a footbath on Thursday afternoons. It's his thing. I don't know why. He just does. It's a ritual of some sort." She wiped tears from her face, smearing her mascara across her temples.

"Hurry up, Meredith. Before the cop comes back."

"He put his feet in, turned on the whirl, and jerked. Then he groaned. He looked like his feet really hurt, and he gripped the arms of the chair. I didn't know anything was wrong. I was so mad at him for lying to me—''

"What were you doing with the electric cord when I came in?"

"I don't know. I wanted to turn it off. But I was afraid to touch the switch. So I unplugged it." She must have seen something in my expression. She stopped, her lip caught in her teeth, tears streaming down her face.

"Why were you afraid to touch the switch on the foot-bath?"

"I don't know. It seemed strange, is all. Everything seemed strange."

"Meredith, everything was strange. Now, think! What did you see?"

Her head dropped, hopeless, like a wilting flower.

"Meredith, you must remember something, surely. Otherwise it sounds pretty feeble."

She whispered. "You don't think I killed him, do you?"

"God, no. I'm just trying to get things straight. Meredith, did he say something?"

"He didn't say anything. I came in just as he put his feet into the water and he just looked at me funny, his eyes kind of bugged, then he closed them and moaned. Like he does when…when we…when he…''

I knew what she meant.

I'd heard him arrange to see someone. Meredith, or some-one else? Balancing Lizette and Meredith *and* yet another would clearly be enough to cause heart failure. "I thought you were going to see him later tonight."

"That was before—'' She caught her lower lip and looked at me quickly.

"Before what, Meredith?"

She didn't answer.

"Meredith, were you on the phone to him around three this afternoon?"

She nodded miserably. "He'd told me he wasn't engaged

to Lizette. She assumed they were going to marry and she bought that ring she wears and she tells everyone they're married, but they're not. But he promised to set it straight. Last night. They had a big fight. He told me he'd broken off with her. But this morning I saw him leaving her house.''

She laid her head on the table, long, silent sobs racking her body.

I wanted to put my arms around her and comfort her, but I knew if I did that she'd completely break down, and I'd never get the details before the officer returned. And I had to find out as much as I could as fast as I could. Stokowski wasn't going to be as sure of her innocence as I was.

The officer burst into the room; I clutched my stomach and groaned. ''The bathroom is right around the corner and down the hall,'' he said.

''Meredith, give me a hand.'' I leaned heavily on her until we were out of the room. ''Meredith, regardless of what Stokowski says, you don't need to answer any questions. In fact, in your shape, you shouldn't. You'll just end up saying something that will sound like evidence to him.'' I stopped. There was a little dazed frown on her forehead, like she'd just remembered something. ''Is there anything else, Meredith?''

''No, nothing.''

She was lying. I can always tell, because she flinches right before she launches into a lie, but there wasn't much more time. It seemed a lot more important then to make sure she understood her rights. I know from experience, Stokowski is very good at questioning.

''Look, if you think you have to talk to him, at least remember this. You can answer some and not all. You can always leave. You can leave anytime so long as you're not charged formally with something. You don't have to go to the police station, or you can go and answer a few questions and you can leave at any time.'' I still wasn't sure she was getting it.

''Will you stay with me?''

"He probably won't let me."

She nodded forlornly. "Stella, all I wanted was to find the right guy. Is it too much to want a family?"

"Is that *really* what you wanted?"

She scuffed the floor with her toe. When she lifted her head, her eyes were puffed and bleary with mascara streaks. "You know what's the worst?"

I shook my head.

"I'm still so mad at him I could just kill him. Now he's dead, and I can't even tell him. That's what's worst of all."

That wasn't the worst, but I didn't tell her so.

STOKOWSKI SPENT VERY little time with Suzanne, maybe twenty minutes total. When they returned, Suzanne was pale and shaky and looked as if she could stand to knock back a stiff drink.

Stokowski refused to make eye contact with me. He had the same I'm-going-to-ignore-you look that Fluffy'd been giving me lately, a very serious sign. "No need for you to stay around, Stella. This could take some time."

That, and the ominous twist of his eyebrows when he left the room with Meredith, told me he was zeroing in on her already. As far as I knew, he didn't have much evidence, but it was only a matter of a few hours before the police discovered my and Meredith's fingerprints on the footbath. That's if she didn't spill her guts right off.

I knew Meredith well enough to know she wouldn't kill anyone, but Stokowski didn't. And he would have her at the scene, having argued and fought, having the motive of a woman scorned. Boxed in.

It was nearly six o'clock and twilight outside. I stood in the silvery splendor of the back hall, partway to the salon waiting room, debating what would be the most useful thing to do. Suzanne brushed past me without a word, pulling on a cashmere, suede, and sequin sweater-jacket. I watched the distinctive, arrogant sway in her gait as she approached the reception room.

She hesitated at Lizette's desk, peered at the appointment book, flipping a page forward and back. Then she glanced around, saw me, and let go of the page guiltily.

"Suzanne, wait," I called. She was whipping down the sidewalk when I caught up with her.

"Detective Stokowski said I'm not supposed to talk to you."

"Well, you know how police are."

"No, I don't know how they are. And I don't know you either."

"Well, I'm not trying to talk to you. How about we get a drink somewhere? Unwind a bit. You must be ready to collapse."

She glanced around again, undecided whether to listen to her manners, which told her to reply to me, or her instincts, which told her to scream and run. She seemed to come to a decision. "Thank you, no."

We were standing at the curb. My car was in the parking lot at the end of the block. I didn't know where hers was, but I figured my best chance to convince her to talk to me was right now, while she was still in shock. "Tell you what, Suzanne. Why don't we go over to Grout's and have a quick drink, even a snack, just to steady our nerves."

"I'm not sure..." She started across the street toward a cream-colored Lexus with gold trim.

I trotted right beside her. She was itching to get away from me, but I was determined to find out what she'd told Stokowski. "We'll go in your car; that way when we're finished you can just go on. It's only a block or so. DeAngelo would want you to have a little comfort. He didn't seem the kind of guy that believed in suffering and abstinence."

Suzanne hesitated with her hand on the car door. "No, I don't—"

"I need to be with someone, Suzanne. Someone who knew and loved him. You're so wonderful to do this."

It should have hooked her. Most people have trouble refusing compliments. She didn't. She looked at me like I was slime mold and said, "Look, I'm not going. Period. If I wanted to help people or listen to their problems, I'd be a social worker."

# NINE

I SHIVERED IN the exhaust of Suzanne's Lexus as she disappeared down the street. I'd left my jacket inside in the locker, along with my purse. If Suzanne had agreed to go for a drink, she'd have had to pay or leave me to wash dishes. Maybe she realized that.

Through the front window I could see David hovering over a client, putting the finishing touches on her coiffure. He held a rat-tailed comb in his right hand, plucking at her curls with the sharp tail end of the comb. His left hand patted and shaped the hair. The artful lighting of the room erased all signs of hollows and wrinkles on the client's face, even erased the sharp relief of David's cheekbones, that had been so noticeable in the parking lot the day before.

The salon smells wrapped around me as I reentered. David's muted voice came through the nearly closed door to the front salon room. Lizette was still nowhere to be seen.

I moved to the reception desk, ran my newly polished fingernail down the appointment page, and copied all the names on the pages from the day before, today, and tomorrow.

I had hoped there would be telephone numbers beside the names, but there weren't, except by mine. The rest of the customers must be regulars. There wasn't a customer file, Rolodex, or book that I could find.

I flipped quickly through the pages. Meredith's name was listed at least once a week and sometimes twice. So were a number of other clients for DeAngelo. Uncomfortably like a harem. Suzanne's name wasn't there at all, but a large letter S was marked twice a week, usually in David's column. I assumed that was she. I was back nearly three weeks when my eyes stopped in the middle of the page at the name Jason. *Jason?* The same Jason I knew and...

Jason! The nerve of him to tell me not to come, after he'd been here himself! I looked again. He had an hour appointment, too. An hour for that short mop of hair, what— I had a swift vision of Gerta, then Lizette and the showers and the cell rejuvenation. I scrambled back through the pages, back three, then four more weeks. He was there again, five weeks ago. Maybe it was someone else. Yeah, right.

I scoured Lizette's desk for her address without success. David's voice boomed near the reception room door. I flipped the book back to today's listing and lifted the telephone receiver to my ear, fiddling with a flashy pencil.

In a loud voice I said, "Yes. I'm sorry I'm late, but there's been an accident and I was delayed. I'll be there soon." I hung up and smiled at David. "I just had to call home. They worry about me, you know."

He frowned.

"Gerta told me you would finish my hair."

David's client came out of the room, shrugging into her coat. "Well, darling, I left a little billy-doo on the counter for you." She held her arms up for a hug. David dutifully hugged. "I do hope DeAngelo will be all right." She beamed fondly at him and slithered out the door.

I had to remind myself that when you're under a hair dryer you can't see much, and you hear even less. He saw her to the door. "You take care. Lizette will call in the morning to schedule your next appointment."

Then he closed the door behind her and sighed. Even the shadow-reducing lighting couldn't hide the lines etched in his face when he turned around. "You found DeAngelo?"

I nodded. He waved at me to follow him. It wasn't until I was sitting with the cape tied tightly around my neck that I remembered how very vulnerable I felt in a hairdresser's chair. A slip of the scissors, and my hair could be crooked, my ear sliced, or my throat cut. At least my feet weren't in a box, or a footbath.

I wanted to get the big questions out of the way first. "What do you plan to do to my hair?"

"What did you and DeAngelo talk about?"

I had to remind myself that he was talking hair. I described DeAngelo's suggestions while David spritzed my hair. After he selected safely short-bladed but very sharp scissors, I hazarded questions.

"You and DeAngelo have been together for a long time?"

There was no change in the snipping. "Most of our lives. We were raised together."

"You must have been pretty close."

"Still are. Like brothers."

For a loving brother he was mighty calm about DeAngelo's death. "Brothers have a lot of fun and a lot of fights."

"Never fought. Only thing we ever disagreed on was the color scheme for the solarium upstairs, and hiring Virgil, the handyman. DeAngelo wanted to do all the work himself. I thought we needed help."

"I didn't know DeAngelo was good at building."

"He's good at anything he puts his mind to."

"Like women?"

He stopped cutting. "Is this all for the article?"

I'd forgotten about my lie. "It's background. You want to talk off the record?"

"Off the record means you aren't going to put it in an article?"

"Promise."

"He really likes women. I mean *really*. Some people like alcohol or gambling, he likes women."

I was beginning to wonder about the use of the present tense for DeAngelo. "An addiction?"

"I wouldn't go that far. He just really likes them. It gets him into trouble. It's no wonder he passed out."

I caught my breath. "Have you talked to anyone about how

DeAngelo's doing?'' I watched as the cutting slowed and he evened off the sides. He moved around so he was standing directly in front of me and snipped at bangs.

"Haven't had time. I'll stop by the hospital after I close up.''

I waited until he finished and stepped back to examine the results. It looked good to me. Safe.

"Then you don't know that the police are here.''

He frowned. "The police?''

"David, I'm sorry to tell you, but DeAngelo died at the hospital.''

"He's dead? But that means—'' David turned around in confusion, blinking rapidly, ostensibly searching for a comb. He picked up first one, then another from the towel on the counter, then finally put them all down and sat in the next barber's chair, his scissors forgotten and dangling from his fingers. "Dead?''

I TRIED, BUT I couldn't get him to tell me what he was going to say when he said, "But that means—'' In fact, he just sat in the chair repeating the word "dead" until Stokowski appeared at the door and asked David to come with him.

"Where's Meredith, Stokowski?''

"I told you to go home, Stella.'' He glanced at my hair, then at David. David rose, looked in surprise at the scissors in his hand, and placed them in the sterilizing container. When David was out of the room, Stokowski turned back to me. "Look, Stella, save yourself some trouble. Butt out for once.''

"Are you taking Meredith downtown for questions?'' I asked. "I want to come with her.''

"No.'' He closed the door.

I threw the cape onto the chair and went after him, brushing the hair from my neck on the way, but he was nearly at the top of the stairs. I decided to try to find Meredith instead and hustled to the kitchen. She was talking in muted tones to Virgil, who was sipping evil-smelling black coffee from a mug that was nearly hidden in his large, encircling hands. "Virgil, it's not your fault. It'll be all right." She looked up at me.

There were little hammocks of fatigue under her eyes, and I could sense her weariness from her posture. I hoped it didn't mean that she'd been careless when she talked to Stokowski. "How did it go, Meredith?"

She hesitated, considering her answer, something she rarely does. "Better than I thought it would. He seems like a fair man."

"You need to get an attorney. Stokowski's a professional. He's good at listening. That doesn't mean he believes you, Meredith."

Her eyes filled with tears, again.

Virgil set his mug carefully on the table and leaned toward me, his jaw belligerently set. "Don't you get her all upset again. Leave her alone." Meredith had conquered another heart.

"Virgil, I'm her friend. I'm trying to help out."

He wasn't convinced. "You were there. You should know." I didn't have time to deal with a smitten, irrational man, so I ignored him. "What are you going to do now, Meredith?"

"I'm going downtown. He has a few more things to cover."

"You don't have to do that, you know."

"He'll think I'm guilty if I don't."

"That's what he wants you to think so you'll talk to him. You shouldn't do this, Meredith. You're not in the right shape for it."

"It's just a few questions."

"Just because you're innocent doesn't mean you can do without a lawyer to advise you. Have you ever heard of the drip torture? One little drop at a time, until you're worn down and saying anything that comes to mind. He's like that. Persistent, until you'll say almost anything."

The kitchen door opened behind me.

"Is that the way it is for you, Stella?" Stokowski's voice had a fine edge to it when he spoke to me.

"You should know. You've grilled me before."

"Ready, Meredith?" Now his voice was calm, even warm and comforting.

I leaned over the table to Meredith. "Meredith, Fluffy's like that, too. Warm. Comforting. He sleeps with his crickets at night to keep them warm. But he eats them for breakfast."

"Go home, Stella," Stokowski said.

"Do you want me to call you a lawyer, Meredith?"

She shook her head. "I'll call you when I get home."

Stokowski led her out the back door to his car, parked on the flattened cement frames. A lump formed in my throat.

Virgil pushed himself up from the table and clumped over to the corner, where he rinsed his coffee cup and put it in the sink. "Police don't like people who mouth off," he said in a nasal drawl.

He was not a large man, but his rough clothes stretched across surprisingly broad shoulders and made him seem bulky. I decided he had some kind of padding beneath his heavy outer shirt that added to his size. "You got a way to get home?" he asked.

"I'll be fine."

"I can give you a lift."

"No, thanks. I've got my car." At that very moment I thought of Suzanne and knew exactly how she'd felt when she was trying to get away from me.

VIRGIL LEFT, SHRUGGING his shoulders indifferently at my refusal of a ride. Upstairs the police were clumping around in the solarium, dusting for fingerprints among other things, no doubt. I finished my coffee, rinsed the cup, and left it in the sink. I was just paranoid enough that although I didn't wash it, I wiped it clean of fingerprints with a paper towel.

I thought of the long slim legs I'd seen go up the stairs, Meredith's legs. DeAngelo must have his *office* up there. No

yellow tape barred the way, so I quietly climbed the back stairs
to the second floor and crept down the hall. Sienna-colored
fingerprint powder stained every surface in the solarium, and
the forensic team was gathering dust particles, threads, any
bits that might point to a killer.

Whatever they gathered wouldn't tell what Meredith had
done beyond holding the plug. And it wouldn't indicate intent.
It wouldn't tell Stokowski whether she'd plugged it in, elec-
trocuting DeAngelo, or whether she'd pulled it out, trying to
stop a murder in progress. The thing that really worried me
was that Stokowski acted as if he had something he was holding back.

All my questions about the electrocution would have to wait
until morning, when I could call a pathologist. The concentration of the crew was so complete, none of them paid much
attention to me. One glanced my way, but went right back to
his task when I said I was just getting my purse from the
locker in the changing room and he saw I had no intention of
entering the solarium.

I retrieved my purse. When I came out there was still no
yellow tape barring the stairs up to the next level. I climbed
the stairs quietly, but not silently, not sneaking. It would attract
less attention and look slightly less suspicious, I figured.

The finished attic space covered only the back half of the
house, and the stairs ended in a tiny landing with doors on
either side and a short hall leading to the very back of the
house. I pushed open the first door, reached for the light
switch, then halted, remembering the sienna fingerprint
smudges downstairs. Using the eraser end of the pencil, I
flicked on the switch. I knew I had that thing along for a
reason.

It was a large room, bare, painted entirely in soft peach
tones and occupied by two tanning beds, two wall hooks, and
a shelf of clean, folded white towels and a stack of eye masks.

On the opposite side of the landing, the room was similarly
painted, bare with only three wall hooks and a speaker outlet

interrupting the pastel surfaces of the walls. A cabinet full of pure white towels and a shelf with a variety of oils stood against the inside wall. A masseuse's couch, draped in white, stood in the center of the room.

Both of these rooms were spartan to the point of ghostliness. I glanced quickly around the room again, making sure I hadn't missed something. As I stepped out I realized I had expected to see mirrors. Everywhere else in this place there were mirrors, lighting, softness. But especially mirrors.

Some sleazy, suspicious corner of my mind was actually checking for one-way mirrors in these two rooms. My mother would be appalled to know I think this way.

The room at the end of the hall was locked with a door of surprising sturdiness. I drew a credit card from my collection of basically useless spent cards. I never throw anything away. It took three minutes to slip the doorknob lock back.

Using the pencil again, I flicked on the light and saw a combination office and love loft, a defiantly masculine room tucked under the slope of the eaves. On one side it was complete with computer, desk, and hardcopy files. On the other side, a sleeper couch lay open, displaying rumpled satin sheets.

Three sealed envelopes, postmarked October 25, two days ago, the top one from an insurance company, lay on the otherwise neat desk. I copied DeAngelo's address.

The door to a closet was ajar. I pulled it open, again using the pencil eraser. Office supplies were neatly stacked on each shelf, except the one at shoulder level. It held two stacks of clean shirts in two different neck sizes.

I turned off the lights and quietly retraced my steps, ending in the kitchen. The cups had disappeared from the sink. I used a paper towel and opened the cupboard. They were there, lined up with several others. It occurred to me that I was overreacting.

Outside I stood on the sidewalk in front of the salon in the twilight, trying to figure out what to do next. Streetlights glowed, leaves scattered before the gusty light breeze, rattling down the sidewalk, across the street, and along the gutter. A faint scent of smoke and dust, barely discernible over the blanket of auto exhaust, the remnants of rush hour, filled my nose. I was tired, discouraged, and in need of a shoulder to lean on.

One brief attempt at glamour, and I ended up in a murder case. Worse yet, my best friend was a possible suspect. And just as soon as the forensic labs examined the footbath, they'd find Meredith's and my fingerprints.

# TEN

IT WAS FRIDAY. Seven-fifteen in the morning. I had overslept. Probably because I hadn't been able to fall asleep until three a.m.

My telephone was ringing. It was Meredith. "Stella, help. I'm in deep shit."

In thirty minutes Meredith was sprawled on my couch, wearing a black headband and a long-sleeved black jumpsuit with a high neck. I'd have thought she was just being histrionic, except her eyes looked like green olives floating in tomato soup, and there were ugly little fatigue pouches on her cheekbones.

"Meredith, what happened?"

"It was ugly, Stella. Stokowski started all gentle, asking about my family, whether I was married, had kids. What kind of shop I have, that sort of thing. He was, like, easing me into it."

"What time was that?"

"About eight last night."

"Where were you?"

"Downtown."

"Yeah, I know, but where downtown?"

"Third floor."

"Come on, Meredith. What room?"

"Why? What difference does that make?"

"It just does."

"Somebody's office, he said."

"With the plants and a desk?"

"Yes, dammit, why?"

"If he thought you were a suspect, he'd have taken you into the interview room. That's the one with the blinds he closes so you won't get distracted and the chairs that he moves real close so he's in your face. Stokowski uses the sergeant's office when he's trying to ease people into talking. So you're all right.''

She swallowed hard. "Well, he moved me into the interview room afterward.''

"Oh. After what?''

"After about ten p.m. After I told him I'd come to the salon to confront DeAngelo and give him an ultimatum.''

"That's all you said?''

She nodded.

"There has to be more, Meredith.''

"I just went over it and over it. Finally, I said I wanted to go home, and he let me go. Her lip trembled. "I went home and packed up and called here.''

"Packed up?''

She nodded. "I can't stay there. The whole time I was there I was peering out the window and listening for police sirens. I can't stand it.''

"Meredith, you're freaking out.''

She buried her head in her arms.

"Where's your car?''

"I left it at home. I didn't want anyone to know I was here.''

My phone rang. I ignored it. "What did he tell you at the very end?''

"Aren't you going to answer that?''

I shook my head. The answering machine clicked on. I heard Jason's voice and turned the sound off. Meredith looked puzzled.

"What's that about?''

"I'll tell you later. Let's get you sorted out first. How bad is it with Stokowski?''

She shook her head again, slowly, her hair moving in shiny ripples on the couch. "I don't know. He told me he'd be in touch. Asked if I was planning to leave town. I said no, but then I thought, maybe I should. Give them a chance to find someone else for a patsy.''

"Leaving town is a real bad idea, Meredith. Stokowski will think you're running."

"He'd be right. I would be."

I walked to the front window and peered into the street. There weren't any suspicious white four-door Fords out there. "How'd you get home from the police station?"

"He had a guy give me a lift." She sat up suddenly, rubbing her arms. "I feel so dirty. I've taken two showers already. They looked at me like I was some kind of rodent from the swamp."

"They don't meet a lot of really nice people, Meredith."

She rose and walked to Fluffy's cage. "Stella, can I stay here with you?"

"Mi casa, su casa. But he knows exactly where I live, remember. From before, if you recall."

She shuddered. "God, I don't know how you do it, Stella. You're so cool about all this. I just want to run and hide. He's going to come after me, Stella." She paced to the front window.

"Yeah, well. We have to do some thinking. I need food. Melted cheese on wheat toast with a swipe of mango chutney. Casein comfort. Primary protein." I found the cheese in the meat drawer wearing a fuzzy blue-green coat. I turned it over in my hand, trying to decide if it could be scraped and resuscitated. "Did you know casein is the chief ingredient in paints and adhesives, too?"

Meredith gagged and leaned her forehead against the glass windowpane. At least it distracted her.

"Stella, there's a white Ford parking outside with a chrome spotlight on the driver's door. I'm blowing this place."

She was halfway across the room before I got to her. "You'll be fine right here, just stay away from the window."

She grabbed her purse and a flashlight that I keep at the door. "I'm not talking to them again."

I grabbed her elbow. "This is nuts! They don't know you're here. And they couldn't possibly be ready to arrest you."

"Yes, they are. I'm out of here."

"Meredith, you can refuse to talk to them. Running makes you look so guilty."

"I already look guilty. Don't stop me." She was almost to the second-floor landing.

I grabbed her bags and followed her down the back stairs.

"They might be at the back, too. Go to the basement," I ordered. At least I could try to contain her, if I couldn't make her see reason.

We fled through the laundry room. I unlocked the door to the storage area and flicked on the light. Each of the tenants has a storage bin in the basement, eight-by-four-foot-square cubicles of plywood from floor to ceiling. Mine held my bike, skis, an assortment of old clothing, lamps, and three bookcases full of books that I couldn't bring myself to give away.

"Oh, no," Meredith said, planting her feet. "I'm not going in there."

"It's safe. No one will ever think of it."

"There's a reason for that. I'm not going in there."

"You'd rather sit in the dryer?" I unlocked the rough pine board door and shoved Meredith and her bags inside.

"There's live things in here."

"Sing to them. Softly."

"Don't lock me in!"

"I won't." I slammed the door. "I'll be down as soon as the cops are gone."

Why was Meredith so convinced she was about to be arrested? Lizette could just as easily have a great motive, and she had more at stake. Even David was more likely.

Back at the first floor, I peeked around the corner to see Stokowski talking to the manager. I sneaked up the back stairs and into my apartment in time to get a buzz from the lobby. I agreed to see Stokowski, thinking that anything less would have been suspicious, and maybe I'd find out why Meredith was so freaked.

Stokowski was wearing his perennial tweed sports coat with a teal tie and brown slacks. He looked tired and cranky, and it occurred to me that he might not have a sense of humor today; not that he was ever overburdened with one. Few things are hilarious in the homicide division.

I offered him a cup of coffee, which he accepted, and then we sat at the kitchen table, shoving the morning papers aside. I waited for him to speak first. That made for a long silence, since he was doing the same thing.

Tension crawled up my spine, arranging all my neurons in a taut rope that reached up my neck and made my head feel like a pumpkin on a stick. I drew in a breath, forcing myself to concentrate on the tiny cracks in the varnish on my table. It's oak, round, and old, so I had a lot to look at.

Finally, Stokowski broke the silence. "I went by Meredith's house this morning. She wasn't there." He paused, positioning his cup on the table, tracing the outline of the parrot on the cup with his finger. "This cup reminds me of Meredith."

"Oh?"

"Yeah, this parrot's poised to fly."

I sat there, staring at the elephant on my cup, wondering what I was poised to do. "Look, Stokowski, it's not personal, it's just that people don't normally rush to talk to homicide detectives. Especially when they've just spent a whole night answering questions."

Stokowski cleared his throat and looked uncomfortably away. He cradled his chin, *Thinker*-like, considering. I figured it was a show to reassure me—as if a homicide detective thinking is in any way reassuring. Especially when he's smart. "Look, Stella, just tell Meredith she's in big trouble."

"As in, it's lawyer time?"

He didn't answer, but the look in his eyes was confirmation. He was slow to speak again, and when he did, his voice was husky, almost warm, the more frightening because of it.

"Stella, you have to stay out of this. I know you and Meredith are best friends. I know you think you can trust her, but you *don't* know, maybe we never really know, what another human being might do, given certain circumstances."

"Bottom line, Stokowski—"

"Bottom line, Stella. We've got her nailed."

# ELEVEN

STOKOWSKI HAD BEEN clear that he had Meredith's death threat to take to the district attorney, as well as her presence at the scene. She had admitted she was there. And she'd given Stokowski hair, fingerprints, and blood samples. All he needed was time to sort out the little details, put together the paperwork, and take it to the district attorney. He said he was appreciative of her cooperation, and because of that he'd put in a good word for her.

He warned me again to stay out of it. "Or else." He hadn't said what the "or else" was, though, but it was probably a charge of obstructing justice.

But I knew Stokowski couldn't have written up all his paperwork this fast. He'd be foolish to; he wouldn't have final autopsy reports for two weeks, minimum. He wouldn't have some of the other forensic lab evidence in either, so he'd risk presenting an incomplete case if he took it to the district attorney this early. Stokowski was nothing if not careful. It was his pride and his success. He was thorough, and when he finally put a case before the DA it was tight. Even if it was wrong, it was tight.

And even if he did take it this early, the district attorney wouldn't begin to read it until Monday at the very earliest and more likely it would be midweek before he did.

I'd learned this because of an incident in the past. It's not nice to have to know this kind of stuff, but sometimes it's useful.

Realistically speaking, I had a good three to five days to find evidence that would convince Stokowski to look further than Meredith for suspects.

I decided to begin with a few calls. My friend at the motor

vehicle department grumbled but finally gave me Suzanne's address from the license registration after I promised an astrology reading. Next I called the pathologist at Denver General, but he wouldn't talk to me.

Finally, I put a call in to my mother's handyman. He was out earning more money than an astrophysicist, so I left a message on his voice mail asking about the nature of electricity.

Then I gathered up all my catalogs into a pile for Meredith. It would keep her busy while I was out. Finally, I switched on the voice of the answering machine so I could hear who was calling.

I checked Fluffy's cage, spritzed it with distilled water, and talked to him for a while. He was hanging by a despondent toe from the ceiling of his cage and refused to blink or flap his lips at me until I started to sing to him. He finally gave in and got a bit excited. Truman Capote maintained that chameleons like Chopin, but Fluffy prefers my lullabies. I can tell because his ribs pump in and out excitedly when I finish. It's lizard applause.

After that I took the catalogs down to Meredith. Frankly, Fluffy was more upbeat. Meredith was too depressed to stay in the storage unit, so I led her back to my apartment and settled her in the bedroom with the catalogs, a diet cola, some crackers and carrot sticks, and Fluffy to cheer her up.

"Meredith, besides the threatening letter and your presence at the salon yesterday, what does Stokowski have on you?"

She shrugged, her glance darting to the closet. "Maybe I left a message or two on DeAngelo's telephone."

"Meredith, I know you're in pain, and I wish I could make it better. But you've got to help me, otherwise Stokowski's going to charge you with DeAngelo's murder. What did you say in the message?"

She bit her lip until it had a little ridge in it when she let it loose. "I told him I'd seen him stay with Lizette. And I'd kill him. That was the first one. The second one I told him he'd roast or maybe I'd just fry him." She looked at me, her eyes pools of misery. "Stella, I couldn't have chosen worse words. And the last time I whispered so it would scare him. I told him he'd die. And a few other little things. I really wanted to scare him. But that was all."

"So you threatened him with death and torture. Anything else?"

She shook her head. "Nothing except a few letters. I don't know whether the cops have them or not. I went to the salon to get them back and whatever else I'd left." She sighed heavily. "I looked all over his room for them before he got there, but I didn't find them. I know he kept them, but damned if I know where. And I've lost the little anklet bangle he gave me. I thought maybe it was in the office in the bed, but it wasn't anywhere. I don't know where it went."

She gazed into the closet again. "You know what I feel like right now, Stella? Like I did kill him."

This kind of talk was going to land her permanently behind bars. I hoped she hadn't said this to Stokowski. "Back up a minute, Meredith. What's this about the anklet?"

"DeAngelo gave me an ankle chain with a little *M* with crushed diamonds on it. It's called…"

"I know. Pavé." I pictured the little *L* on Lizette's ankle even as Meredith stuck out her ankle with the empty chain. I wondered if DeAngelo gave each of his lovers an anklet bangle, as his own little harem symbol. "Where do you think you lost it?"

"I don't know. I noticed it Thursday morning. That was one of the reasons I came to the salon."

"Changing the subject—did DeAngelo ever talk to you about the shop?"

She refocused on me, puzzled. "Some. Usually only in general terms. When he was really stressed out."

"What stressed him out?"

"When the renovation didn't go right. He was trying to do

it all himself. Sometimes the clients. He had this one—you wouldn't believe how women fell for him—''

"Meredith!"

"Money. He was always short of cash."

"Coke is expensive."

She ducked her head, rubbing her temple with her thumb. "He didn't use it as much as Lizette said he did. Only when he was really down or stressed. He said he was quitting. Mainly he used the footbath and meditation to lift himself out of it."

"Where's his family?"

"He didn't have any."

"And David?"

"David's a good guy, a hard worker, and he's great at hair colors, better than DeAngelo. The best thing David ever did was insist they hire Virgil so DeAngelo would get off the renovation kick. It was a godsend when Virgil came on."

"Okay, changing the subject again. Was DeAngelo married to Lizette?"

"No! He couldn't have been. They didn't live together." Her gaze dropped guiltily to the bedspread.

"Meredith, are you sure there isn't something you haven't told me?"

"God, what else?"

"Like, if I go to DeAngelo's place am I going to run into Lizette?"

"More likely you'll run into cops." Her eyes were no longer brimming with tears every time I asked her a question, but there was a veiled quality to her gaze, as though she'd pulled a curtain over her thoughts and feelings, keeping them tucked inside where only she could see them.

"There's still something you haven't told me. I know it. You keep glancing away from me."

She looked at me, her eyes startled and large with dawning comprehension, the first sign I'd seen that she had engaged her left brain and was returning to reason. "Help me, Stella, please. I'm so scared."

IN HALF AN hour Meredith had fallen asleep, curled in a desperate, semifetal ball in the middle of my queen-size bed, a pillow clutched in her arms. At least she didn't have her thumb in her mouth.

I left a note on the telephone telling her I'd be back midafternoon and to wait for me. I'd never seen Meredith in such a state before. Usually she was a laid-back, open, go-with-the-flow woman—a little eccentric perhaps, but solidly in reality. This tense, panicky Meredith with the closet full of secrets was new and a little unnerving. I could hear Stokowski's husky warning about not knowing what someone else will do under "certain circumstances."

I drove to Meredith's attic apartment in Capitol Hill, wondering what he thought the "certain circumstances" were. My first thought was to check on her mail and pick up anything that might mislead the police. That wasn't illegal, since she hadn't been charged.

I parked a block away and approached her place from the west. I figured I'd head down the alley and go up the back way. When I saw the anonymous white Ford with the side spotlight parked across the street from the front door, I turned and strolled up the sidewalk past it. The car was locked. An empty clipboard lay on the passenger seat. Blue Freedent gum wrappers littered the ashtray and the dashboard.

I sauntered to the end of the block, crossed the street, walked halfway down the block, and entered the alley. Hers was the third house in, with a garage at the rear and outside wooden steps leading to her kitchen. I squinted at the little window. The yellow kitchen curtain moved abruptly. I was sure the police were searching her place.

My chest constricted and quickened my breath. I thought of the old saw. Just because you're paranoid, it doesn't mean they aren't out to get you. Maybe Meredith's anxiety wasn't as far-fetched as I'd thought.

I walked around to the front door. Silence and the scent of freshly applied lemon furniture polish greeted me. I climbed the oak stairs to the second floor. Mrs. Poland, in her flowered apron, was polishing the woodwork in the hall, working her way to the third floor. She had wound a kerchief around her spry white hair, noticeably leaving her ears and her barely discernible, state-of-the-art hearing aid uncovered.

She was listening in.

She moved industriously to the top step, just short of Meredith's door, and flapped the dust rag at me to tell me to stay put.

Heavy footfalls sounded from inside Meredith's apartment. I wondered if they noticed the scent of orange blossoms, Meredith's favorite. The door swung open. Mrs. Poland dusted on.

Stokowski emerged, glanced at her, chewed his cheek, and then caught sight of me. He stopped beside Mrs. Poland. "I think the woodwork looks fine now. You can stop."

He put a hand under her elbow and gently turned her around. He waited until she started down the stairs, then followed her to me. He leaned close to my ear and kept his voice low. "What is this, Stella? An obsession? Stay away from here, or I'll charge you with obstruction of justice."

"I'm standing in the *public* hallway, Detective. Minding my own business."

"I seriously doubt it." He tromped on down the stairs.

Mrs. Poland grinned at me and adjusted her hearing aid. "Stella, dearie, you watchin' out for killer vans? Any more near misses?"

A little chill ran over my shoulders. I had managed to put it right out of my mind until she brought it up. I shook my head.

Stokowski stopped on the steps below. "What near misses, Stella?"

"Nothing. She's talking about something long ago."

"I'm not. Detective, you should spend your time getting real killers like that van. Nearly killed this girl last Sunday. Instead you're out here wasting time chasing after innocent people. Big mistake. Now come on in here, Stella." Mrs. Poland swept me into her apartment and slammed the door. "Can you believe it? That dear girl." She carried the lemon furniture polish to the cupboard and placed it on the shelf. "Pepsi?" she asked.

"Sure," I answered and sank into her goosedown-cushioned chair. The seat puffed up around me and threatened to swallow me in comfort. I loved its warm security.

Mrs. Poland placed a glass of Pepsi on the table beside me and plumped herself down on the love seat. "I said all that in the hallway to put it to him, chasing after innocent girls, indeed. When there are dangerous goons on the street. I mean it when I say it isn't safe for you. That van was going for you and you need to be more careful. One of these days something real bad could happen."

Strangely, her concern seemed to banish mine. "Mrs. Poland. Trust me. I'm very careful."

"You don't even look when you cross the street most of the time. You young people think you'll live forever. When you get my age you know better." She took a sip of her Pepsi. "Caffeine keeps me going. I even give it to Bud when he's sleepy. The vet said it would kill a parrot, but Bud thrives on it. He's hooked, if you ask me. Now tell me all about it."

She had mellowed me, massaged my brain, and talked me into a near stupor. It would have been a pleasure to tell her, to lay it all out, facts, fiction, the whole thing, except that anything I said would be broadcast throughout her incredible crony network, so I chose my words carefully. "Meredith's all right, the police are just doing a thorough job."

"The police think she's done in that gorgeous hairdresser, dear. They're here gathering evidence, and you know it. Now, what are you going to do about it?"

"Well, I sure can't stop them."

"That's not what I mean." Her lips closed with a visible snap. She rummaged in her apron pocket, pulled out a crumpled picture, and handed it to me. It was a match to the picture of DeAngelo on Meredith's end table last Sunday night. Only now it had voodoo needles stuck in it. I held it loosely in my hand.

"Where did you get this?"

"I found it on the ground by the Dumpster this morning. I always do trash early."

"So does Meredith—"

"If I thought she'd done it, I'd have given this to the police," she said. "But I don't think she did. She was so taken with that man. She talked about him endlessly. She said she thought about him all the time. Wanted to have his babies." She put both gnarled, veined hands on her knees and leaned forward on them. "I don't think she would have harmed a hair on his head. I've seen this sort of thing before. Leads to heartbreak. Now you're her friend. Her best friend. And you have to do something. Or it'll be the end of her. She doesn't have anyone else, you know."

I did know. Meredith's only family was an aunt who lived in South Dakota. They weren't close. I and my family had been Meredith's for the last ten years. So why had she talked to Mrs. Poland about him endlessly? Why not talk to me?

Some of this must have shown on my face, because she immediately began to answer the question. "Sometimes we talk to people more readily when we don't know them well. That way we can present whatever truth we want."

When I left Mrs. Poland ten minutes later, she was sitting with her parrot Bud at the front window, her "eye on the world," as she called it. Her words, "whatever truth we want," rang in my ears as I turned the corner to walk to my car.

Meredith had been telling one truth—hers—but it wouldn't necessarily be *the* truth. The trouble with perceptions is that everyone has one, and they're not all the same. Like the blind men describing an elephant, each one perceives the truth as the part they feel.

I was still thinking about that and how I'd know when I was seeing things clearly when I passed the mouth of the alley that ran behind Meredith's apartment house. Stokowski and three other officers were gathered around the Dumpster for the block. A photographer was taking pictures of a black plastic bag. I sidled up, my stomach rolling nervously. This had all the earmarks of finding evidence.

One of the officers spotted me and motioned for me to stay back. I could still see.

The photographer lowered his camera. Stokowski squatted and, using a pen, lifted back the plastic bag, revealing a peach-colored-towel-draped bundle, the approximate size of a foot-bath. My heart began to beat heavily.

Stokowski waited patiently each time for the photographer to nod, indicating he'd finished, before he lifted the towels away. When he finished, I saw the footbath. I groaned.

Stokowski heard me and turned. "You need to leave, Stella."

"Anyone could have dumped it here. It could be anyone's footbath. They were a favorite Christmas gift, and they've all worn out at the same time."

He didn't say a word, just looked at me impassively.

"It's a frame-up, Stokowski, and you know it."

He just shook his head.

I SAT BEHIND the wheel of my car for several minutes, organizing my thoughts and calming myself. My breathing was shallow, my heart racing.

It *had* to be a frame-up. It *had* to be. Meredith was a be-liever in nonviolence. Hitting DeAngelo was a fluke. A once-in-a-life-time thing. She could *never* hurt anyone.

But Stokowski looked like he bought it, completely.

They'd been all over the salon when I left last night, but it seemed ordinary, almost casual. What changed that? What made Stokowski so suspicious? It must have been something Meredith had said.

Meredith hadn't helped herself one bit. God knows what she had said to Stokowski. She could have, in fact must have, incriminated herself right up to her pretty eyebrows. There are some people who have a proclivity for guilt, and she's one of them.

Mrs. Poland's words came to me like a judgment. I was Meredith's best friend; I had to do something, or it would be the last of her.

What if I couldn't do anything? My palms went cold and damp. I curled them into fists for warmth.

Not only would Meredith be charged, the real killer would be loose. Maybe to kill again. No, certainly to kill again. I thought about it some more. Sweat broke out on my brow. I started to shiver, started the car, and turned on the heater.

I'd been there when DeAngelo was electrocuted. I was a witness—except I wasn't, because I was wrapped up and strapped down with my eyes and ears conveniently covered.

What if Meredith hadn't been there? DeAngelo would have been dead, I would have been there, presumably a witness that no one was in there, and it might have been quite a long time before anyone even suspected murder. It would have been listed as accidental. A perfect murder.

But Meredith was there; she pulled the plug, and almost saved him.

So what made Stokowski think it wasn't an accident? I'd told him I thought it was murder, but that wouldn't be enough.

Could they have been looking specifically for a footbath? If so, why?

Meredith and I had fingerprints on it, but we'd have to. We had shoved it to the side when we started CPR. Unless it didn't have fingerprints on it. Didn't have...

She and I had done CPR, nearly reviving him. Maybe it was intended for her to be there, not to interrupt the murder, but to be a suspect. If DeAngelo was the victim, and Meredith was being framed as the fall guy, what was I? Nervous sweat trickled down my back and sides.

I scrubbed my face with my hands, trying to generate answers, I guess. My car rocked from passing traffic. I opened my eyes. Half a block away a white van was turning the corner. I shivered.

I had to do something. I couldn't just sit and wait for justice to ride down from the heights and rescue us. Besides, action always makes me feel like I'm going forward.

I decided to start with DeAngelo. Why would anyone want to kill him? The letter I'd seen on his desk in the love loft had been addressed to Anthony DeAngelo. I was pretty sure I could remember the address. He was dead, so he at least couldn't hurt me.

And if Lizette were really his wife and had been there, that would be okay, too. Because she was next on my list of people to find and grill.

I started the car and pulled into traffic, paranoid enough to watch my rearview mirror for cars following me.

DeAngelo's address was on East Virginia in Glendale, a little community located in and completely surrounded by the city of Denver. I parked on the street, got out, locked the car, and faced a rabbit warren of townhouses with shingles and raked roofs à la Cape Cod. A little out of place, since Denver is a desert, where grass is maintained only with careful, continuous watering.

I located DeAngelo's house up a flight of open wooden steps, quaintly twisted above a rock garden. It was all very picturesque, and probably deadly in an ice storm. The front door, painted cottage blue, echoed hollowly with my heavy knock. I shamelessly peered in the front window and saw a tastefully decorated room in various shades of cream and burnt orange, with a very large ginger tabby snoozing in a pool of sunshine on the floor. A matching cat. My estimation of DeAngelo's perfectionism rose another notch.

My stomach growled. Who was feeding the cat? I knocked

again. The cat stretched, yawned, and jumped solidly to the windowsill, meowing at me. He pawed the windowpane with clawless paws. Meowed again. He could live a long time without food, but he'd need water. I peered in, looking for signs of a water or food dish. Not likely in the living room. I tried the front doorknob and found it locked.

At the back of the units, a similar but less picturesque set of stairs led to the kitchen door. I climbed them and knocked on the back door. The cat answered with a pitiful meow.

Food and water dishes stood on the floor by the kitchen sink, but both were empty. I tried the doorknob. It was unlocked. Maybe the police had already been there and left the door unlocked by mistake. I pushed the door open and stepped in.

It was a very tasteful condo kitchen, clean and remarkably tidy for a bachelor pad, with only a mug, a spoon, and an ashtray soaking in the sink. And remarkably free of police fingerprint powder. Maybe they hadn't been here yet.

The cat immediately rubbed himself against my ankles, arching his neck, begging. I patted him, filled his water dish with water, and replaced it on the floor. He lapped it up without hesitation. I found a bag of dry cat food in the lower cupboard next to the sink and poured a dishful. He buried his head in the bowl, crunching as though starved. "Good kitty," I said, and rubbed his ears. He growled. He wasn't as affectionate now that he had his food.

If Stokowski found me here, he'd jail me. I straightened, told myself to leave, and took a step toward the door. My gaze fell on the telephone answering machine. The message light was blinking.

I punched buttons, finally hitting on the right combination. The machine wasn't too unlike the one my mother had. A beep sounded; the message was from the day before yesterday. A breathy whisper, Meredith's voice, filled the room. "De-Angelo. It's me again. I'm going to call until you answer me—"

A door banged.

The cat, startled, raced out of the kitchen to the living room. My heart stopped, then thumped. I glanced first to the back door, expecting to see the stolid navy form of the police. Nothing. I peered around to the front door. Nothing. I strained to hear. Nothing.

I sidled back to the answering machine, turned down the volume, and idly began to go through the stack of paper messages by the phone.

The toilet flushed. Someone was in there with me.

The cat raced in from the living room, vaulted to the kitchen counter, and skidded, knocking a plastic glass to the floor. I stepped to the back door, yanked it open.

"What are you doing here? What do you want?"

My hair stood up on end. I turned.

David stood barefoot, in wrinkled polo shirt and jeans, his hair ruffled, eyes sleepy, and a sleep crease on his left cheek. Dark smudges beneath his eyes made him look mean and debauched, and the smell of stale alcohol hovered around him. He scrubbed his face with both hands to clear his brain.

My brain was in cell-lock from fright. For a long moment the only sound was the cat, crunching the nibblets I'd poured for him. "I thought this was DeAngelo's place."

David noticed the blinking light on the answering machine and punched it off. "How the hell did you get in here?"

"The back door was open. I thought this was DeAngelo's place—"

"It is. Was. It's mine."

The cat snorted and snatched another mouthful of food. "I thought the cat was starving."

"He is. He's on a diet." He glanced at the cat's nearly empty food dish, frowned, and grabbed it away from him. "He's not supposed to eat. He's too fat."

"I didn't mean to. I thought—"

An angry flush was creeping up his neck. "This is a *two-*

bedroom condo. DeAngelo shared the place. But we're not gay.''

"I didn't say—"

"You thought it. Everybody does. Hairdresser equals gay."

"Hey! Don't get defensive. I was just terrified. I thought DeAngelo lived here alone."

He glared at me, then drew in a breath, and some of the latent tension in his face eased. "How *did* you get in here?"

"The back door was open. Unlocked, I mean."

"And you just walked in?"

I didn't want to get into all that. "David, listen. I need your help, badly—"

"Help what? He's dead."

In spite of his blurry-brained act, there was a gleam of intelligence peeking out from under his eyebrows. I weighed the possibility that he'd strangle me on the spot and decided to risk it. I slid into a chair opposite him, still close to the doorway. "The police suspect Meredith killed him, and they're building a case against her."

He shook coffee into a filter basket, filled an automatic drip coffeemaker with water, and flipped the switch on before he slumped into a chair, scratched his chest, and focused his bleary brown eyes on me again. "I happen to think so, too. So why would I help you?"

"The point is, she didn't. That means the police are not looking for the real killer. And that means there may be more murders. You don't want that, do you?" God knows, I was praying he wasn't the real killer. "And I think you can help."

Hostility lay so close to the surface I could almost feel it. He seemed to be grinding his teeth. "What do you want to know?"

I thought he'd talk more easily if we started on the easy stuff. "Tell me about DeAngelo. What kind of guy was he? Why would anyone kill him?"

He gazed over my shoulder, focusing on some happier distant place for several moments. "He had charisma, you know what I mean?"

I nodded and murmured. He'd said this before in different words. He was stalling for time, thinking. The brewing coffee smelled good and very strong. "A lot of people who are charismatic have a depressed side—," I prompted.

"Sometimes he'd get real down. Mostly, he'd stay incredibly busy, but when things were slow, then he'd dream up some new thing to do. That's how we got into the salon. Tony got depressed, and one day he went out and bought the place. It was like it gave him a new purpose, for a while anyway. Like he was always on stage. We used to do plays together as kids, but he needed to hear the applause, really needed it, to know they liked him, I guess."

"He'd sort of outrun depression? By distracting himself?"

"Yeah, kind of like that."

"And women were one of the ways he distracted himself?"

David shrugged. "I guess. He was always attractive to women."

"Did any of the women ever get mad? Threaten him?"

"Sure. Meredith. She was something else. That babe is scary." His answer was a nanosecond too fast, blaming.

"You don't like Meredith?"

"Don't care one way or the other. But the things she thinks of..."

I waited, but he didn't complete the thought. "What do you mean, 'the things she thinks of'?"

He shrugged. "You heard her on the tapes. That's just part of it. She's obsessed. She calls him maybe twenty times a day. Here. And at the salon."

"But he was pretty serious about Meredith?"

"He might have married her, eventually. He was talking about kids—to take care of him in his old age." He laughed. "Talk about a delusion. You know what a delusion is? A dangerous illusion—get it?"

I decided to move off this subject. "He'd been dating Lizette, too. Meredith said he was breaking up with her."

David frowned. His voice dropped a notch. "Yeah, he said he was going to. 'Bout broke her up. She was real upset. I don't know, she's not going to get over this very soon."

"Lizette said she and DeAngelo were married."

David rose, got out mugs, and poured coffee for each of us. I watched closely, making sure I wasn't going to be poisoned. He was using it to give himself time to think. "No, he wasn't married to her."

"She has that huge ring."

He replaced the coffeepot on the warmer, sat, and took a sip before he replied. He was definitely considering his words. "He wasn't married to her."

"Maybe he wouldn't tell you."

"I'd know."

I tasted the coffee. It was strong and rich. If it was poisoned, at least it tasted good. "You two were pretty close?"

David tipped his chair back on two legs and began to look restless, glancing pointedly at the clock. "Like brothers."

"Did you notice whether Lizette left the reception desk at any time yesterday?"

"I think she was there. I can't see her very well from my station, so I couldn't swear to it."

The interview was nowhere. I'd been sidetracked. I was nervously gripping the mug so tight my fingers hurt, but I didn't know why. What was it about David? After all, I hadn't exactly lied and he hadn't threatened me. So why was I having trouble?

I took a couple of deep draws on the coffee and decided we'd been nicey-nicey too long. "How careful was DeAngelo about dosing his coke when he did the footbath?"

"I don't know what you're talking about."

"I know he used. Lizette and Meredith have both confirmed."

He banged his chair down. "He was very careful, and he wasn't using much anymore."

"But you worried about it?"

"No. He was quitting."

"You argued with him, too, didn't you?"

"No!"

He was lying. His gaze faltered. The hollows of his eyes deepened, like he was looking out from a great depth at something turned sour. "Did you fight over Meredith as well as money and drugs?" I asked.

"Time to go."

"DeAngelo is the one who was the shop draw, right? He was the big name. He got the women, he was the magnet." David's jaw was clenching. I remembered the envelope on DeAngelo's desk from the insurance company. "Without him, you're now owner of the salon. Jealousy and money are powerful motives."

"Get out!" He rose slowly, barely controlled, more menacing than if he'd leapt up. He was six feet tall, a lot of muscle.

I got up and backed down the hall to the front door, glad I'd left it open. I realized I still had the half-full coffee mug in my hand.

I glanced behind me, making sure I wouldn't squash the cat in my getaway, and ran my gaze over his living room one more time. The cat was batting at something beneath the chair. He pushed it into view. It was a pink spike-heeled shoe.

I grinned and stepped over the threshold. "Mending poor Lizette's broken heart?"

A flush rose on his chest and neck. He brought up a hand in a fist. Then he caught himself, flexed his fingers, and gripped the door. His eyes were narrowed, hostile.

"You're pretty scary yourself, David."

He slammed the door shut.

I left the mug on the railing.

# TWELVE

I'D LEARNED A little more about DeAngelo: that he and David had argued, presumably about money and Meredith and coke and who knows what else. And now suddenly David would get it all. And the "widow" Lizette had spent the night with David—grieving, no doubt. It wouldn't be the first time a partner killed to get the business and the woman.

I was sure it was Lizette's pink shoe, and I figured she would use the back door, since I'd left by the front. I got in my Taurus and moved it to where I could see David's back door.

Someone had alerted the police even before they got to the hospital. The police officer had left but returned to the salon within moments. If Lizette had accused Meredith, or me, in the ambulance with the emergency medical technician, that would account for the rapid police involvement. Or maybe just the mention of coke was sufficient.

My impression of Lizette, if I could rely on it, was that she wasn't the swiftest. But that could be what David called a delusion—a dangerous illusion. I rather liked that. When I thought about it, everyone at the shop was in the business of illusions. I had the illusion of puffy, vibrant hair. I wondered who else had illusions—and then I thought about Jason's appointment. What was he having done to his hair? Color? What illusion did he have running? And most of all, why?

I was still pondering illusions when Lizette came tripping down the back steps in her pink shoes, wearing an enormous sweater that reached midway to her thighs, and carrying a ridiculously large pink purse. She got into an elderly little blue car.

Lizette drove only about eight blocks, to one of the three-storied yellow brick apartment buildings ubiquitous in southern Glendale. It was an L-shaped building with pool-steamed windows in the first floor of the el and a tattered awning over the front door, fluttering in the breeze. It stood in the shadow of the sleek, elegant Giorgio Hotel, providing contrast.

I marked her address as well as her license tag number in my little log book and followed her into the building. The building roster didn't list apartment numbers, only door phone numbers. I scanned the roster. Lizette Lewis. I rang. Instead of an answer I got a buzz from the door. Lot of good that security measure did.

I didn't know her apartment number, so I entered and walked down the hall on the first floor to the back stairs. Up those to the second floor, then the third. A door opened at the front. Lizette poked her head out.

"Oh, you!" She glared at me, opened the door wider, and stood on the threshold, her mahogany hair moussed to little spikes. She had shed her heels and her enormous sweater and wore a sweater as snug as paint over a leather microskirt and opaque tights. Her lower lip puffed out in a pout. "I don't want to talk to you. You made David mad. What do you want?"

"May I come in?"

Her eyes narrowed to vaguely blue slits. "You're the reporter, aren't you?" Wheels were turning in her pretty head. "I suppose you can come in. But I'm very busy. I have things to do, you know. It's been a tragic time for me."

I'd almost forgotten about that little lie. The trouble with lies is, it's so much work remembering them. "Won't take much time."

It was a very feminine place, done nicely but inexpensively in southwestern colors of faded aqua and mauve with dark turquoise accents. Several magazines, topped by *Self,* lay primly on a little table at the end of the couch. Lizette closed the door behind us and let out a long-suffering sigh. "Now, what do you want?"

"Lizette, I see you as one of the…principal people at the salon. You're at the reception desk, and you must see everyone who comes in. You're the first person they meet at the shop, and you make the first impression. So—let's start with you. Were you with David and DeAngelo before they opened this salon?"

"Well, let's see." She lowered herself gracefully to the couch and rolled her eyes in coy blue calculation. "I met DeAngelo at the Puss N Boots Bar. Happy hour, you know. I was a waitress there. They had the cutest outfits for us, little lacy bra tops with leather miniskirts and leggings that looked like hooker's boots you could put right over tennies. Saves your feet, you know." She looked at me speculatively for a moment. "You probably don't know. Anyway, I waited on him, and he was there until closing. He hired me the next morning. He said I had the right presentation of self for the salon. He meant the right look. He always used classy language."

She hadn't actually answered my question. "Lizette, did you—"

She gushed on. "I was a leg model—you know, stockings and shoes mostly." She stretched out first one and then the other of her legs as proof. I wasn't sure which she wanted me to notice, that she didn't have roller-skating scars on her knees, or that there was not a single razor nick on her ankles, or that she had a new ankle bracelet, a gold heart with a tiny diamond. "Nice bangle."

"Oh, that old thing!" Preening. "Now, where was I? Oh, I wasn't looking for anybody special. But I'd been talking to my guardian angel 'bout how I need to find a guy. And then I saw DeAngelo, and there it was. Like magic. He fell for me on the spot. He never could stay away. Some things are meant to be. He couldn't resist." She shrugged whimsically and admired her ring, glinting in the light. "Fate."

"Yesterday you said DeAngelo gave you that ring. David said you weren't married."

Her chin rose. "We would have been...soon."

"And your ring?" I asked.

She stared me straight in the eye. "DeAngelo wanted me to have it."

Her defiance, her careful, odd wording, and an air of wistfulness made me wonder how to ask her if she'd made up the whole marriage story.

I was about to try when she rose, glided to the window, and posed in the sunshine, letting the light illuminate the mahogany color of her spiked hair and her high cheekbones. Very photogenic. And very convenient; I couldn't see the expression in her eyes.

She raised her face to the sun. "Sometimes when I close my eyes in the sunlight I can see the light of my guardian angel. I'm a real spiritual person." She turned suddenly to me. "Am I talking too fast?"

"Too fast?"

"You're not writing."

"Photographic memory."

"Oh. Cool."

"Lizette, let me get straight what you do. When a client calls in, you make the appointments, take down their name, telephone number, and address, and note it in the computer."

"I print it in the book and on a card and give it to whichever stylist is going to see the client."

"You write their name and phone number in the appointment book?"

"Nope. It's a special book. DeAngelo keeps it."

"What else do you do? Manicures? Hair washing? Computer?"

"I'm the receptionist, the hostess, and sometimes I help out Gerta with manicures, depending on her schedule. I'm real good with polish."

"And the computer?"

She smiled. "I'm just the receptionist. Davey and DeAngelo take care of the computer stuff."

"How long has Gerta worked at the salon?"

Lizette returned to the couch, frowning. "Gerta? Maybe a couple months. Are you going to have her in the story?"

"Do you know where she lives?"

She shook her head.

"And Suzanne? What's her last name?"

"That's confidential information. I can't give it out. Besides, I don't know." She was lying, of course. Just two days ago, when I was scoping out the place and Suzanne breezed in, she'd used it. I was pretty sure she had said Suzanne McAllister.

"Well, I figured you and Suzanne would want to be featured in the story. Picture—?" I'd caught her attention now.

She wavered, touched her hair, what there was of it, spikes and all. "And a full write-up—?"

"Lizette, remember, you're key at the salon, so the story depends on you."

"Well, maybe—"

"But I have to have a little on the others, or it won't be balanced. You know—"

"Oh. So, what else?"

"I thought Virgil—how do you spell his last name?"

She looked at me with sympathy. "I'm not great at spelling either," she confided. "J-o-h-n-s-o-n."

"And he does...?"

"Virgil mostly does the building stuff."

"Yesterday he was picking up in the solarium."

"Well, he does the heavy stuff, like any lifting. Those wet towels are nasty, and the footbaths get heavy." She arched her back. "I have back trouble."

"I heard DeAngelo and you had a fight the other night."

She shook her head nervously. "It was nothing. And we made right up again."

"Meredith said he was breaking off with you. That he was planning to marry her."

"She lies! He wasn't. She was just another one of his clients. Like Suzanne. And all the others. That's just the way he was." Her cheeks flushed. "He'd tell them they were gorgeous and talk them up. He didn't mean it."

"Lizette, did you mention to the ambulance crew that DeAngelo used drugs?"

She drew up in righteous indignation. "I'd never snitch!"

"The cute EMT, what was his name?"

She frowned. "I didn't think he was all that cute. They don't really earn much, you know? I mean when you think they're almost doctors and all."

"Was his name Bob?"

"Dan. I'm pretty good with names."

I made a note of Dan's name. I could call him later. "I'll bet he was surprised to hear DeAngelo used coke with his footbath, wasn't he?"

"You know, he was! He said he thought he'd heard it all. And he wrote it right down. I'll bet he hears a lot."

"I'll bet he was surprised to hear about Meredith, too."

Her eyes narrowed. "Is this part of the story?"

"That's up to you."

This time, when she glared straight at me, I had the sense she wasn't lying. "Well, she *was* there. She's the cause of all this. She's why DeAngelo is dead. I saw her with the electric plug in her hand."

So Lizette had fingered Meredith. "That's why it was so important for you to be in the ambulance. So you could alert them."

Her chin trembled. "And so I could be with him."

"And you were at David's last night for...comfort?"

Her face clouded over. "DeAngelo was my very best friend in all the world, and I was so lonely I couldn't stand it. And David was pretty bummed, so we just hung out together, you know what I mean?"

"Awesome."

"Yeah, awesome."

I LEFT HER in the doorway, mourning DeAngelo in her own special way. I felt depressed and grizzly, and not just because I was starving. I'd seen something in Lizette's eyes that I recognized. The terrible need to love and be loved. It was a drive that I knew personally was a terrific force, strong enough to propel me into a lousy situation in the past. What might it have driven Lizette to do?

I started the car and pulled into traffic, still toying with the notion of illusions and the illusion Lizette had been creating. On the surface she appeared to be so polished. Perfect. Then she opened her mouth. Meredith looked perfect, too, in a different way. Was that what attracted DeAngelo? Perfection? And when the illusion shattered, was that when he left? Had Lizette killed him when the illusion of his love crumbled?

I kept coming back to illusions. Why were they important? And what were mine?

I slowed for a traffic light, then signaled and changed lanes. A van ripped alongside of me, the driver waving a rude finger in my direction. I thought about my illusions, that I was competent, capable, smart—and safe. At least I was damn good at writing an astrological lovelorn column and running across white vans. I was beginning to dread seeing one.

I stopped at a 7-Eleven for a hot dog and a Super Big Gulp and phoned in to Zelda. The hot dog was great. It gave me indigestion before I'd even finished it. Zelda made it worse.

"Gawd, what have you done now? Gerster's threatening to pull your column." The rest of what she said was a confused blurr involving Stokowski and Jason.

By the time I got to the office, Stokowski and Jason had left and Mr. Gerster was in his office with his door shut. It's an unwritten rule that no one interrupts him when the door is shut, but I didn't think I could wait. I knocked, remembering the first time I had come to his office, expecting to see the Clark Gable of small-press publishing.

Mr. Gerster grunted, and I pushed the door wide. "I understand you have a few questions for me." I wished I was wearing a sober outfit from my former life as an accountant. It's so much easier to emanate power from navy blue than from pink and orange.

"Sit down, Miss Stargazer." He used my title like my mother used my full name after an enormous sin, such as floating pillow feathers through the fan to make a snowstorm.

"Mr. Gerster, I'd—"

He held up a hand, halting my mouth. "Miss Stargazer, this hurts me worse than it does you—" I'd heard that old phrase several times as a child. And I still didn't believe it.

"Detective Stokowski told me you were at a crime scene again. I told you on Monday that I was concerned about you being in danger, and it seems to me that this column of yours is leading you into trouble. Detective Stokowski said a van nearly ran you down. I refuse to be a part of anything that will endanger you—in any way."

"Mr. Gerster, this has nothing to do with my column. Nothing whatsoever. It's a total freak accident, a complete coincidence I was even there, either time."

He rubbed his mouth, his lips totally disappearing into his face. The chill of his soul-deep disapproval settled over me, raising goose bumps on my shoulders and down my arms.

"Miss Stargazer—"

"Stella, please." His wife had even given me an afghan last May; surely he could call me Stella.

"Stella, I know you think you're invincible. Jason has told me you have complete confidence in yourself. But we both think you'd be safer if you were—"

"Jason has told you to pull my column?"

"He agrees that you're in some kind of crisis—"

"I am not, *not*, in a crisis. Jason doesn't have the right to say a thing about it! How dare he!"

"Now, Stella, you are overreacting again—"

"I am not overreacting, Mr. Gerster. I am furious! This is so unfair. Why would Jason have a thing to say about this?

Do you consult him on everything, or just on my life? Do you ask him when you can take a—lunch hour?''

''Now, now—''

''No. It's not 'now, now.' My column accounts for more readers than the whole rest of the paper now. How can you even dream of pulling the column? You don't—''

''I do what I think is best. For the paper, *and* for you.'' He rose from behind his desk and edged toward the far wall for safety, keeping his nervous hands in front of himself. Anyone else would have jammed fists onto hips, but Mr. Gerster doesn't have hips. Fluffy has better hips than he has. He glowered at me from the corner behind his desk. I glowered right back.

''Does this mean you're firing me?''

''No. It means your column won't appear in the paper until I'm satisfied that you're safe.''

''And just what do I have to do to achieve safety? Get a written statement from my mommy? Maybe permission from the great god, Jason? Or Detective Stokowski? Just what asinine excuse do I need to have? A suit of armor, perhaps? Bulletproof vest? Sex change?''

Mr. Gerster was blinking rapidly.

''That's what I need—testosterone. Maybe a testosterone patch under my skin to give me that leaner look, biceps, and a five o'clock shadow on my face, so I can sashay around this office and be a guy.''

I think that last line did it. I wish I could say that I regretted it as soon as it was out, but I didn't. I was so upset and angry I was shaking, but I was determined to hold my own and proud of it. I wasn't going to back down.

Mr. Gerster raised a trembling finger and pointed at the door. ''Go.''

*Now* I was going to back down. ''Mr. Gerster—''

''Go.''

I was halfway out the door when he cleared his throat. "Stella?"

I turned, hopeful he was changing his mind. "Yes?"

He held out a bundle of envelopes. "Your correspondence."

# THIRTEEN

I WAS GLAD that Jason wasn't there. I sat at my warm, lovable oak desk in the corner of the back room at the newspaper office and stroked it, feeling the tiny splinters, the grooves from wear, the old familiar stocking-snagging slivers, all now quite precious to me.

Resting my head in my hands, I stared at the doodles on the desk pad. Endless loops and swirls. Little tornado funnels. By squinting and tilting my head to my left shoulder, I could see a black blot, myself in miniature, storm-tossed and upside down in the midst of the largest funnel. Bleak.

The mental list of my life's mess included harassment by white vans, my car damaged, my bank account undernourished, my column—and thus my meager income—on hold because of Jason's perfidy, my best friend inhabiting another ozone layer, my love life in limbo, and worst of all, the best hairdresser I'd ever had electrocuted in a footbath while I snoozed on a hard bench in the same room. I was fine. Really.

And as soon as I could calm down Mr. Gerster, discover who really killed DeAngelo, get a paycheck, and sort out my life I would be in great shape. If I could just live long enough.

My phone rang. It was Jason. "Stella, I have to talk to you. I heard what Gerster is doing—"

"And I heard you said I was in a crisis. Well, I wasn't in a crisis until you stuck your nose in. Are you deliberately trying to undermine me?"

"Not true. I just said I was afraid someone was harassing—"

"You're jealous of my column's success?"

"Of course not—"

"Oh, I know. A hidden desire to wear dresses and write to the lovelorn!"

"Stella—"

"And for that I should stop writing my column?"

"I offered to stay with you all the time to protect you."

"That's it! The great testosterone solution! Why on earth didn't I think of that? I can call my friendly local gynecologist and remedy my shortcoming, so to speak."

"Stella, I'm sorry—"

"Your conscience pricking you?"

"You're just looking for an excuse to blame it on me!"

"Of course I am. I feel like sin, and you, who are supposed to be a friend, have made things worse."

"There's a message for you on my desk—and chocolate in the bottom drawer.... Peace?"

"Only one piece?"

I FOUND THE message for me. It was my mother's handyman, returning my call. I dialed him immediately.

"Oh, sure, yeah. You could kill with household voltage, for sure. But those footbaths are made to be safe, Stella. It'd take some real tinkering to bypass the safety device. It's my guess something else killed him. He have a weak heart?"

"Say it's normal. Could a footbath work if you took the safety box off the cord?"

"Depends on who took it off. If someone knows what they're doing it would, pro'bly. Who you gonna kill?"

"So suppose that I figure a way to wire it. What would the electrocution look like? Would I hear noise? Smell anything?"

"Well, look. Electricity is powerful stuff. It knocks out the human body's electrical timing. So if anything's wrong with his heart, he's likely to die easier. If it's a vigorous healthy man...this gets really gruesome here. Well, if it's a high-voltage jolt, you're likely gonna get some noise, some burning smell, and it'll go to ground, so the bottoms of the feet would be burned. Maybe even a scorch mark on the floor or tub. If it's low voltage you'd pro'bly not get any noise, maybe not any smell. You might not even get external burns.''

"So what you're saying is that there's a range of possible injuries, and unless it's a huge jolt, or a long time, or there's some other factor, like a weakened heart, the amount of electricity alone probably wouldn't kill him.''

"Well, it could—it's just everyone's a little different.''

"What if there was a load of cocaine on board?''

"Now, that could do it. Enough coke, you don't need the electricity.''

"Thanks.''

"You get any more questions, you call, hear?''

I cradled the receiver and looked down at the drawer where I'd been rummaging for Jason's promised chocolate. I found it right under a Burberry College alumni magazine, the autumn alumni fund drive edition. I'd heard of Burberry somewhere. Smart, exclusive, Ivy League private college stuck in my memory.

I flipped through it. Rolling hills, vivid autumn hardwood trees, pristine paths, residence halls covered in ivy. I started to put it down, and then the address label caught my eye. Jason Paul Gordon.

The telephone number and address for Burberry College was conveniently printed on the back cover and three inside pages, just in case you were bitten by the contribution bug. I telephoned them. They were courteous and finally gave me the address of the family of Jason Paul Gordon, so that I could reach his sister to invite her to her class reunion. No wonder Jason was the way he was. His family lived in a New York post office box.

The alumni office was not forthcoming with any other information about Jason, except for his class year. Assuming he was eighteen as a freshman, he was twenty-eight now, older than I'd thought.

So why was Jason here under half his name? Hiding out from the family fortune? Or banished because of some little sin? It sort of explained where he'd get the money to buy a Miata on a DDO salary. It didn't fit the image I had of him. It left me feeling uneasy. I had preached to Meredith about how she didn't really know DeAngelo, and I'd been much too right. Now here I was interested in someone I apparently didn't know very well. It might well be nothing, but it might not. I could feel myself building an emotional wall around myself. I left the magazine on his desktop, address label up. He'd get the idea.

I returned to my desk and put in a call to my buddy at the motor vehicles department. There were no Virgil Johnsons listed with the department.

I fanned out the correspondence Mr. Gerster had handed me. One of the envelopes bore my mother's return address. It was stiff and a little bulky. I slit it open and shook it out. A postcard, addressed to my mother, fell to the desktop. I picked it up and turned it over. There were three sentences and the instructions, "Check all that apply."

I am alive, well, and thinking of my loving mother.
I am on my deathbed and need my mother to comfort me.
I will telephone my mother right now so she will stop worrying about me.

I felt a great wide rubber band squeezing my chest, so tight it was hard to draw a breath. I was in way over my head.

Stokowski and Gerster were right. I had no business being involved. I didn't have the foggiest notion of how to investigate a crime, especially a murder. I had overreacted to everything except DeAngelo's death, which I'd conveniently stuffed away so I wouldn't get scared and upset. Instead of grieving like any normal person, I'd blundered all around, merely irritating people and possibly causing even more trouble for Meredith.

The worst thing about confidence is how fast it can desert you.

My phone rang. I stuffed my thumbs in my ears and closed my eyes. I needed to organize my thoughts, get the little that I knew clear, make sure Stokowski had the information, and trust in him and in…and in… The word "justice" wouldn't pass my lips, even in a whisper.

"Stella!" A hand shook my shoulder. Slut-red nails and Passion perfume. Zelda. "Stella, it's your mother. She's fixed extra tuna casserole, and you're to bring Meredith with you." A thin line of worry lay along Zelda's forehead, making her eyes look a very deep, sad blue-violet.

"I wish *I'd* thought to call and ask for tuna casserole. Thank you, Zelda. My mother loves you, too. Want to come?"

She shook her head. "Nah. This is my night to do my toes. Feet are real sexy, you know. Gotta keep ready. I never know when a stud will tear down my door and lick my toes."

"You do your own toes?"

"Course."

"In a pedicure tub?"

"Dr. Scholl."

"Little motor and all?"

She nodded, the line on her forehead deepening in puzzlement. "Yeah. Why?"

"Describe the electric cords."

Her face wrinkled up. "Cord. Short, simple, and with a little safety box. Just one cord. You fill the thing with water, put it where you're going to do your feet, plug it in, and stick in your footsies. Twenty minutes later you've got the happiest feet in town. Wanna try it?"

"Not two cords?"

Zelda frowned. "You're not supposed to get into this, Stella. Call Stokowski and tell him about the second cord." A sly grin grew on her face, erasing the worry lines. "Better yet," she said. "I'll call him. I'll get him to my place and demonstrate the tub for him. With my naked feet.'' She left, moving so fast her feet barely touched the ground.

I called my mother to tell her I'd be there and felt better after hearing her voice. I shoved the letters into my purse and gave my desk one last loving stroke. On the way out I heard Zelda leaving a message for Stokowski.

It was four-thirty, and the sun was hanging close above the mountains. Cloud wisps trailed across the sky in chilly mare's tails. Twin silver contrails streaked the sky from east to west, reminding me of…the *two* electric cords I'd seen leading from the footbath where DeAngelo's feet were immersed, to the wall plug.

I was *positive* there were two electric cords. That had to be how the footbath was rigged. It would be simple just to run a live, bare-ended cord into the tub. But Stokowski hadn't said anything about a hole in the footbath. Maybe there wasn't one. Maybe there weren't any fingerprints on the footbath they found in the solarium. Maybe it was what *wasn't* there that made him suspicious.

At a stoplight I closed my eyes, picturing the whole scene again. Two cords. Plain as day. It didn't prove who did do it, but for me, it proved Meredith didn't. She is so technologically illiterate she cannot change an electric plug. Barely changes lightbulbs. Has been in fact afraid of electricity ever since she jolted herself in a high school physics class experiment on series and parallel wiring. She still uses a ledger for her shop's accounts.

It wasn't far out of my way to go past the salon, and chances were good that Stokowski was there. I could talk to him about the hole in the footbath and Meredith's electricity fears. Then maybe he'd start looking at all the other suspects seriously.

Yellow police tape crossed the front door of the salon, and two white police cars were parked in front. Curtains were drawn across the windows, and vague shadows moved inside. I wondered if the police were looking for something specific…like a footbath with two cords.

I circled the block and drove down the alley. Yellow tape also barred the back door, but not the garage. A light burned inside.

I parked beside a battered red Yugo and stepped from the car, my car keys in hand. I was guessing the Yugo belonged to Virgil, because there was a toolbox and carpenter's apron in back. I couldn't picture the ladies of the salon driving around with that on the backseat. With any luck he'd be in the garage. He was sullen, but at least he liked Meredith.

Trying to look casual, I approached quietly and peeked around the corner of the garage. The door was barely ajar. I knocked softly—softly enough that a wild bird wouldn't have heard it, then leaned in the door.

The garage was stuffy and dim, but surprisingly spacious. The windows, one centered on each wall, were covered with opaque paper, and the whole thing was lit by a single overhead lightbulb hanging from a cord in the center of the ceiling. Metal shelving lined the walls, with boxes stacked floor to ceiling across the garage, dividing it into two rooms. The only thing I could see beyond the boxes was a dingy gray metal filing cabinet.

Virgil was head down in a deep box, reaching for something. I held my breath, trying to decide whether I wanted to speak and let him know I was there or just wait and see what he came up with. I tapped on the side of the door, again barely audible.

Virgil grunted and straightened up, holding a roll of heavy black plastic. He turned, caught sight of me, and glared, first at me, then at the roll of utility plastic in his hands, then back at me. Suspicion flooded his face. I waved and said the first inane thing that popped into my mind. "Hi! Is that your Yugo?"

"My Yugo's around behind."

"I may have blocked you in the drive. I can move if you need to leave." I inched forward. "Looks like you found something."

He swung the plastic to him protectively. "How come you're sneaking around?"

"I knocked! There wasn't an answer, so I just leaned in. What's that?"

"Heavy-duty plastic. Just putting things away. Neat, like he liked it." He set the bundle down on the top of one of the boxes and pushed his hair back from his eyes. "Don't think you should be here."

"Oh? How come you're here?"

Virgil shifted his weight from one thick cement-splattered boot to the other. "They was lookin' for anything out of place. So I come out here. They got the salon all tight." He rubbed his jaw. A band of pale skin ringed the base of his third finger, brighter because of the thick freckles on the back of his hand. "Whatcha doing here?"

"Was that out of place?" I asked, pointing at the roll of plastic.

"Course. Whatcha doing here?"

"I'm looking for Stokowski. Is he here?"

Virgil's eyes flickered, and the freckles on his face deepened in color. "I dunno." He glanced around the little room. "Whatcha doing here?"

I ignored his question again. "How'd you get this job, Virgil? I heard DeAngelo didn't want a carpenter."

His gaze slewed uncomfortably to the side. "I dunno." He rubbed the back of his neck with his hand. "Guess he saw how much he couldn't do. Maybe I should tell the guys you're here."

The guys. Like he, Virgil, was one of them. Buddies. So I'd better be properly respectful of him. I watched him trudge to the back door of the salon and knock heavily. A face appeared, and I heard Virgil's slow, indistinct drawl.

Overhead the light swung, making gauzy semishadows and highlights dance around the room. Outside, Virgil was still speaking to the officer.

The overhead light swung again in the breeze. A glint of light shone on the floor near the box where Virgil had been.

I walked over to it. It was a tiny gold and diamond pavé, *M*. Meredith's lost anklet bangle! How did it get out here? And why did Virgil have access, as if he lived there?

The drone of Virgil's voice continued.

I glanced around the garage, strangely homey even with the boxes and utilitarian shelving. What was in the other half of the garage? I sneaked to the end of the row of boxes. Behind it was a narrow cot with blanket and pillow. There was even a lamp on a bedside box. All that was needed to complete the cozy picture was a chest of drawers.

Virgil was still talking to the police, gesturing toward the garage. The filing cabinet was two steps away. Chances were that it held only old invoices, but you never knew. There were several pennies and a dime along with a folded credit card receipt lying on top, as if Virgil had emptied his pockets there. I jammed the receipt into my pocket and yanked on the drawer. It yielded with a squeal.

"Hey!" Virgil yelled.

I glanced inside.

Neatly folded men's laundry. T-shirts, size XL, pairs of rolled-up men's socks, an alarm clock. I closed the drawer. I figured the second and third drawers were shorts, shirts, and trousers. And if he were like me, maybe a chocolate bar or two. Virgil was doing more than stacking boxes in this garage. He had set up housekeeping. He did live here. I wondered if that was part of the deal for his work—free housing.

"Hey!" Virgil ran toward the garage. I jumped to the metal shelving and grabbed a side support.

Virgil filled the door, puffing. "Whatcha doing?"

I leaned over, huffing loudly. "Sorry. I was feeling sick. When I grabbed the shelves they screeched." I jerked the shelving, hard. It squealed. All the boxes jumped, rattled, and shifted on the shelves. I couldn't tell whether Virgil believed me or not.

Stokowski's face bore the marks of seeing too many ugly things, and there was an indelible shadow beneath his eyes from lack of sleep. Nothing in particular in his expression was menacing, but the way he flexed his fingers as though he was trying to keep them from strangling someone told me he was really pissed. "What in hell are you doing here?"

"Actually, I stopped to see if you were here—"

Virgil snorted and stalked to the back of the garage and pulled on the second file drawer. It opened without a sound.

"Why would you want to talk to me?" Stokowski asked.

I shifted to my left foot so I could see around Stokowski and keep Virgil in sight better. "We were all upset yesterday after...well, and I forgot about seeing two cords coming from the footbath. And I wanted you to know..."

Virgil opened the lower two drawers of the file cabinet in succession; neither squeaked. He seemed reassured that nothing was disturbed and returned to stand next to Stokowski and glower at me.

I put a hand on Stokowski's arm to get his attention. "You do understand what this means, don't you? The two cords mean it wasn't Meredith. It would take knowing more about electricity, planning ahead. She couldn't string two extension cords together, and she was in love, planning to stay that way."

He steered me to the chilly outside. "Stella, stay out of my way. If I find you messing around in this one more time, your ass is grass."

"Listen! That rigging was so simple anyone could have done it, not just Meredith! A second wire runs into the tub and straight into the water from the wall plug. ZZZZT. Dead."

"So simple, even Meredith could do it—in a hurry."

# FOURTEEN

THE WIND WAS blowing from the northwest, bringing a hint of winter, but at least it was blowing the day's accumulation of smog out of the city and across the eastern plains. I was cold, tired, and hungry.

I'd proven to Stokowski that anyone could have crisped DeAngelo, but it had backfired. And with the bangle, even as circumstantial as it was, Meredith was even more a prime suspect. I did not look forward to telling her.

I always think better with a happy stomach. Any meal someone else fixes is seventeen times better than anything I make, and my mother's cooking is far better than that. Even Meredith eats her cooking. I dialed Meredith from my cellular phone. It rang four times, then switched to the answering machine.

"Meredith, pick up the phone, it's me. We're going to Mom's for dinner." She didn't answer. "Meredith!"

I told myself Meredith could be anywhere in the apartment, tied up with something. She could be in the bathroom and unable to come to the phone just then. She could be sleeping. But when I opened my apartment door, I recognized the silence of an empty apartment. Meredith was gone.

I followed my feet through the living room, heard the creak of the bare hardwood floor, smelled the close, stuffy air. The front window was shut. The pillows on the couch were tidied, Meredith-style, one piled in front of the other.

The bedroom was pristine. The odor of fingernail polish lingered in the air. Meredith loves long, polished nails, but she'd had hers done recently, so that was puzzling. But everything else was in place. The bed was smoothed, the catalogs stacked neatly at the side of the bed, the side stand dusted. Meredith's telltale apology; she dusted and tidied everything before going. There was even a faint hint of her favorite scent, orange flower, in the bathroom.

In the kitchen a note dangled from the fridge by a butterfly magnet, one that Meredith had made and given me for my birthday last year.

Stella

I can't stay...they're watching me. I didn't kill De-Angelo. I didn't. Believe me, please. Don't worry about me. Have Jan cover the shop, I'll be in touch.

Love,
Meredith

I did the only thing I could think of to do. I called Meredith's place and left a message on her answering machine for her to call immediately. Next I called Mother and told her not to hold dinner. Then I put my head on my arms and tried to think.

The footbath had been found in the Dumpster behind Meredith's place, and Mrs. Poland had seen her out there this morning. Although Meredith was a notoriously tidy person, Stokowski would add her presence at the Dumpster to the growing pile of circumstantial evidence against her.

And then there was her bangle in the garage. What did that mean? She said she couldn't remember where she lost it; she thought it would be in the office cum love loft with the letters, but neither bangle nor letters were there.

Initially, Meredith called me to ask for help because she was scared and she wanted her letters to DeAngelo back. She was still scared and still wanted the letters, so where would she go? The most logical place was DeAngelo's home—David's place. With any luck I'd find the letters and Meredith.

I quickly checked on Fluffy and found him a dark, moody brown, hiding under the log in his cage, sleeping with a cricket I'd put in there for food. He turned his back on me as if to say he'd rather sleep with his food supply than play with me.

When I tried to pick him up, he jumped away. Fluffy was depressed. And angry. I turned off his light and closed the cage, to keep the cricket in.

I circled the area looking for Meredith's car with no luck, then drove to David's. His front door was locked, the apartment dark, and no one answered my knock. Not even the cat.

I retraced my steps, hesitating on the landing of the unit directly below David's. I knocked. The front door swung open, and sounds of television news trickled out the screen door along with the smell of hot dogs. A young woman barely twenty years old with tired blond hair, tight jeans, and a crying toddler on her hip looked belligerently at me. I couldn't tell if she'd been crying or merely wore contact lens.

I smiled with as much warmth as I could muster. "I'm looking for David. The guy who lives upstairs. Do you know if he's around?"

She gaped at me as if I'd asked her if he wore water wings to the pool.

"Maybe you noticed a tall girl with long chestnut-colored hair going up there?" I added.

"Do you think I've got time to watch a neighbor? When I've got a kid and a job and a thousand bills? Get a life." She slammed the door in my face.

At the back of the unit David's garage was shut tight, evidently with an automatic door opener. I ran up the back steps. The screen door was shut but not locked, and the kitchen door stood open.

This was the second time David's door had been open. The last time he'd been in the john and hadn't heard me. He probably wouldn't buy it happening again. I stuck my head in and yoo-hooed, like Auntie Ess always did before she walked into our house. We never locked our doors then, either, but that was a different time. There was no answering call.

I pushed the door open. Maybe David was incredibly sloppy, or maybe someone else was rifling through stuff and left in a hurry, perhaps when I knocked at the front door. A little chill ran over my neck.

I took a deep breath and entered.

The last of the daylight illuminated the kitchen and the cupboard doors, open as if someone had hastily gone through them. The cat's dish was full. David must have planned to be out.

Where was the cat? He wasn't one to leave a meal untouched. I tiptoed through to the hallway and David's bedroom and flicked on the light. Dresser drawers were ajar, the closet open. It could have been David's usual decor, but I didn't think so. It looked picked over.

In the corner, papers littered the top of a small desk, and some had slipped to the floor. I stepped over them, peering closely, and recognized an envelope from DeAngelo's desk in the attic office cum love loft. One sheaf of papers on the floor was covered with tiny print, which I recognized from my former career as an accountant. I looked more closely. It was a mutual insurance policy on Anthony DeAngelo and David Christof.

I'd seen policies like this fairly often. They're taken out to ensure that the business continues even if something happens to one of the partners. I peeked at the beneficiary line. Two surprises. The beneficiaries were listed as Suzanne McAllister and Victoria DeAngelo.

Who the hell was Victoria DeAngelo?

Given the number of women in his life, maybe it should have been spelled Victim DeAngelo. Was there a woman alive, other than myself, who had *not* been involved with this man?

A faint, baleful meow made my heart jump.

I took a deep breath and pulled a tissue from my purse, wishing I had brought a pair of rubber gloves. I went to the other bedroom door, the one DeAngelo occupied on the rare evenings he was home. The meow was louder. The door was shut.

A sickly anticipation crowded up my throat, a pre-gag, as I put the tissue around the doorknob and twisted it. *Please, don't let me find David in here on the floor.*

I opened the door. The cat darted past me. I flicked on the wall switch and glanced around, checking the floor. The scent of orange flowers lingered in the air, as though Meredith had barely left.

The room was starkly modern in utilitarian brown and gold, with absolutely no attention to style and no hint of passion. It was reminiscent of 1970s Holiday Inn, and so unlike his love nest in the attic of the salon.

There was a double bed, a small bookcase with several books on house repairs, a dresser, and a nightstand, the drawer of which lay on the floor.

The room wasn't trashed, but drawers were open, contents rumpled. The closet was open, clothes pushed to one end, and the bed was wrinkled as though the mattress had been checked. This looked like a Meredith-type search to me. Tidy but thorough. The cat must have been accidentally locked in the bedroom.

So where was Meredith? And for that matter, where was David? And why had Meredith left the back door open? The only thing I could think of was that she had left in a rush. I pulled the door to DeAngelo's room closed, then hesitated and reopened it.

The bookshelf held paperbacks and one hardback volume, which lay on top. One. It seemed odd. I wondered just what one book DeAngelo would find so fascinating he'd have it in hardcover. I crossed the room and picked it up. *Treasure Island.*

I opened it. The center of the pages had been crudely cut away to leave a three-by-four-inch hiding place. Whatever else may have been in there, now there was only a small white cardboard jewelry box. I lifted the lid. An antique-looking pocket watch and a plain gold man's wedding band lay inside. The band was inscribed. I held it up to the light and squinted.

*Gerta & Tony.*

I WAS CERTAIN Meredith had been there. Whether she had found her letters or not I couldn't tell, but undoubtedly, she had found the ring. That could account for her leaving in a hurry.

Resentment toward DeAngelo coursed through my veins. If he'd been there, I might have killed him. His life had been a regular *I Led Three Lives,* except for him it was *I Misled Three Loves.* Meredith thought he was in love with her; Lizette claimed to be married to him; and now it looked like Gerta actually was married to him. Victoria was probably married to him, too. Meredith would have made him a quatrigamist, at a minimum.

I was so angry about DeAngelo that I was determined not to leave a scrap of evidence that either I or Meredith had been there. It took me five minutes to wipe down everything with the tissue, check the living room, give the cat water, and shut and lock the doors. I couldn't leave it open. Just anyone could come in. I didn't know what kind of shape Meredith would be in at this point or what she might decide to do. I almost wished she'd turn herself in to Stokowski so she wouldn't be a target for the killer. It seemed clearer and clearer to me that I had to find the killer as soon as possible, but I had to be careful not to jeopardize Meredith in the process. She was the appointed scapegoat.

I came back to the simplicity of the murder. And simple made me think of Lizette. Did she know this Victoria De-Angelo?

I drove straight to Lizette's place, keeping a wary eye out for looming white vans, but for once there weren't any. I drove around the block and through the alley to check for David's and Lizette's cars and found Lizette's, with a space open next to it. I parked. On the off-chance, I felt the hood of her car. It was cold.

A soft light glowed orange against white drapes, pulled

across the casement window. One of the window panels was open and the curtain blew gently in and out with the cool air.

I went inside and rang the bell. I didn't expect an answer, but I rang a second time anyway.

"Yeah? Who is it?" Lizette's voice piped out of the answering tube.

"Stella, the reporter."

There was a hesitation, then she let me in.

Lizette was immediately visible, leaning out of her apartment door, by the time I reached the third floor. She was wearing a unitard with flowered fetish straps where all good fetish straps go. Her lips were carefully outlined with mahogany lipstick and filled in with the same color of red as her fingernails. She had an overall ready-for-the-camera look. "So what's up?" she asked, leaning out her door. "Did you come for pictures?"

How lies cause trouble! "Um—I'm looking for David. Have you seen him?"

She shook her head, eyes wide. "No. Why would he be here?"

"Can I come in?"

She looked at me with disappointment from beneath her considerable lashes, then stepped back and let me in. A cigarette burned in the ashtray on the coffee table. There wasn't a smudge of lipstick on it.

"Lizette, I'm confused about things."

"You're not the only one." She threw herself dramatically on the little couch. She was coordinated enough to do it without knocking herself out.

"Looks to me like you have company."

"No!" she protested. "Why do you say that?"

"You usually smoke?" I asked. "I don't remember the smell of tobacco on you before."

She shook her head. "I'm just too upset. Thought it would calm my nerves. You know, I'm like, too upset for company tonight. I'm, like, in grief, you know, so you should, ah, come another time.''

She took a long drag on the cigarette, held her breath, then blew the smoke out slowly. Lizette was different tonight than she'd been earlier in the day. There was a sort of street-smart, watchful look in her eyes that reminded me of Fluffy stalking a fly. Maybe Eve had the same transformation after she'd taken a bite of the apple.

"Lizette, the afternoon DeAngelo died, were you at your desk the whole time?"

"The whole time. Didn't leave once."

"Until the lights went out, then you came upstairs—"

"Right. I heard Suzanne yell, then I came upstairs."

"Did you see either David or Virgil?"

Lizette stubbed out the cigarette with awkward little jabs, then left it in the ashtray, bent at right angles, with a little smudge of lipstick on the end. She leaned back, her chin tilted, lips pursed.

"Well, Virgil must have gone to the breaker switches to fix the lights, and David was cutting hair. What does any of this have to do with the article?"

"Uh...background. I'm just trying to sort out all the people at the salon."

"Well, maybe you'd better forget the article for now. Things are real...crazy right now."

"I promised the paper a story. Tell you what, skip David and Meredith. Tell me about your customers. Nothing special, maybe a little about the oldest regular one."

Her pointy little tongue slicked down her lips. She was tempted. "That's confidential."

"You're going to need the good publicity. You'd be doing the place a favor. And yourself. We've got subscribers in Aspen, even. Some of them are even in films."

She weighed the possibility of an Aspen, Colorado, reader being a movie producer. "Well, DeAngelo and David both have clients from a long time ago, even from the other places they've worked. Mostly they tried to bring along the rich, influential ones, of course."

"Such as Suzanne?"

"Yeah, like Suzanne." Lizette's eyes brightened, and she came to life. "Did you see the rock on that woman's hand? It's real. Not like—" She involuntarily glanced at her hand, then back at me defensively. "So, what did you want to know?"

"Suzanne McAllister's address is…"

"Number two Bellevenue Street. Do you know she has a lap pool indoors *and* a Jacuzzi? Turns her hair blue. Why do you need this for your article?"

"She seemed to be a big regular. I thought I'd get her to comment on how great the place was, that sort of thing. She acted like she was right at home."

"She was at home, all right." She burst into a series of sharp, cynical little fox-yip laughs. "It *was* her home—once. She owns the place."

"The building?"

"The salon. The building. It."

She rose and walked into the kitchen. I followed her. A glass sat in the sink, but she took a clean one from the cupboard. She dropped ice cubes into it and poured in two inches of Red Label. I wondered if I'd interrupted someone who might this very minute be lurking in her bedroom, waiting for me to go.

"Are you all right, Lizette?"

"You need to leave." She tipped the glass to her lips and took a deep drink.

I waited for her to choke on the alcohol, but she handled it fine. She strolled back to the couch, deliberately ignoring me. "I thought I told you to leave."

The fact that she was beginning to be uncomfortable seemed promising. "Where's your family, Lizette? Who helps you and watches out for you?"

"I don't have a family. What's left of them are in Tennessee, in the hills, grubbing in the dirt for a living. What's wrong with a girl wanting better? I left there, soon as I could. So I watch out for me. And I'm doing a damn good job, too."

There was a pathetic childishness in her tone of voice, as though she was convincing herself as well as me. The only hint of her Tennessee background was in her pronunciation of "Tinnasee." I smiled. "You've pretty well erased the southern accent."

"I've pretty well erased Tinnasee, too."

"Tell me about David. Who are his friends?"

She took a deliberate swallow of her drink, then set it by the ashtray on the coffee table, delaying her answer. She tilted her head back. "I don't know."

"Where is his family?"

"Doesn't have any family. His mother dropped him off at an orphanage in Denver when he was a baby."

"And he wasn't adopted?"

She shrugged. "I don't know. DeAngelo never knew where his mother went, either." She tapped a cigarette from the pack impatiently and lit it, blowing the smoke in my direction. "DeAngelo wasn't an angel, you know. He had his problems. He always wanted things his way. He didn't let David in on the glamour end of things, and he was always spending money. That coke was just one of the things. And his moods— you can't imagine how hard they were to live with."

Her sudden change of attitude toward DeAngelo nearly left me openmouthed. This from the grieving almost-widow.

She continued. "He couldn't stand criticism, you know. Once this woman insisted he do her hair a certain way. He told her it would look awful, but she insisted. Insisted! Then when he did it, she complained and said it was awful and wanted her money back and said he had to fix it. He sat her down, put the cape on her, and cut her hair all off. All of it! Now, how wonderful is that?"

The corners of my mouth twitched. I had all I could do to keep a straight face. "Pretty bad."

"You just ask David sometime. He was about to pull out of the shop, he was so fed up. DeAngelo made promises he never kept. Like Meredith. He wouldn't have married her. I'll just tell her so, too."

It sounded to me like she had heard from Meredith and was expecting to hear again. "When did Meredith say she'd be by?"

"She didn't."

"What did she want when she called, Lizette?"

Lizette sprang up from the couch, knocking her drink across the coffee table. She ignored the spreading amber flood and stalked to the window, yanking the curtains to the side.

When she turned back to me, her face was pale, her cheeks mottled. "I'm not talking about Meredith. She's nothing. He never loved her."

"Who told you so?"

"Suzanne. He never was going to leave me, and he never intended to marry Meredith. And I told Meredith so."

Her chin was set defiantly, her hands on her hips and her feet planted, toes seeming to grip the floor.

"Lizette, who is Victoria DeAngelo?"

Her chin trembled. Tears splashed onto her cheeks in a stream that dragged mascara after it in dark streaks. Her whole body seemed to sag momentarily, then stiffened. "None of your goddamned business. Now, get out!"

I left Lizette's apartment building, scuffing through the leaves, the crisp air cooling my cheeks. I was puzzled by two things. First, her reaction to the name Victoria DeAngelo. She had changed from defiance to wounded vulnerability in seconds. So many mood changes, so many sides to Lizette. It was hard to know which was the real Lizette, if any of them were. When her facade slipped, Lizette's vulnerability revealed her sad little soul. Of course, that didn't mean that she was innocent or harmless. Yesterday she had pointed a finger at Meredith; today, Suzanne.

The second thing that puzzled me was the cigarette. It

wasn't lipstick-stained until she puffed on it in front of me. That, and the glass in the sink, made me think someone was in there with her. I waited in my car half an hour to see if anyone I'd recognize emerged. No one did. And no one's shadow fell across her window curtains either, but that didn't prove much.

My stomach was growling and churning. I made one last circle of the block, then turned toward Colorado Boulevard and my mother's house in Park Hill. It was close to nine. Barely thirty hours since DeAngelo was murdered.

I called my answering machine one more time. This time Meredith had left a message.

# FIFTEEN

MEREDITH'S MESSAGE WAS short and, for her, remarkably to the point. "I'll call back at nine-thirty."

It was already two minutes to nine.

Mother wasn't thrilled to hand over tuna casserole without any significant conversation or murmurs of appreciation, but she was understanding, and very concerned about Meredith, whom she regards as one of her own.

The phone rang just as I unlocked the door. I didn't bother with lights; I grabbed the living room telephone. "Where are you?"

Meredith's breathing was ragged as if she'd run a fast quarter mile. "If I tell you, then you'll be aiding and abetting. I've thought this out. You'll be in even bigger trouble if I stay with you. Stokowski will know I'm there, anyway. This last three weeks I've been nuts. Strange things have been happening. Like I told you Sunday. He's been an obsession. Now that he's dead, I feel released."

My own voice wasn't that steady. "And now?"

"I have to have time. If I talk to Stokowski now, I'll incriminate myself. Maybe I already have."

I was trying to hear what she was saying and at the same time concentrate on background noises in order to locate her. But there aren't a lot of distinguishing noises in Denver—no handy seaport with buoy and bells. No nearby airport—now. Nothing that really identifies one place over another. If a siren would sound I might have some luck. "What did you tell him?"

"I don't remember much of it. I told him I'd rather De-Angelo was dead than with someone else. But I didn't kill him.'' Cars went by in the background. She was probably at an outside pay phone. That did not narrow it down.

I set down the tuna casserole and lowered myself to the couch. "Did you go to David's house this afternoon to look for your letters?"

She hesitated, then answered. "I didn't find them."

"Did you leave fingerprints?"

"Nope. I polished my fingertips. Stella, I think I know who has the letters."

I closed my eyes, remembering the smell of polish in my bedroom. "Who?"

"Has to be Gerta."

"Gerta! Where does she come in?"

"She'd have a key. DeAngelo was married to her. Maybe he still is—was."

"How do you know that?"

"I found it all in a book while I was there. It was all there—''

"Meredith, did you go to the garage anytime after De-Angelo died?"

"No. Why?"

"I found your diamond pavé M on the garage floor."

"God, no."

"You're sure you were never there?"

"Positive. Stella, do you know the police are watching your place?"

I frowned at the telephone. She seemed to be getting flaky. "What are you talking about?"

"Look, I've got to get off the phone. Your line's probably tapped."

"Wait, one more question. Did you go to Lizette's anytime?"

"Hell, no. She'd kill me."

"Mom gave me the name of a reasonable lawyer for you. Do you want me to call him?"

"Not yet. Just find the letters, before Stokowski does. Oh, I borrowed your credit cards."

A little shudder ran down my arms when I heard that, but she's my friend. Besides, I'd done it to her before. "Meredith, they're at max—" She had already hung up. That should teach me to leave the cards in my desk. Somehow I'd have to make extra payments now. I decided to think about it later.

Meredith had sounded on the verge of paranoia, talking about a stakeout and wiretapping, and yet now I listened for telltale sounds of wiretapping myself. Paranoia is so catching.

The light from the street shifted through the leaves of the tree in front of my building, scattering vaguely sinister shadows on the walls of the living room.

I rose and tiptoed to the front window, careful not to step on the weak board in the center of the room. I scanned the cars parked along the curb on both sides of the street, still listening hard.

East Capitol Hill is congested, and after six-thirty in the evening it's impossible to find a space to park. A stakeout would be a challenge. Not because sitting in a car at curbside is unusual in this neighborhood. In this neighborhood, no behavior is all that unusual. But it *is* hard to park a car. Unless they parked in the daytime and then changed watchers. I drew in a soft breath and pulled a miniblind slat down to see better.

Unmarked police cars tend to stand out in my neighborhood. They're usually substantial, four-door, undented, and pastel, if not white. Most of the inhabitants of this area drive small older, two-door foreign cars of the insubstantial, easily dented variety. A different kind of Civic center.

I peered through the miniblinds. There weren't any substantial road hogs, but there was a crumbling white van halfway down the block, like the one driven by the jerk who had smashed my rear fender Sunday night. Little goose bumps rose on my arms.

I released the blind and went to the kitchen. The chill glow of the full-spectrum light over Fluffy's cage spilled across the kitchen floor. Fluffy was perched on a log, snoring.

I double-checked the front-door lock and headed to bed, wishing I'd left the blinds in the bedroom—the darkest room—open so I could see better. I was halfway to the closet when I stopped, holding my breath.

There were breathing sounds. Not mine. A snort and snuffle. A body, head lolling, was silhouetted in the little chair by the window, sleeping. I backed silently away, keeping my eyes on the figure.

"Stella?" Jason's sleep-softened voice rumbled out of the chair. My heart changed pace, not necessarily slower, simply different.

"How'd you get in here?"

"Used Meredith's key."

"So she *is* staying with you. At least she's in a secure building." I reached for the light switch.

"Don't! We think someone's watching the place."

Shadow imps danced along the walls. Jason rose from the chair, moving awkwardly in the unfamiliar room. He beckoned to me. "Stella, come here. I'll show you."

I joined him at the side of the window. He put a hand on my shoulder and leaned close to my ear. When he whispered, it blew my hair. "See the white van across and down the street?"

I nodded.

"Meredith said it drove up and parked this afternoon about four-thirty, and it's been there ever since."

I pulled away, much too aware of the warmth of his skin so close to mine. "Jason, Meredith's getting outright paranoid. And so are you. There are a zillion white vans in Denver. Have you looked into it?"

"No."

"Well, go down there and knock on the window or something. If anyone is there, tell them you need a parking space and ask when they're moving."

"What do you think I am? Nuts?"

"Well, then, I'll do it. I'm not going to run away from things. And while we're at it, just who are you? And what is it you're running from?"

"You know who I am."

"Then why are you getting mail from your alma mater addressed to Jason Paul *Gordon?* You know, a hungry college is more accurate than the IRS."

"Just trust me."

"Why should I? Does Gerster know you go under a false name?"

"It's not a false name."

"Half name, then. It's still not honest."

"What you see is what you get, Stella. You just have to trust me."

"I don't have to do anything, Jason. And I sure don't have to make a fool of myself over someone who won't trust me enough to even tell me his name. And besides that, I don't ditch my friends the minute trouble hits."

"Stella, I'm not ditching either you or Meredith. But I am very worried about you. Stokowski told me that the case against Meredith is overwhelming, and you're the only one who doesn't understand that. She had the motive, she told him she'd kill him, she even admits she's left letters that incriminate her. She was there, she'd fought with him, he's murdered right after meeting her in the attic room. To top it off, she tells me a footbath mysteriously showed up in the trash barrel behind her apartment house. She saw it there this morning and took it down the alley and pitched it in the Dumpster."

"Stokowski already found it. This morning. I saw them all huddled around the Dumpster. A trash bag on the ground, and it turned out to be *the* damn footbath."

"Don't you see what Stokowski's case is like?"

"It's a frame. She didn't do it."

"I'm going to help her as much as I can, Stella, but I'm not going to break the law for her. It won't help her in the long run. She's in this up to her navel. And at this point, so are you. Trust me, Stella."

"'Trust me' and 'It's in the mail' are the two biggest lies ever told."

Light from the streetlamp flashed over him as he walked to the door, falling across his face and highlighting his brow, his cheekbones, and his chin. The musky scent of his anger and the smell of his leather jacket lingered seductively in the air. He stopped with his hand on the doorknob and turned toward me. His golden hair was dark in the shadows, his eyes hidden in his frown. "What do I have to say, Stella, to convince you?"

"I know Meredith is innocent, and it seems she doesn't have anyone else in her corner. Certainly not you, even though you're giving her a place to stay."

He stared at the floor for several long seconds, then met my gaze darkly. "I'm just worried about you. I don't know what else to say. Call me if you need me."

If he'd stayed around for another half hour, I'm sure I'd have come up with something clever and cutting to say.

I never did turn on the lights. I stormed around the apartment for an hour, trying to cool down until I was tired, and then I flung myself, fully clothed, on top of the bed and fell asleep. I didn't even remember to turn off Fluffy's full-spectrum light. Poor guy had to sleep with the lights on.

I was dreaming about diamond pavé bangles when I awoke in the dark, shadows of the tree leaves outside fluttering silently on the walls. I called them night butterflies when I was a child, a million-odd years ago. A light breeze blew in from the window, open a bare inch, and the mournful woo-woo of a train made the night seem as old and miserable as I was.

It was slightly after five o'clock in the morning. I'd been asleep for maybe five hours, just long enough to make further sleep impossible.

I shucked my musty, wrinkled clothes in a heap on the floor and stepped into the shower. Sometimes I think better with water spraying on my head. And I needed to think really well, because if I didn't come up with another hot suspect or the real killer, Meredith, with or without her letters, was going to be charged. Stokowski had been quite clear that he was building the case against her.

I turned the water to hot and the showerhead to pulse, hard, and stuck my head under to wake up my brain cells and charge my synapses.

Meredith was searching for her letters for some reason. I'd been talking about Ami's declaration-of-independence letter to her when she told me about DeAngelo. Letters seemed to lie at the bottom of everything that had happened since then. And thinking about it, I hadn't heard from Ami for a while.

Chasing Meredith's letters implied breaking-and-entering activities. While I don't mind strolling into an unlocked, essentially open place, true B&E makes my nerves zingy. Furthermore, the letters wouldn't change Meredith's status as favorite suspect. I decided to scratch the letters for now.

I turned the showerhead to needle-hard spray.

The old hell-hath-no-fury-like-a-woman-scorned motive might apply to Meredith, but it fit Lizette even better. She was the one being jilted. Lizette's motives seemed the strongest. She was more open about them, and I'd spent more time with her and so knew how changeable, even labile, she could be. Furthermore, I was sure she was lying when she swore she never left the reception desk.

The thing that stuck out in my mind was that this murder had taken some planning; it must have been done by someone who knew DeAngelo's footbath regime, knew he would use coke for a boost, and therefore knew the amount of electricity going through the cords would be fatal. That was a whole lot of planning and knowing. More than I associated with impulsive Lizette.

Then there was Gerta—cute, smart, and previously married to DeAngelo, possibly still married to him. How did she like seeing DeAngelo with other women? Perhaps she was carried

away with a sudden jealous rage and killed him. Since she'd
been married to him, she might know who Victoria DeAngelo
was, and she might know about his relationship to Suzanne—and why Suzanne and Victoria were named as beneficiaries, not she. The trouble was, I liked Gerta. I didn't want
to find that she was the killer. Anyhow, I needed to find her,
but I didn't have a clue where she lived, or even what last
name she used.

David, Virgil, and Suzanne were the only other ones actually around when DeAngelo died. And I didn't know squat
about them, except that Suzanne owned the salon building and
was listed as a beneficiary in the mutual insurance plan. I
wondered what, or who, else she might own. She, or her relationship with DeAngelo, seemed pivotal.

Enough shower; I'd become a wrinkle. I toweled off.

I put on my black satin teddy with the lacy keyhole, black
jeans, a turtleneck, and a black sweater. I was dressed for
skulking, from the inside out.

In the kitchen I turned out Fluffy's light and took a spoon
and the telephone book to the living room to eat the tuna
casserole I'd forgotten to refrigerate, hoping I wasn't poison-
ing myself with salmonella. Gerta wasn't listed under De-
Angelo.

By a quarter to six I was still wide-awake. I snagged a diet
Pepsi from the fridge, locked my door, and started down the
hall. Halfway to the stairs I stopped, returned, and set a tiny
piece of paper in the crack of the door, three inches up on the
hinge side. It's called projection. Whatever you are doing, you
suspect others of doing. Since I was skulking, it made perfect
sense that someone might try to slither through my place. At
least this way I'd know it.

My car was parked down the street and around the corner.
I started to go out the back door, then changed my mind and
went out the front.

Capitol Hill is very well lit with orange streetlights, a crime-
prevention effort that has had some success. The lights were

still on, even though the dawn was showing on the horizon. It felt like an orange-glow movie set under surveillance cameras. Or someone's heavy gaze.

My neck felt dangerously exposed. I walked lightly on the pads of my feet, avoiding the larger clumps of leaves on the sidewalk. I shivered and pulled the collar of my jacket up around my ears. The weight of someone's gaze still lay on my shoulders.

The white van stood across the street. Its headlights were in perfect condition, but they could have been repaired. The license began with A, and the left front bumper was dented, but so was the right front bumper and the whole of the driver's side. I couldn't see that any of my Taurus's paint was embedded in it. I debated whether to peek inside. Then I did it, knowing that I'd always wonder about it if I didn't. I waited until a car was coming, so that if I was shot by some monster in the van, there'd at least be a witness.

The front seats were battered and worn, the dashboard dirty and cracked from age and exposure. Sandwich wrappers and crumpled beer cans littered the floor of the passenger side. I couldn't see into the back. I wrote the whole license number on my palm and moved on.

I reached my car, key in hand, and jammed the key into the lock, wrenched open the car door, checked the backseat for muggers, and slid inside. My heart rate was two hundred. The price of skulking is paranoia, and it will kill you.

By the time I was cruising the genteel streets of Hilltop, trying to figure out which of the houses might be Suzanne's, I had begun to think I'd lost my mind. The lawns and homes still slept under a wide, innocent sky that was growing lighter by the moment.

I turned down a street empty except for a Corvette parked in front of number two Bellevenue. There were only two homes in the block, tall, graceful trees standing guard over their rooftops. Both had walks that wandered in a leisurely way from the street up to the front door. The implication was clear: if you have to rush, you shouldn't live here.

I drove by slowly. The 'Vette's license plates read DAV-EED, and the huge Spanish-style house it was parked in front of was flanked by tall old blue spruce, their sheltering branches sweeping down to a lawn that looked as if it had been combed by hand.

A light was on at the back of the house. I drove discreetly down the alley to peer in, but the six-foot privacy fencing blocked the view.

I parked down the block and power-walked down the street to look vaguely like a genuine inhabitant out for early-morning exercise. Here my feet were nearly silent because the lawns, including the gutters, had been swept, vacuumed to near perfection.

The driveway and garage were on the near side. I ducked under the spruce, found myself completely hidden, and edged toward the window.

At that moment the front door opened. David's voice floated out in the stillness of the dawn: "I'll see you later."

The reply was low, too muffled to hear. I crept forward under the tree branches and saw David, his arms circling Suzanne awkwardly, as though he wasn't sure he wanted to hold her but felt some obligation.

I waited until he'd left, then stole from the tree and rang the doorbell. The door flew open as though she'd been close by.

Suzanne had aged since I'd seen her at the salon yesterday. The hall light shone harshly on her, accentuating the hollows of her eyes and fatigue lines in her cheeks. I guessed her age at late fifties to early sixties, some fifteen years older than she had looked yesterday. My sister always said love aged you, but I hadn't thought it was this bad.

She assessed me in a glancing sweep, and her expression soured, as if I'd just emerged from the swamp. She started to swing the door shut. I stuck a foot out, blocking it. She wasn't going to talk to me unless I could find some incredibly good reason, or a threat.

"Suzanne, talk to me or talk to the police—because that's exactly where I'll go next."

She hesitated, then let me in and closed the door. I followed her into a museum-piece living room of polished wood, thick carpeting, and expensive furniture, all in peach hues. It was like stepping into a peach compote, except for the lingering odor of furniture polish and burned coffee.

I glanced over the walls. The wall decoration was noticeably minimalist. In fact, there were shadows of former pictures. She had recently removed them, I assumed. But why? There was no sign of preparation for painting.

She settled herself on a couch next to a sheaf of papers. I sat with her, glancing at the papers, trying to read upside down. She pulled them away, but not before I read "Fairmont Cemetery" across the top and a decidedly feminine signature.

"You are arranging DeAngelo's interment?"

"David and I. He's all the family DeAngelo has."

"But you're not family, are you?"

"What are you getting at?"

"Lizette told me you own the building."

"I'm a casual investor, you might say."

"That's a bit much for a casual investor, isn't it?"

She shook her head, adjusting the large yellow diamond solitaire on her ring finger. "David needs someone, so he turned to me. I don't find that so odd."

"You know, I find it odd that not only do you own the salon but you act as though you own David and DeAngelo."

Suzanne grew absolutely still, as though waiting for the bomb to go off.

"There are mutual insurance policies so the business will continue, and you are listed as one of the beneficiaries."

Suzanne flinched when I said, "one of the beneficiaries."

"Do you know who the other beneficiary is?"

"I didn't know I was one."

"Who is Victoria DeAngelo?"

She blinked and frowned. It looked like the first genuine expression I'd seen on her face, except for the irritated look she'd given me when she first saw me. "I don't know who Victoria is. I've never heard of her."

"You loaned David and DeAngelo a significant amount of money, and you don't know who Victoria DeAngelo is? I find that hard to believe."

She lifted her gaze to mine. "Well, that's not my problem. I'm a business partner, that's all. I don't know why that should be your concern."

"With DeAngelo dead, David assumes all of the business."

"Of course. And all the debts. It's not a free ride."

"But since you are a beneficiary, you'll get your loan money back from DeAngelo's insurance."

Her shoulders stiffened. "I would get more from the business with DeAngelo alive."

"Over time. And only if the business goes well. Whereas this way, you get your money now, guaranteed."

I looked around the room, lovely, yet quite bare. "And if you got your money fast enough, it would be in time to get your paintings and valuables out of hock. Perfect, and perfectly simple."

"Rubbish."

Her sudden flush told me I'd hit on the truth. She was in a cash crunch, but I'd have to pull her fingernails out one by one before she'd own up to it. "It wouldn't be the first time a person murdered for money."

Suzanne blinked rapidly, then the corner of her mouth twitched. She laughed, long and mean.

I walked back to my car. A persistent feeling of being watched chilled my neck, and after I climbed in my car I locked the door. No cars followed me out of the area, but I felt edgy. It could have been caused by chocolate withdrawal, but I didn't think so.

# SIXTEEN

WHAT I KNEW of DeAngelo now amounted to very little more than before. He had been married to Gerta, promised to Lizette, and in love with Meredith, although that might have lasted only as long as she didn't expect anything from him. And there was still Victoria. Whoever she was.

Motive was the key to the killer's identity, and I kept coming back to two motives—money, the root of all evil, and jealousy. Hell hath no fury like a woman scorned.

Gerta had had the most access to DeAngelo, and to all of us, at the time he was killed. She'd strapped me down so I couldn't easily move. She'd put Suzanne in a footbath like DeAngelo, so unless Suzanne dried off her feet, she'd have left wet footprints. There hadn't been any wet footprints, only a bit of sandy grit on the floor. Gerta had been taking care of Suzanne, but Suzanne had howled for her—so Gerta hadn't been with her then, or with me. Where had she been? Plugging in DeAngelo? Or somewhere she hadn't mentioned?

It was still too early for the sticky bun place that I loved so much, but the Belcaro King Soopers was open, and they had coffee and some mighty fine chocolate-glazed doughnuts. Sugar and chocolate are the building blocks of the brain.

I picked up a few other staples—a six-pack of diet cola, corn curls, and some extra-fine dark chocolate—and one weapon, a purse-size canister of hair spray. This is my basic surveillance survival kit. I paid for them, returned to my car, unwrapped the hair spray, and slipped it into my purse.

Hair spray is a miracle weapon. It immobilizes attackers by temporarily blinding them, shellacs their faces, and removes ballpoint ink stains, all at the same time. A woman's best friend, and my personal favorite.

The sky was clear blue, promising a good weather day, and the air was crisp. I leaned back and considered inhaling my breakfast on the spot, then thought of poor old Fluffy, alone and lonely, and drove back to my apartment.

I parked behind the building and climbed the front stairs. The building was Saturday-morning silent except for the squeak and scuff of shoes rapidly descending the back stairs. I wondered who it would be. Mine is not a building known for athletic people.

Five feet from my door I spotted the slip of paper I'd left in the doorjamb, lying on the floor. Had Jason used Meredith's key to my place again? Or was someone else there?

I peered at the face of the lock and saw there were tiny scratches on it. They could be lock-pick marks, but they also could have been made by me anytime, jamming my key in.

Good sense said to call the police. But I'd feel like an idiot if it were Jason.

I set down my groceries, doughnuts, and coffee and took my canister of hair spray and a can of cola from the six-pack. I could spray with my left and smack with a can in my right. Deadly.

Thief-silent, I opened the door. I stepped forward and peered through the crack to make sure no one was hiding behind it. No one was. The living room was empty. I stepped inside, leaving the door wide behind me as an escape.

The mail stacked on my hall table littered the floor; the contents of my desk were strewn across the desktop.

The bathroom was empty, the toilet seat cover was down, but the water was running in the stool. I shuddered.

I stole to my bedroom, hair spray ready, praying I wouldn't find anyone. The room was dim, the blinds closed. I flicked on the light.

All my gorgeous undies were thrown everywhere, and the dresser drawers lay on the floor. I checked under the bed and in the closet, but no one was there. They'd have been strangled in the coat hangers anyway.

I moved to the windows to open the blinds and let in fresh air. My hand was half raised to the window blind cord when I saw it. A crude doll made from towels, with a lipstick smear for lips and draped with my turquoise teddy, hung from the blinds by a thin cord around its neck.

I sneaked to the kitchen, my heart pounding. If anything had happened to Fluffy...but he was wedged up along the top of his cage, bright green. Eyes open, ribs pumping. Frightened. Even his little feet were cold. I cuddled him while I called Stokowski.

Stokowski arrived within minutes and brought a finger-printer from the lab who looked as if he'd been up all night. He had. So had Stokowski. It was a bad night for Denver.

I expected Stokowski to lecture me right away on the danger I was in and how I should be more careful, but he ordered me to go through the letters and the few files that I'd brought home from the office while he wrote up his report.

I made coffee and gave Stokowski my doughnuts because my stomach was jumping around. I've been through a break-in before, but this still left me pretty frightened, even a little depressed and angry, although I didn't want to admit it.

"Stella, why in hell did you come in here? I've told you time and again—"

Fortunately Stokowski was interrupted by the print man, who said the prowler had left several smudges but no clear, identifiable prints. He packed up and left for another crime scene.

A half hour later I'd gone through everything and found nothing missing. Not even the Snickers bar I'd stashed two months ago before my last diet. The thought of eating anything that might have been touched by the intruder was repulsive. It hit the wastebasket with a clang. It was a little stale anyway.

Stokowski poured a third cup of coffee and settled on the couch, watching me put things back in the desk. His eyes were an earnest, crystalline blue, almost without guile.

He leaned forward. "It's okay. *Most* people feel scared and violated when their place has been tossed."

I looked at him for a long moment, then sighed. I was wrong. The intruder had taken something from me. The last of my security.

Stokowski took a long sip of coffee while I took in enough oxygen to bolster myself, then set down his cup.

"You noticed there was no sign of a break-in. Someone used a key."

"Or a set of lock picks."

"You know anyone who has lock picks?"

I shook my head.

"Stella, why didn't you call the police in the first place? Why'd you come in here by yourself—with only a can of cola and hair spray, for God's sake?"

"I thought maybe I was being paranoid."

"Really? It wasn't because you thought you knew who it was?"

I shook my head. I *had* that nasty little feeling that comes when I've been found out. I had thought it might be Jason. In fact, I'd kind of hoped it might be. "I did think it might be Jason," I admitted.

"Or perhaps Meredith?"

"Meredith is *not* here. I do not know where she is. I am not trying to hide her from you. Why can't you be more open-minded? Look, Stokowski, you could paint this picture another way.... Sunday my car was hit by a white van. Meredith was at home. Thursday my hairdresser was electrocuted while I was in the next cubicle, and today, Saturday, my apartment is broken into *and* a totem is left hanging by the neck. These are things that could be done by anyone, even several anyones." The room felt suddenly very cold. I didn't seem to have convinced him, but I'd scared myself nearly to death.

"And Monday you got a menacing letter." He held up a hand to quiet me. "A letter that only *you* say isn't menacing."

My stomach twisted.

Stokowski finished his coffee, rose, and stood for a moment, then walked to the kitchen, his shoulders stiff and always a little too large for his tweed sports jacket, so that it pulled across the back. He put the cup in the kitchen sink, then returned to stop in front of me at the desk. "Do you have any other letters anywhere else?"

"At the office, in locked files." I looked up at him. "Oh, and a few here in my purse that I haven't had a chance to read, since you and Jason convinced Mr. Gerster that my column was lethal."

He was silent.

I pulled my purse around onto my lap and pawed through the contents until I found the stack of envelopes I'd swept off my desk yesterday afternoon. I held them up.

"Are there any from that Dick person?"

I fanned them out on the top of the desk and ruffled through the envelopes. My hand rested on one. The handwriting looked familiar. I picked up the letter opener and slit the envelope.

My fingertips began to tingle. My lips grew stiff, and the room grew dim and cold. I blinked repeatedly, trying to clear my sight, but it didn't work. The room darkened. I felt a tremble begin in my chest and radiate out through my body.

A thin, acrid ammonia smell filled my nose and mouth, chilling my cheeks and tongue, followed by a cold, metallic taste. I was having another spell.

A distant pinprick of light pierced the curtain of dark in front of my eyes and moved steadily toward me. A rustling, whispering, susurrant sound filled my ears, crescendoing, then diminishing until silence and dark ice wrapped around me, suffocating me.

Air burst from my lungs in a long, soft whoosh.

I saw the light become a shoe box, then a coffin-shaped box. It came closer and closer until it was in my face. Cold, crushing, strangling.

It slowly began to move, change; finally it morphed into a person wrapped in gauze, arms crossed peacefully in front, mummylike. Gauze covered its face. It moved. It reached out to me, asking for help. At the last moment, those dead hands grabbed my throat and squeezed. I choked, gasping, throat aching.

Large, dark, baleful eyes stared at me. Desperate, dead eyes.

# SEVENTEEN

ALL I COULD think was to try to breathe, draw air through my burning throat. Rip at the icy hands cutting off my air.

"Stella?" A soft voice far away. "Stella?" A hand shook my shoulder, patted my cheek, slapped my palm. The room warmed, the light returned, the smells and tastes faded.

"Stella, are you there?" It was Stokowski, his hands on both sides of my face, cradling my cheeks. "Stella!"

I looked at the envelope again, crumpled in my fingers, then handed it to Stokowski.

He took the envelope from me, holding it gingerly between his thumb and forefinger. He was watching me closely. "Are you going to faint?"

My eyes welled up under his scrutiny. An ache in my throat kept me from speaking. The twin feelings of sick and scared seemed to permeate my head. I would have been glad to faint. To not feel what I felt.

"Stella? Were you having one of those, uh, spells?" He waited for me to answer, but I couldn't yet. He seemed to understand. "Stella, did you see something?"

"A coffin... A body that asked for help, then tried to strangle me."

There are a lot of things about Stokowski that irritate me, but I am forever thankful that he listens to me and never, ever laughs at me. Of course, he's only seen one other spell, but even then he was considerate. That counts for a lot with me.

"Do you know what it means?"

I scrubbed feeling back into my face with my hands. "Something bad. Don't know what." The chill had worn off now. I pointed to the letter in his hand. "What's the letter?"

Stokowski used my tweezers to pull the letter from the envelope and carefully spread it on the desk.

Wednesday, October 26

Dear Stella,

I know you said to be careful, but I'm leaving him. I told him after supper, and he took it better than I thought he would. He just stared at me and turned a weird color. He's been in the work shed ever since.

I don't know why I'm writing a letter. I guess it's because I'm so excited. I feel like I've been freed. At last.

It's late, so I'll call you at the paper tomorrow and tell you where I'm staying. I don't have kids or any family, so I sort of see you as my family. Hope it's O.K. Call you tomorrow.

Ami

I looked at Stokowski. I think he had the same thought I had. "This is Saturday. Her 'tomorrow' would have been last Thursday, when DeAngelo died," I said, and drew in a deep breath. "I think something bad happened to Ami."

The lines at the corners of Stokowski's eyes deepened, and his eyes looked cold and faraway; a curtain had dropped over his feelings. "Is that what you...saw?" He seemed to have trouble saying the words.

I shook my head. "Just a feeling."

He searched my face as though he'd find something else I hadn't told him. "Do you know where she lived?"

"We corresponded only via the column. She didn't want her husband to know she was writing to me."

"What is that on your palm?" He pointed to the license number of the van that I'd jotted down. I'd forgotten about it. I told him.

He walked to the front window. The van was gone. "You feeling all right?"

"Great. Splendid."

He rested a hand on the top of my head, sliding it around to my cheek, suddenly tender. "You want me to call someone?"

"Who?"

"Maybe Jason."

Jason's face came to mind. His warm smile. My vulnerability. His secretiveness. "He isn't who he says he is, either."

Stokowski stuffed his hand in his trouser pocket. "Who does he say he is?"

"He says he's Jason Paul. His college alumni office says he's Jason Paul Gordon. He says, 'Trust me.' You think I should trust him?"

Stokowski looked me hard in the eyes. "Tough call. I think you'll have to trust yourself."

Everyone is a therapist. "Great."

Stokowski continued to scrutinize my face, chewing thoughtfully on the inside of his lip. The tenderness I'd seen in his eyes was gone. "Are you holding out on me, Stella? I don't believe for a minute that you have no idea where Meredith is. I don't believe you are staying out of this mess." He leaned into my face close, so I could count the pores on his nose. "Stella, so help me God. If I find out you're holding out something—"

"I'm not! I'm not. I'm friggin' innocent for once. Honest to God."

Stokowski quit, but he wasn't convinced. He packaged the letter and envelope from Ami to run through the lab. He paused in the doorway, his brow an angry line. "Stella, if you want to stay healthy, get smart. This is no game. It's goddamn dangerous. Be careful. And change these damn locks."

I went to the kitchen, spritzed Fluffy's cage with distilled water, and sat down to talk to him. He was clinging to his miniature tree, a succulent he particularly likes. I smiled at him. He turned away from me.

"Hey, Fluff. What's the matter? You want to come out for a while?"

He burrowed under the log in the far end of his cage.

It occurred to me that maybe I had bad breath. I headed to the bathroom to gargle. Then the phone rang, and Jason's voice came over the answering machine. "I'll come over if you don't pick up the phone, Stella."

I picked up the telephone. I didn't tell him that his voice warmed my heart even though I didn't want it to. I also didn't tell him about the break-in or Ami's letter and my worry that she was dead. That would only have convinced him he was right, he would tell Mr. Gerster, and I'd never get my column back.

"Do me a favor?" I assumed his silence was acquiescence. "Dig up all the information you possibly can on Suzanne McAllister. Everything, especially her bank account. And most important—find out about all the insurance policies she and/ or David might have had on DeAngelo. You know the stuff."

"Stella, you're not supposed to do this."

He is very susceptible to the lure of a big story. "It's part of a huge story, Jason. Another byline to share with me." I paused for a moment to let temptation eat at him. "You can leave messages for me here and at the paper. I do still have a telephone there, don't I?"

His voice was very unhappy when he said yes, but I knew he'd get the information.

I whipped into the bedroom, straightened the covers on my bed, and gathered up the musty clothes I'd left on the floor when I showered in the a.m. I dropped all but the jeans in the laundry hamper. The jeans I held on to to check the pockets. Nothing is worse than a tissue shedding all over your clothes in the wash.

I jammed my hand down into my right front pocket and felt a searing pain in my index finger.

The diamond pavé *M.*

The *M* that incriminated Meredith—which I'd found in the

salon garage and should have turned over to Stokowski. I must've thoughtlessly stuck it in my pocket.

I was dead meat. Worse. Roadkill.

I've been a careful, law-abiding citizen 100 percent—well, maybe 99 percent—of the time, and now I'd committed a felony or something. I couldn't even think straight. I couldn't believe I'd done it. I swear that *M* burned its outline in my palm.

How *could* I have put that thing in my pocket?

If I told Stokowski now that I had the thing, he'd immediately decide Meredith had tossed my place looking for it. He'd be furious. I would lose whatever credibility I had. He might even charge me with interfering with a crime scene, secreting evidence, hindering the investigation, and maybe seventeen other rule infractions. No amount of whining, protesting innocence or stupidity, would get me out of this one. Unless I trapped the killer. Then it wouldn't be important. Or *as* important.

Very few burglars steal dictionaries. I taped the *M* to the inside back cover of my Webster's and stuck it on the bottom shelf with my photo albums, another low item on burglary lists.

I might have stayed there, all curled up on the edge of my bed, mentally massaging myself, for I don't know how long, but the phone rang again.

It was Zelda. Her voice crackled over the answering machine. "Are you ever returning to this place? I have correspondence, telephone messages, and complaints tit-deep around here, and this is a Saturday. Stokowski told me he was around your place because of a break-in, and when Jason heard he lit out of here so fast his feet were smoking. Do you hear me? I mean it! Get your bod in here." Then she dropped the phone.

Jason was on his way here. The thought of having to face a self-righteous, overprotective, testosterone-laden, too-attractive male in my vulnerable state was too much. I stuffed the remainder of the crickets, a few underthings, my still-unpacked bag of grocery basics, and a sweater in the top of my purse. I put Fluffy into his travel cage and snatched a soda from the fridge and was out the door and down the back stairs in four minutes flat.

There is parking along the rear of my building. The rest of the alley is lined by garages for the other apartment buildings, except for three homes that have yards and six-foot back fences. The alley is one long narrow canyon through the block. Very utilitarian.

My car was parked close to the back door. I had partially backed out of the parking space when the building manager came racing out, waving his arms.

"You've got a package," he huffed. "You want it, or you want me to put it in your place?"

"I don't have anything on order—" I remembered Meredith and the catalogs. "Oh, give it to me." I put the car in park and stepped out.

He handed me a shoe boxsize package with a typed postal label. The return address was a post office box. That didn't quite make sense. All the catalog companies use large-print labels to advertise their names and addresses. I shook the box. It felt like something slipped around inside. Good companies pack their stuff so it doesn't shake around. I looked at the manager. "What did the deliveryman look like?"

"Didn't see him. The phone rang, so I was in the back. When I came out, it was there on the counter."

I noticed the paper was old, well handled. I squinted at the postmark. Denver, Colorado. September 2. Nothing takes *that* long to deliver in Denver.

I hadn't ordered anything in August. I was too broke then. Stokowski's warning rang in my ears. Call me paranoid.

Adrenaline pumped into my bloodstream. My heart started to pump, loud and fast. A bomb!

I threw the box as far down the alley as I could and yelled "Duck!" at the same time.

I think it sailed about sixty feet—terror is a terrific muscle builder. The manager and I hit the ground at the same time, behind the car.

Nothing happened. My palms burned, pain from my banged knees ached up my legs. Still nothing happened.

The manager cursed and rose, brushing off his trousers. I peeked out from under my arms, under the car, and saw the package down the alley. He turned and, still cursing, went inside. I got to my knees, feeling the most foolish I've felt in a long time. I wasn't quite standing when it blew.

A flash of light. Then a deafening explosion.

The smell of black powder, sulfur, and seared paint filled the air. The garage doors near where the package had landed were scorched and blistered. The car rocked gently on its wheels. I peeked out, still on my knees. Nothing was left of the package.

My ears were ringing so loudly that I couldn't hear. My voice was loud and funny inside my head when I tried to yell for help. I rose to my feet and glanced around, searching for someone, anyone, who was out of place or watching too closely. No one.

Gradually the shock wore off. My elbow stung and prickled, sticky with blood and grit. A survey of my body systems revealed all more or less okay, but stunned. My hearing cleared, but my emotions were numb.

I staggered to the rear of my car and ran my hand over the trunk, feeling the damaged surface. The rear window was shattered in a million crazed lines, with a gaping hole where something had flown through.

Across the alley fifty feet from the explosion site a window in the second floor had shattered. I inched forward.

The other side of my trusty, rusty Taurus was pockmarked where rocks had slammed into it. The paint was blackened and bubbled. The rear side window was shattered. My stomach flopped over sickeningly.

Above me the sky was a deep, brilliant blue. The pavement

at my feet sunlit. Across from me, grapevines trailed over the ordinary wooden privacy fencing.

Normal, except someone had tried to kill me.

I swallowed. If I'd eaten in the last hours I would have thrown up. Since I hadn't, I tasted bile in my throat and swallowed repeatedly.

A chill shook me briefly. Like a rabbit sensing the enemy, feeling the danger, smelling disaster, I reexamined the alley minutely for movement, odd things, any indication of—but I wasn't sure what I was looking for. Just looking. Quaking inside. Like the rabbit.

A siren warbled in the distance, cutting through my immobilization, pumping a fresh flood of adrenaline into my veins. I slid into the Taurus, turned the key in the ignition, cranked the engine, and heard it croak and die. I tried again. It shuddered and died again. Whatever the problem was, it wasn't going anywhere.

I grabbed Fluffy and my bag and darted down the alley. Fast. All I could think was, *Escape.*

I couldn't run, because my legs weren't steady enough, but I walked fast and felt better with each step farther away. My cheeks were wet with tears I barely realized I'd shed. I was scared. A car horn blared in the street beside me.

"Hey! Where do you think you're going?"

It was Stokowski.

# EIGHTEEN

IT WAS THREE in the afternoon before Stokowski let Fluffy and me go. I was tired and discouraged, but at least Stokowski had grudgingly agreed that Meredith wouldn't use a bomb to get rid of me. It just wasn't a Meredith MO—modus operandi.

Jason had come as soon as he heard and telephoned my mother so she wouldn't panic if she saw it on the news. And then he and his melt-your-heart brown eyes had waited for me.

I slid into Jason's little Miata convertible right over the door and hunched down in the seat. "No questions. Drive."

He pulled away from the curb, concentrated on the road, and waited a full ten minutes before he asked what was wrong.

At Washington Park he turned in and parked beside the lake, turning off the ignition. "Before you say anything at all, Stella. I want to tell you, whatever has happened, most of all I'm just so glad you're all right. Now," he said, and wrapped a warm arm around my shoulders, rubbing my ear with his thumb. "Talk to me."

"Where is Meredith?"

"She's staying at a motel. She's fine. Meredith will be all right. She's grown up. She can handle herself, Stella."

"Except for men and romance. In every other aspect of her life, Meredith is a smart woman."

He nuzzled my neck. "You smell like black powder." He put a finger beneath my chin and pulled my face around to look into my eyes. "Tell me again what happened."

The more I talked, the more unreal it seemed, but the more I began to shake. He rubbed my shoulder while I talked.

"Jason, I can't count on Stokowski being fair. He has a job

to do. He's bound by facts. And so far too many of them connect to Meredith.''

"You know, jail's not the end of the road, Stella."

"Oh yeah? You've been there? You know? Think on this one. The expense of a lawyer."

Neither one of us had the kind of bucks it would take to defend against a murder charge. "Being innocent can be just as expensive as being guilty, or more. And no one pays you back for the money you spend for bond or to prove you're innocent."

"Stel, slow down. There isn't a thing you can do right now."

"I don't even number a private investigator among my acquaintances."

"Stella, you do know a lawyer, and—"

"And that's how I know neither Meredith nor I have the money to hire one."

He nuzzled my neck. "The *good* thing is, you look great. Your hair, the way your eyes *show* up—would it *kill* you to say you liked me a little?"

"Probably."

"Then how about a little kill?"

"How can you make fun? I damn near died, and you're snuggling like it was some kind of picnic. How can you even think I'd feel like—?"

"Stella, all I can think of is, you're alive. And here. Safe. It…it makes me happy. I don't want to think about the rest of it." There was a gentle, laughing spark deep in his eyes, right back near the dark part that looked into his heart. I meant to tell him he was an insensitive boor, but he kissed me. Full on the mouth, with a whisper of caressing tongue across my lips, teasing them. He asked for it. I kissed him back.

And that was just the beginning.

What bizarre, out-of-this-world kink is it in me that made me amorous in the presence of death? Or is it that some primal urge impels us all to make one last attempt at continuing life even as we see its extinguishment?

And perhaps we are so terribly vulnerable in death's presence, so overwhelmed with mortality, that lovemaking is suddenly no longer the risk it was before. If you're faced with death, can cellulite really be so horrible?

I'm sure I'd never otherwise have skipped a meal to end up in his arms, wrapped in his love, feeling it, riding it, wishing it would go on forever.

I WOKE UP in the early-morning light, nicely tangled in Jason's arms. My head on his chest, half lying on him; the rhythmic rise and fall of his rib cage, the steady beat of his heart, was solid, reassuring.

Nothing else was.

If this turned out to be a bad case of lust, like the last relationship, gonads on parade, I was going to puke. I had sworn to myself never, ever, to put myself in a vulnerable position again. I had vowed to operate as an independent woman, to deal from strength. And here I was, like Meredith, a jellyfish caught in the web of love, so to speak. At least, I hoped it was love, not merely hormone rush.

There was a change in the rhythm of Jason's breathing. He was waking. He stirred. He moved his arm, ran his fingers over the side of my face, curled them under my chin, lifting gently.

"Give me your face."

I squeezed my eyes shut tight, pretending I was asleep. I wasn't ready to see the expression in his eyes if he was disappointed this morning. It would hurt so bad.

"I know you're awake. Your eyelashes blinking on my chest woke me up." He tugged gently. "Come on."

I let him lift my chin while I searched his eyes, looking for even the slightest hint of fatal hesitation or indifference.

He smiled gently. "It's morning. Do you still respect me?"

He was looking real good, just about perfect. I nodded. "Kiss me. I want to make sure you're real."

There wasn't any hesitation.

I was still snoozing when Jason announced he was going out for a minute and would be back with bagels. Nothing felt quite real. It was too good. Jason was perfect. Handsome, caring, sensitive. I slipped on my hyacinth teddy and over it my navy jumpsuit, from my bag of clothes.

I shook my head and inspected my hair. David had done a spectacular job. It fell nicely into place, shorter than I was used to, but full as though it actually had body. I'd have a hard time pulling it back to put up and hide under a hat, but I didn't need to hide it anymore.

I pulled the bed together and came out into the rest of Jason's apartment. Now that I took the time, I saw that it was quite nice, although sparsely furnished—brown leather couch, chair, ottoman, lamp, and a television. On the wall was an enlarged aerial photo of green, rolling-hill country estates, with trees, gardens, horse paths, and stables. I squinted at it, expecting to see Ralph Lauren on a polo pony in the right front corner of the photo. Seemed an odd picture for him to have.

The only other furniture consisted of a glass dining table and three chairs. Like the couch and the chair, they weren't new, but they were very nice pieces. The refrigerator was a wasteland. The cupboards were descendants of Old Mother Hubbard's. No wonder Jason had made a bagel run. I poured a cup of coffee and slumped into the leather chair with the morning paper. The headline blared, "Bombing in Capitol Hill." The coffee in my cup sloshed. I got up and went to the kitchen and ripped off a paper towel, blotting the hot spot on my thigh.

I crossed to the trash, lifted the lid of the bin, dropped in the soaked towel. Several envelopes were scattered there. I picked them up, turning them over. Reading other people's envelopes is *not* as bad as reading their contents.

Three were empty window envelopes, the kind I try never to open until they're threatening me. The fourth was addressed to Jason Paul. The fifth was from Burberry College, Alumni Office, again. They were tenacious as limpets. The envelope was addressed to Jason Paul Gordon IV, *and opened*. He wouldn't open it if it weren't for him.

Why was he using a different name? Was he hiding a history as a thug? A felon? A witness in the protection program?

What was I going to say to him? Hi, honey, who are you? I was just plowing through your garbage and I happened to notice your mail was all addressed to someone else?

I drew in a deep breath. He had said to trust him before when I asked him. I hadn't, but he had come through for me when I needed him. The least I could do was trust him now. Or maybe I should trust in my own ability to tell when someone was genuine. I dropped all the envelopes and closed the lid.

BY TEN O'CLOCK we were buried in the Sunday papers in Jason's living room, the bagels we'd eaten were swelling, and I was plagued by worries about Meredith. "Jason, Lizette sits right at the front desk, like a gate monitor. She sees anyone who goes up those stairs—"

"Remember the back stairs."

"I guess you know the place pretty well—"

"I've been there. Haircut, you know."

I bit my tongue. I was *not* going to start in grilling one of my few remaining friends. "Okay. Except the back stairs. So if—Wait! She couldn't see Meredith there unless she went to the back or was already upstairs."

"But Gerta was upstairs. She could have seen Meredith. And you said Lizette was upstairs when DeAngelo was assessing your jowls, so she probably goes all over the shop all the time."

"Right. But any one of them could have got hold of a footbath, maybe weeks ago, planned it out and drilled a hole for the killer cord, then just waited until there was a handy fall guy.''

"Or some other precipitant—"

"Like Lizette's argument. We only have her say-so that they were patching things up. Meredith says DeAngelo was breaking up with Lizette. When I was there, he just seemed to be trying to placate Lizette. And when he talked to Meredith, he was placating her. You know how you can usually tell when someone's just saying things but doesn't really mean them—" I stopped. I couldn't continue.   Jason looked at me. "Yeah, I *do* know. Why are you looking at me like that?"

"Nothing. I was just thinking about Gerta. I found a wedding ring at David's place yesterday, inscribed 'Tony and Gerta.' He'd kept it. I was thinking about how it must have been for Gerta all these times, seeing him with other women, hearing him schmooze them, knowing he was with some of them.''

"Maybe she left him. Maybe he was the lovelorn one. Trying to fill that big empty spot with other women.''

"Hmmm. I don't think so. The one consistent thread in all this mess is DeAngelo as victim of his own irresistibility to women and his need for affirmation. A kind of fatal attraction.''

"Maybe he just loved himself so much he imploded. He curled up and died. In another year, all that sucking up would have permanently puckered his lips.''

"You're jealous!''

"Am not.''

"Are too.''

He was grinning. "Am not.''

"Jason, look at this from another angle. Who benefits?''

"Stella, you've been over this until my head hurts. Give it a rest. Let Stokowski figure it out. He's good. He'll get the right person.''

"Suzanne and David benefit. Suzanne lent them money. Suppose she needs it back right away. There's a mutual insurance policy so that if anything happens to David or De-Angelo, the other gets the business and cash to pay off the debts. When I mentioned that to Suzanne, she about burst.''

"Stella, is there anyone you haven't talked to?"

"Gerta—and Meredith, of course." I ran my hand lightly over my face, as though that would clear away the cobwebs of worry. "If I could just see Meredith and be sure she's all right."

Jason dug out the comics section. "She's fine, believe me. She needs a little alone time—to think."

"I think I'll go to the gym and work out a little bit." Jason lowered the papers and raised his head. "You belong to a gym?"

"A health club. I joined several months ago. In the midst of a fat frenzy."

"You think Meredith might be there, don't you?"

Meredith would rather die than miss her workout. Especially her Sunday one. "Maybe. Jason, true love is lending me your car."

He looked at me like I'd sprouted snakes from my ears. "I'll rent you a car."

I was actually disappointed, although I shouldn't have been. Jason is very fond of his Miata, and I don't have a very good record with cars. Fluffy's eyelids were very green, and he flapped his jaws at me to say he was in need of some quality time. I decided he was jealous of Jason. I took him with me in his travel cage.

Meredith wasn't at the health club. I fiddled around on the weight machines for twenty minutes, then fell off the treadmill. After that humiliation I went straight to the Little Nothings lingerie boutique. That's the other place Meredith loves to go. There is nothing like a little retail therapy to calm the nerves.

Eventually, through a complicated inheritance, I may own this shop, but right now I'm on a very strict budget. I can't afford most of the things I like the best, but I still find it therapeutic to fondle the garments.

I think of them as the least for the most. The least material for the most dollars. But they are gorgeous. Magnetic, for a lingerie addict like myself.

Cleota Banks, the shop manager, said Meredith hadn't been in for several days, but she had called earlier this morning and placed an order. I was relieved. Meredith was alive and ordering.

I was trying on a nightie with a price tag five times bigger than the size of the nightie and three times bigger than my checking account. A piece of magenta lace perfection, the only one in the shop, it was an original I couldn't possibly afford. The telephone rang, and Cleota answered in a voice, rich and mellow, which carried clearly into the dressing cubicle. If she hadn't said Jason's name, I'm positive I'd never have listened in so carefully.

"Well, sure, Jason. I've got the perfect thing. A piece that is absolutely irresistible. Oh, if she likes lingerie she'll like this. It's one of my favorites. Deep magenta lace. I only have one, though—"

I looked down at the magenta lace nightie I was trying on. That was the nightie she was describing. And *Jason* was buying this nightie—*for who?* Me? I slipped the nightie off and held it up.

The words "*if* she likes lingerie" rang in my head. The whole world—everyone at the newspaper, my bank, my credit card company, and especially this shop—knows full well I am in serious debt over lingerie. Jason definitely knew it. But he couldn't be buying it for me. We weren't on lingerie-swapping terms—were we? It must be some other Jason.

I looked at the nightie. It was made for me, me.

I pulled on my clothes and went to the cash register. Cleota had completed her conversation and was looking through the rack where I had found the nightie. She is a big woman, nearly six feet tall, with long arms and dark hair pulled severely into a bun at the nape of her neck. I peered over the counter to the notepad.

"Jason Paul" was written in block letters, along with the words "hold magenta." And right beneath was the person to whom it was to be sent. Bipsie Lotts, 4324 Clifford Street, Los Angeles, California. I didn't get the zip code because I was seeing too much red.

Cleota turned, frowning, then saw me and smiled.

I held up the nightie. "I just have to have this, Cleota."

"But—" She paused. Her face mirrored her struggle to find a way to say she had just promised it to someone else.

I felt momentarily ashamed of myself, but only momentarily. The thought of Jason buying *this* for someone *else* swept all shame away. I whipped out my credit card and slapped it down on the counter with authority.

She smiled bravely and drew in a deep breath. "It's the only one like it," she said.

"I know. It's beautiful. Tell Jason it looks better on me than on Bipsie."

WHY DON'T THESE guys come with a mark on their foreheads so chumps like me could have half a chance? Maybe if I was lucky he was only a distant cousin to Rick the Ick, or the other two notably bad choices in my prior life. Where was my psychic intuition when I really needed it? Out with the trash fairy?

What would Jason tell me? More lies? And then what? Would I challenge him and say—what? I caught you? After all, who was caught, him or me? I knew the answer to that by the weight on my spirits.

I didn't want to hear him tell me some feeble excuse. I didn't want to hear a lie. I didn't want to hear anything. I was so damn disgusted and disappointed, I guess in myself, I just wanted to go home and…and get on new clothes and a new life. But home wasn't safe. And I couldn't switch lives, not now.

It was one o'clock. Gerta was at the top of my list of contacts for several reasons, but the only way I knew to locate her was at the salon. I wanted to know what she knew of Lizette's whereabouts when DeAngelo was killed and where she'd been at that time. She hadn't been with Suzanne or with me and there hadn't been any other clients on the floor that I knew about. And finally, I wanted to know who Victoria DeAngelo was. The sooner I could find her, the better.

I decided to leave the car in the Cherry Creek Mall parking garage for the time being. With any luck Foley's would have a sale, and the car wouldn't be noticed for days.

With a little ingenuity I could get to the salon and find Gerta without being recognized by a cop or a cruising mad bomber and maybe even avoid the salon staff identifying me. I knew I was suffering rampant paranoia at that point, but that didn't make it one bit less real.

If I take pains with makeup, great clothes, and a spectacular hairdo I stand out, but with a pair of glasses, nondescript hair, and basic brown clothes, I'm invisible. I slicked back my hair into a tiny ponytail at the nape of my neck and pulled on my sweater.

I spread my resources out on the car seat. One sulky lizard in a travel cage, two credit cards, several department store charge cards, a library card, and a bag containing a clean change of underwear and a few snacks. And thirty-seven dollars.

Fluffy was huddled in the corner of his cage, already cold. I lifted him out, slipped his little harness on, and pinned him to *my* teddy.

I left my other stuff in the car and set off at a good clip. The salon was only a few blocks from the mall, and I got there without meeting a single police car. Best of all, it was open for business—on a Sunday, no less. It seemed odd that the only sign of mourning was a black wreath and an announcement stuck to the front door that they would be closed tomorrow, Monday, in memory.

David's car was parked behind the salon, along with three

others. Lizette's little car wasn't there. I jotted down the license numbers of the cars with a ballpoint pen on my hand, noting time of day. If anything happened to me, Stokowski would find the numbers. The hair on my head seemed to be standing on end from sheer nervousness, or maybe it was amazement that the salon was open on Sunday.

Now that I was here, I realized I wanted far more than simply to talk to Gerta. After all, I could have telephoned her. What I really wanted was a chance to get into DeAngelo's office and snoop into the salon's accounts; money is the root of all evil, and a person needs roots.

The garage was locked, and Virgil was nowhere to be seen, but the back door of the salon was open. Coffee was brewing on the counter with a plate of oatmeal cookies next to it and cheery little cocktail napkins at the side. Someone was trying to feed the place back to normal. My stomach growled, and I started to take one, then thought better of it and moved into the hallway.

Ahead of me, the reception desk where Lizette usually sat was empty. A pencil lay next to the telephone message pad as though she'd just stepped away, but the chair was pushed under as if it hadn't been used lately. Since the salon usually wasn't open, David might be the only one there. That would make it easier for me, at least.

I dodged up the back stairs to the upper hall, my footfalls muffled in the carpeting. Quiet filled the hallway like cotton, muting voices, absorbing the sounds of the salon. DeAngelo's fierce energy, the life force of the establishment, was gone, and the result was eerie.

I eased along the hallway as a solitary female voice murmured from a room up the hall, Gerta's room, the room where Suzanne had been when DeAngelo was killed.

At the room I remembered as Gerta's station, I peered in, expecting to see Gerta's dark head and bright blue eyes. Instead I saw Lizette's mahogany spikes. She was hunched over the hands of a nervous young woman wearing a gold-embroidered cap, whose feet rested gingerly in a footbath. She was braver than I would have been.

Immediately I glanced around the room for Gerta's license to get her address. Beside the mirror, a solitary nail stuck out of the wall, and faint scratches marked the paint where the frame had been. "Lizette, may I talk to you for a minute?"

Lizette looked up, her eyes first rounding in surprise, then narrowing as she recognized me. She resumed filing with a vengeance. "In a moment," she replied. She buffed the nails for a busy minute, then rubbed them with oil and instructed the woman to relax for a minute before her hand massage.

Lizette's face twisted impatiently as soon as she emerged from the room into the hallway with me. "What do you want?" she asked irritably.

"Where's Gerta?"

"She called in sick today. Sounded like she had a terrible cold."

"Do you know where I could reach her?"

She refused to meet my gaze. "Check with David."

"This *is* Gerta's station, isn't it?"

"Yeah, why?"

"Her license is gone."

She turned impatiently, then an exaggerated puzzlement filled her face. "Well, for heaven's sake. Where do you suppose it is?"

"If I were Gerta and I wanted to disappear, all I'd have to do was erase my name from the computer, pick up my license, and go. I'd be traced, but it would take a while."

"Gerta doesn't know a computer from a calculator," Lizette said.

"Where does she keep her client file?"

"Locks it in her bottom drawer. She's, like, absolutely jealous of it."

I made a move toward the drawer, and Lizette jumped ahead of me, pulling on it. It flew open. "Well, I'll be! I'll bet she's gone for good.'' She couldn't have looked more pleased if she'd eaten a canary.

"Do you know where she lives?"

She smiled sweetly. "Sorry, no idea." She lied, of course, but I couldn't very well strangle her in front of a witness.

The door to the solarium was closed. I turned to DeAngelo's room, slipped inside, shut the door, and flicked the light switch on a mausoleum-like atmosphere. For a moment there was even a waft of carnations and roses, funeral bouquet scent.

DeAngelo's scissors were lined up on the counter, one at an angle, a wisp of hair in the blades. His hair dryers were racked up like pistols ready to be drawn and fired. Even the bowl where he'd mixed my hair color was still in the sink. No one had cleaned.

I picked up the telephone receiver and turned it over in my hand. It was a private line—why? Had DeAngelo been suspicious of his own staff? His partner, David? DeAngelo had phoned Meredith from there. I pressed the redial button, expecting to hear Meredith's answering machine. A soft, older, feminine voice answered. "Hello?"

This wasn't Meredith. But this was DeAngelo's telephone, and a private line. While someone else could have used it, most likely he was the one who dialed this number. All kinds of possibilities jumped forward—it could be a sales rep, it could be yet another woman in DeAngelo's life, it might be the mysterious Victoria DeAngelo. And if it was Victoria, I wanted to get an address without scaring her off the line.

I crammed the phone to my ear and plunged in. "This is the Communications Satellite Corporation calling to tell you that you've possibly won the grand prize in our drawing. Now to verify that you're the correct person, I need to know whether you're married or single."

"Well, I don't think—"

The last thing I wanted her to do was think. I rushed her. "You're on the verge of winning a magnificent trip to the destination of your dreams. We only need to know whether to plan on a single or a double room.''

Cartoon sounds from a television jangled in the background. ''Oh, how exciting! I've never won anything before. My husband will be so amazed. I'm Mrs.''

I was careful to use authority words like ''verify'' and avoid questions that would cause her to stop and think. ''Great. Now I need to verify the correct spelling of your last name. It is…''

''Oh, let's see. Uh, W-a-l-l-e-e-n. Walleen. Dorothy Walleen.''

''And where should I send the prize notification?''

''To 10094 Lincoln Street, Arvada, Colorado. People are always calling it Arv*ay*da, but it's really Arv*ah*da. But I guess you know that, don't you? Oh, I'm so excited. Now, who did you say you were?''

I snatched up a pen and a scrap of paper from the counter and scribbled down the address. Now for the crucial information. ''I believe you know a Mr. Anthony DeAngelo?''

There was a sudden hush at the end of the line. A child's squeal of delight and cartoon music were all I heard. I had almost concluded that someone else had used this phone to call when, in a much changed, lower voice she spoke. ''Uh, yes. At least formerly. Before he died.''

''Well, I'm so sorry to hear that. Mr. DeAngelo gave us your name for the drawing. He must have known you rather well.''

Again there was a long pause, then a somber reply. ''He…knew my granddaughter, Vicky.''

Vicky….*Victoria. Victoria DeAngelo?* I wanted to ask about Vicky, but I figured that would blow the interview. But if I hurried, I could get to her by late afternoon. Maybe even catch up with Vicky, who could well be the last person DeAngelo spoke to. ''Well, I appreciate your cooperation. You should receive final notification any day. Thank you.'' I hung up, feeling like a scuzzbucket, but an incredibly successful one. I was sure I'd found the mysterious Victoria, but I'd conned a nice, decent woman like a pro. The line between crusader and flimflam artist was looking mighty narrow.

I shook myself. There was no time to wallow in regret; someone was out there trying to kill people. Hell, to kill me.

I folded Dorothy Walleen's address and stuffed it in my pocket. The pen I recognized. It was the pink-and-lavender ballpoint I'd seen Lizette use the first day I'd come to the salon. I remembered its distinctive laser carving. What I hadn't noticed before was that it was from the Hair Spa, DeAngelo's rival—something to ask Lizette about the next time I saw her. I shoved it in my back pocket. As I did, I remembered how I had shoved Meredith's bangle into my pocket the same way. It was an ugly little memory.

I was nearly out the door when I remembered DeAngelo's card file. He'd had me write my name and address on a three-by-five card with a little *DA* in the upper corner, which he'd filed in a gray metal file box. I looked for the box. Everywhere. I couldn't find it, although there were two cards lying on the supply cart. I checked the supply room again, and found nothing except for a suspiciously empty space at the back of the counter where a file box would have fit nicely.

Lizette had claimed she didn't have customers' addresses, only phone numbers. DeAngelo kept them locked in his computer.

The voices in the room down the hall had dropped to a soft murmur. I stole down the corridor, peeking into each room as I went. The changing room on my right was empty.

The stairs to the third floor were on my immediate left. I took them two at a time, remembering how I'd seen Meredith's legs as I sat in the chair at DeAngelo's station.

Upstairs I silently eased open the door to his office, flicked on the lights, and closed the door behind me. The police had clearly been through the room, leaving behind the telltale rusty smudges of sienna fingerprint powder. The window blinds were still pulled shut, but DeAngelo's love couch was folded up, and the pictures on the wall were just enough out of adjustment that I knew even they had been examined. Nothing had been overlooked.

The envelopes I'd seen on DeAngelo's desk were gone, but I was pretty sure I'd seen them at David's place. The desk drawers were locked. Even the closet had been searched. I wondered what had been found.

DeAngelo had programmed his telephone with all the employees' telephone numbers and conveniently written in their names. I punched in Gerta's. It rang five times, then switched to an AT&T answering service. I didn't leave a message.

I turned on the computer. It asked for a password. I tried DeAngelo's initials and David's, TDA, DND, Daveed, Ubetcha, and an assortment of words, then the telephone number to the salon; finally I tried the names of the women in his life.

"Victoria" worked. Poor Meredith. As far as I was concerned, this was just another indication of his perfidy.

DeAngelo kept his wedding ring with "Tony & Gerta" inscribed in it; he used "Victoria" for his computer password; God knows what he used to memorialize Lizette and Meredith. My mother's cat had a trophy system, too. He saved a small portion of each creature he caught and laid it on the doormat. Not too different.

The computer directory held all the information I needed after that. Lizette had stressed that DeAngelo locked up the confidential information, but the lock hadn't kept me out for more than a minute. So who in the salon knew computers?

I went to the employee files first. Curiously, Virgil's address was given as the salon. Gerta lived in northwest Denver. I copied her phone number, then dialed it. No answer. I printed out the listing, then went to the customer files.

I searched the list for the name Ami and found nothing.

Finally I scanned the accounts. The billing was rudimentary; the accounts were hopelessly scrambled. From the little I saw, this shop was headed for financial trouble. However wonderful DeAngelo was at hairstyling, he was terrible at books. I flipped to the last entry—my payment—entered after DeAngelo died. But of course, David would have access to the account file.

I closed the files and returned to the second floor, slipping along the hallway. All the usual hum of a busy salon was muted, hushed, as though the business was holding its breath. I was even holding mine.

As I came down to the first floor I saw through the glass French doors that David was in the midst of a final comb-out and swirl. I caught his attention and waved, but he shook his head, refusing to be interrupted.

Since I had to wait, I twirled on Lizette's chair at her impeccably neat desk. I have always suspected that a clean desk is the sign of an empty mind.

I pulled open the little drawer. All the pencils were sharpened, the pens lined up, and every paper clip lay the same way. I stirred the paper clips to give her something to do later and rolled the pens, remembering Lizette's Hair Spa pen in my pocket.

It was a long shot, but I dialed the number and, to my amazement, someone answered. In my best officialese I said, "Hello, this is Dorothy Claybanaugh with the Polyburg Technical Assistance and Service agency. May I speak to the manager, please?"

"I am the manager."

"I'm calling to verify employment and earnings of Lizette, Elizabeth Lewis."

There was a long silence, the murmur of a busy shop in the background. Finally, the receptionist spoke up. "She left here six weeks ago."

"Can you verify her position?"

There was an even longer silence before the woman cleared her throat and spoke. "She was a…a consultant."

"And her duties included computer skills?"

"That was her best skill."

"Would you describe her as competent, excellent, or in need of further training?"

"Quite competent."

"I see. Well, thank you very much."

"Wait a minute, this is Sunday! What agency did you say you were with?"

I hung up. So Lizette was quite competent on computer. Given the elementary business files DeAngelo set up, she probably had full access. Interesting, but I wasn't sure where it went.

I stared at the telephone messages, thinking. Lizette was in a position to know a great deal about DeAngelo, David, and the salon. She was the receptionist, so she took down all the information that eventually went into the files! I wondered if Lizette's "consulting" was in the form of selling customer lists and other information.

David's client finally gave him the obligatory hug and tip and "ta-ta."

I waited until she was through the front door, then darted into his room.

He was sweeping crescents of damp hair into a dustpan in jerky, irritable movements. In the far corner a woman was tucked under a dryer, sipping coffee and reading *People* magazine. The smell of permanent wave solution clung to the room. Despite the indirect lighting, fatigue shadowed his eyes and hollowed his cheeks.

He turned to me so the client couldn't see his face. "Please smile, I don't want the client upset by you. I don't have the slightest idea where Gerta is. Lizette said she called in sick. Didn't even cancel her clients, so Lizette had to fill in for her. Not that she minds, since she was dying for Gerta's space, but still— The clients are pretty pissed."

David continued in a rush. "Fine thing! Gerta wasn't in love with him anymore. She just loved the house he bought for them. Bunch of shit, if you ask me. So, what do you care?"

My lips stretched in an imitation smile. "Her client file is gone. Do you know anything about it?"

He tossed a soggy towel into the bin. "Probably means

she's cleared out. You'd think she'd at least wait for the money!''

"Her paycheck?"

He laughed bitterly. "Hell, no. Her flaming inheritance. They never got divorced. She'll get everything, but she'll have to fight for it, by God.''

I'd seen the insurance papers *and* the business accounts. Inheriting the shop was a probable disaster, whereas the insurance, if paid up, was worth something. And Victoria DeAngelo was the number-one beneficiary. If Gerta killed DeAngelo it might be for revenge or jealousy, but it wasn't for money. "DeAngelo's file is missing too."

"I've got it. We don't leave client listings around; you never know who'll be prying into them.''

"Shameful. May I look at it?"

"No. It's locked up. There's all kinds of sneaks in this world.''

"Of course, all this information comes through Lizette. I guess it's not terribly secret.''

"Lizette wouldn't divulge client information."

"Of course not. She's incredibly loyal. Like Gerta."

He slammed the door after me.

I was in the back hall heading for the back door when Virgil emerged from the basement.

"Whoa!" he exclaimed when he saw me. His face was damp with the sweat of his brow. He backed up toward the basement. A wave of sour armpit smell followed him.

"Virgil! I'm trying to find Gerta. I'm worried about her. Do you know where I can find her?"

He shook his head.

"She always liked you, treated you well. You'd help out if she was in trouble, wouldn't you?"

He scowled. "But you're the trouble she's trying to get away from."

"Look, Virgil. I know you and I didn't hit it off, but this is important—to her."

He backed into the basement doorway, took a stumbling step down. I followed him. "Look, I'll help you out if you'll tell me where she lives. I'm not going to hurt her."

"How're you gonna help me?" He moved down another step on the basement stairs.

"Well, I could clean your garage apartment for you, tidy the place up. Maybe come to the basement, help sort supplies, that kind of thing."

"You stay outta there. Stay away from me." He shut the door in my face.

I was so frustrated I was half tempted to throw the brass bolt on the door and lock him in there for good.

I thought about leaving a message for Stokowski, pointing out that Gerta was not to be found, but that would tell him I was messing about in his case and further enrage him. Since I couldn't locate Gerta, I decided to follow up with Dorothy Walleen and Victoria, and then swing by Gerta's house afterward. Between the two of them, I might be able to find out who Victoria was and why DeAngelo had called her.

As soon as I left the salon I felt eyes on the back of my neck again. Fluffy seemed to sense my nervousness, crawling up so he could see out the neck of my sweater.

After I reached my rental car I drove circuitously to Arvada. I couldn't spot anyone following me.

Dorothy Walleen lived in a one-story, sage-green house in a neighborhood of thirty-year-old ranch-style homes with gently curving cement driveways, old enough to have medium-size trees in the front lawns. She had a two-car garage whose door was open, showing labeled boxes stacked to the rafters and a wall with tools hung on pegboard.

I knocked, the blare of a television coming through the front door. A child's voice called out, then the door abruptly swung open. "Mommy?"

A little girl of perhaps four years of age stood before me, with long, dark hair in a thick bunch on her back, tied with a vivid blue ribbon that emphasized the blue of her eyes and her tiny winglike eyebrows. She was a miniature Gerta. She stared at me for a moment, then turned and called over her shoulder. "Gramma, someone's here."

I leaned toward her. "Is your name Victoria?"
She nodded.

Another twist. Victoria was Gerta's daughter. And, I thought, odds on she was DeAngelo's child, since Gerta had been married to him. However, so far none of the relationships in this group had been straightforward.

"Gramma" was a young-looking forty-something woman in tennis shoes and a powder-blue sweat suit that set off her short, prematurely white hair. She was small, striking-looking, with a trim figure and the same distinctive, winglike eyebrows as Vicky and Gerta. The family resemblance was unmistakable, grandmother, mother, and daughter. She looked at me guardedly through the screen door, worry at the back of her eyes. "Yes, what can I do for you?"

I was so sure this was Gerta's mother that I risked it. "Mrs. Walleen, I'm trying to locate your daughter, Gerta. I know she's been upset about the death at the salon, and I wanted to talk to her. Can you help?"

She frowned, eyebrows drawn together. "Well, she isn't here right now. I can take a message."

"I really need to talk to her personally."

Mrs. Walleen licked her lips and glanced down at the child, who was staring at us, wide-eyed and alert. "Vicky, dear, run see if the kettle is boiling on the stove for me, thanks." She waited until the child had left, then spoke in a hushed voice. "Gerta hasn't been home since she dropped Vicky off yesterday morning. I don't know what to tell you. I've called the police, but they won't take a report yet. She was going to go to work, then to the funeral home, and promised to pick up milk on the way back. She would never forget Vicky. I know something's wrong." Her lip trembled, and her eyes filled with tears.

I'd forgotten all about DeAngelo's funeral. "Which funeral home was she going to?"

"Kinsey and Mulholland. But I've already called there, and they haven't seen her."

"I'd be more than glad to drive by her house and check there to make sure she's not there."

"That might help. I've been reluctant to take Vicky with me—"

"Gramma—" The child appeared at the doorway to the kitchen, swinging her leg back and forth. "Gramma, the stove's not on."

"Okay, dear. I'll be right there." She turned back to me. "Do I know you? You sound so familiar."

"I met Gerta at the salon. I'm sure we haven't met."

She looked dubiously at me until I began to be uncomfortable. I wanted her to think about something else, fast. "It must have been a terrible shock when DeAngelo died."

"Oh, yes. Very sudden. I know I haven't seen you before, but your voice sounds so familiar, like I just know you from somewhere."

"Gerta was married to DeAngelo, for what, four years?"

She pursed her lips. "Seven years, more or less. She wanted a divorce three years ago, but DeAngelo kept stalling. Said he didn't want to lose his only family—" She jerked her head toward Vicky, who had draped herself over the arm of an easy chair and was watching the television upside down.

"But Gerta wanted a divorce?"

"At first she said it was for her. For her independence. She wants to change everything, even her job. She wants to go into real estate sales. She figures she'll have more time for Vicky and a better income."

"What did DeAngelo say to that?"

She rolled her eyes. "It was odd. At first he was opposed, then he agreed. He didn't really have any say in it anyway."

So Gerta wouldn't inherit, and she didn't want to stay with

DeAngelo, and he was willing to give her a divorce. It was looking a lot more likely that she was a victim than a killer.

"Does Gerta have a white van?"

"No, she has a little blue Honda, about ready to fall apart. She couldn't afford a second car. We've tried to help her, but—" She glanced toward Vicky again, then, reassured that the child wasn't listening, turned back to me. "Tony was devoted to Vicky, but he wasn't a great provider, although he tried." She glanced at her watch again.

I had the same nasty feeling about Gerta's safety that she had. "Mrs. Walleen, if you'll call this number and talk to Detective Stokowski, he'll listen to you." She opened the door and took the slip of paper.

Vicky appeared at the door, her nose pressed against the screen, making little squares of flesh. But it was her eyes that caught me. Luminous blue depths, and troubled. A terrible feeling of desperation welled up in my chest, followed by a tremor that started in my heart. Time was running out.

Gerta's home was in Northwest Denver on a side street of well-kept 1920s bungalows that were set a few feet farther back from the street than the norm, giving the block a certain graciousness. Hers was a small bungalow with a dormered roof facing south. A tall, narrow Siberian elm grew on the parking strip, and twigs from it littered the lawn. It needed a good trimming. Siberian elms always need a good trimming.

In the yard next door, two little boys around five and seven years of age were digging dirt with a bright yellow Tonka earth mover. Their eyes, solemn and round, followed me as I got out of the car. The afternoon sun was warm on my back, almost hot, and the unraked leaves smelled warm and sweet and crunched under my feet.

The house looked sleepy, uninhabited. The morning newspaper lay on the porch and a *Watchtower* pamphlet from the Jehovah's Witnesses protruded from the screen door. I knocked on the door. The boys inched closer, staring. One of them stuck a filthy finger into the corner of his mouth. I knocked again and smiled at the kids.

"She ain't there," the taller one said. "She ain't been there, neither."

"Where'd she go?"

The smaller one edged toward me, a finger exploring his ear. "Vicky's not home." The bigger one punched him, whispered fiercely in his ear, then looked at me suspiciously.

I leaned against the porch railing. "Where's her mommy?"

The older boy elbowed the smaller one into silence, grabbed his shirt, and dragged him to their house.

I felt sick and knocked again. Then I tried the doorknob. It was locked. I walked around the house, peering into the windows. All I saw was a tidy house, well kept, with a kitchen sink containing a few dirty dishes. A garage at the back of the yard looked as if it hadn't been used in fifty years. The door sagged with age, and there was a line of trash blown against it. Old trash.

I knocked on the front door of the neighboring house where the boys had gone. The younger of the two boys opened the door solemnly, sucking on the same dirty finger. A woman called out roughly, then appeared, wearing torn jeans and a soft flannel shirt. "Yeah?"

"I'm trying to find Gerta," I explained.

"Haven't seen her since yesterday."

"Did you notice any strange cars at her house, maybe in the drive?"

She shook her head, but the older boy nodded.

"What'dya see?"

"A white van."

His mother frowned. "Oh no, you didn't. I'd remember that."

"Yes, I did. I seen it. Last night. You were talking on the phone again."

I tried to keep a bland response. "You don't remember the license number, do you?"

He studied the floor and the toe of his shoe, thinking. The phone rang in the kitchen, and his mother trailed off to answer it.

"Did something happen to Vicky?"

"She's fine. She's at her gramma's for a little while."

He smiled, so suddenly and obviously relieved it warmed my heart and made my eyes sting. "Are you sure you don't know the license number? It's really important."

He shook his head. "I just remember Chevy."

# NINETEEN

To THE WEST a bank of clouds had piled up over the mountains, smothering the sun and leeching the heat out of the last of the daylight. The wind chilled my neck, and I pulled my jacket closer, wondering how lonely I could possibly get.

I started the engine, then sat for a moment, trying to sort out my next move. There was little safety left; the margin of error had shrunk to zero, but my brain seemed to be dulled with fatigue and depression.

A sudden prickle on the skin of my neck startled me. The hair on my head rose. I reached gingerly to scratch and felt a cold body. Fluffy.

My heart lightened immediately. "Hey, buddy. I'd forgotten about you." I dragged him out. He was cold, disgusted, and grumpy, but he was company. I had to have a place for Fluffy, preferably centrally located, with heat, light, telephone, and toilet, and all for free. I held him in my hand to warm him, but my fingers were so cold he flapped his lips at me and blinked. He was asking for a warm cage and a wiggling meal.

"I don't *know*, Fluffy—we're not really homeless-shelter material, I don't have enough cash, and I can't risk charging a room, in case Stokowski has a tracer on my card."

I thought of Jason. If I had to, I could go there, but that would be just before hell froze over. I was still hurting over the nightie for Bipsie Boo or whatever her name was.

I passed a Kmart. The parking lot was full of cars, the mart windows glowed with Halloween decorations, and the lights were bright, cheerful, and innocent. I wheeled in.

Inside, Kmart-scented air burst onto my face, warm and warehouse-cozy. Overhead, a piercing nasal voice called Housewares to answer on line three. They have tryouts for that job. I smiled at the shoppers and considered the possibility of spending the night in the fitting room, or slipping into the back room and hiding among the boxes. Or in the ladies' rest room. I could lock the stall door and prop my feet up until everyone went home.

Sweat suits were on special. I selected the largest they had. If I had to spend the night on the streets, at least I could stuff it with newspapers—insulation *and* a disguise. I also picked up a fresh supply of chocolate and a pocket flashlight.

I found a checkout counter and slid in behind the only other customer. A rack of midnight gossip tabloids stood in front of me. Headlines screamed out. ''Grief-Stricken Bride Spends Night in Morgue.'' ''Sex-Starved Ghost Drives Couple from Home''—this seemed familiar, maybe a rerun, back by popular demand. But it was the last one that got me. ''Snake Oil Cures Acne, Obesity, Impotence and Infertility.'' So does death.

The papers sparked an idea. I still had the key to the *Daily Orion*, if I could just get there. I hadn't been fired, and Mr. Gerster hadn't told me not to be there, he'd only said he was pulling my column. And if I got bored, I could go through my files and check my mail. Maybe there would even be contact from Ami.

The most important thing now was to get into the office, where Fluffy would be safe. I slung my purchases in the back of the car and drove to central Denver, where I located an apartment building three blocks away from the office with unassigned parking in the rear.

After I pulled the sweat suit over my clothes, I stuffed my emergency supplies, corn curls, and chocolate into the sweat suit, changing my shape considerably. Lowered recognizability.

It was barely past six o'clock, with a cloud cover reflecting the streetlights in a hazy twilight. Cars lined the street, dark and vacant. A block from the office my sweatpants sagged, threatening to spill my stuff. The corn curls chafed the skin on my ankles. I slowed my waddle and lingered at the corner, looking for signs of someone hidden in the shadows of a darkened front seat, watching. Nothing.

A catalpa tree waved its branches in the wind, its beans rattling hollowly in the branches like so many bones. I shuffled on, feeling as conspicuous as a neon sign in a cemetery, a crawly feeling on the back of my neck.

The street was too quiet. I wasn't sure whether it was paranoia or the normal level of silence. I glanced left and right, scanning for telltale movements. A sudden gust of wind broke the quiet, pushing leaves and a paper bag before it. Two houses away, cotton ghosts for Halloween flapped from the tree branches, and a cardboard skeleton shuddered on the porch.

I lumbered past the office on the opposite side of the street, then stopped, pretending to examine a special garbage treat in order to scrutinize the street once more. I couldn't see a thing, not one person, yet the feeling that someone was watching persisted.

At the intersection I crossed the street and debated with myself whether I really wanted to go through with this, but then I felt Fluffy's little feet, cold on my skin. He wouldn't live through a night in the car alone in his cage. I had to get him inside and warm. I started toward the front door.

I was still two houses away from the office when headlights appeared in the street, down the block. I hesitated. The streetlight shone on a light rack, flashed on the door badge. It was a squad car. A siren howled. The squad car came on, fast, racing through the intersection, the light rack flashing red, white, and blue.

My heart tripped, and a slick of sweat broke out on my cheeks and palms. I was in front of a two-story house with dark windows and a tall hedge. It was too late to run for shelter in the alley. Running would only draw attention to me; besides, I couldn't run with my sweatpants full of provisions.

The siren fell; the squad car slowed, drew up opposite me,

and braked, pulling to the curb. Its spotlight beamed over the *Orion* office, back and forth across the front of the building.

The front door opened. The thin figure of Mr. Gerster appeared, waving to the officers.

I shoved myself tight against the scratchy hedge, trying to look like part of the windblown rubbish. A dog barked, then howled. My skin crawled. Fluffy dove for my shirt pocket.

Two officers emerged from the squad car. Barely noticing me, they strode to the front door of the office, flashlights out, beams ready. Another squad car drove by, turned the corner, and disappeared down the alley.

I swallowed, took a deep breath, and went straight back the way I came. My awful outfit kept me from running and attracting attention. I lumbered away.

Fluffy was cold, and I was exhausted. I had done everything not to involve and possibly endanger friends. But I couldn't think of anything else to do. I dug my cellular phone out from the bottom of my purse and punched in the numbers. Nothing happened. The battery was too low.

It was a bizarre coincidence that the police were there just as I was arriving. If I'd come a hair sooner, I'd have run right into Gerster and the police would have been all over me. Bizarre coincidences occur, true.

I stopped a half block away from my rental car and changed directions. Even the slim chance that my rental was spotted was enough. There was even the possibility that Jason had told the police about renting the car for me. My paranoia was rampant.

It was three blocks to a 7-Eleven with hostile bright lights and a telephone. I called my answering machine first. There were two messages. First, a breathy, unimaginative whisper that made me choke. "That was for fun. Next time I won't miss."

The other was from Zelda, telling me to answer my phone. I'd hoped to hear from Jason.

I called Zelda, and she arrived in less than twenty minutes.

The car door opened, overhead light flashing on her bright blond curls. "Stella! Hurry!" She reached up and killed the light. "Come on!"

I fell into the car, and she gunned the engine and sped away. "Where are we going?"

"Home. You can get out of that stupid outfit, comb your hair, and do whatever you need to do. Mine is the one place Lee won't come."

"You'd better slow down. Don't need a ticket now."

She lifted her foot from the gas pedal. "I just get so damn mad." She stopped for a light and turned to me. "I heard all about the bomb on the television news and from Jason. Now the office has been broken into."

"When?"

She glanced at me. "Not sure. Mr. Gerster went by for some reason just a little bit ago, and found it. He called me after he called the police."

I started to ask why he would call Zelda, then I stopped. After all, Zelda virtually ran the place.

Zelda continued. "He's absolutely convinced this has to do with that Big Dick guy of yours." She glanced at me. "You don't suppose it does, do you?"

I shook my head. "I don't believe in coincidence, Zelda, but...Nah, probably just some desperate burglar looking for petty cash."

"Then why throw the files around?"

"My files?"

"Guess so. First the bomb, and now the burglary. I was afraid you were hurt."

"Zelda, I'm fine. I don't want to talk about the bomb. Or about the burglary. Now, tell me, why are you mad at Stokowski?"

"Lee figured you'd give Meredith a credit card in order to hide, so he traced her to the motel. I told him he shouldn't arrest her, she's as innocent as a goddamn lamb, but he just looked through me like I wasn't even there. I think he did anyway.''

"You're doing this, picking me up and all, because you're mad at Stokowski?" She didn't reply. "And when you forgive him, then do you turn me in?''

"No. I don't turn people in. I don't rat on them, and I don't believe in threatening people with jail so they'll talk."

I was relieved to hear Meredith was safe, even if in custody.

"It's his job, Zelda. And maybe he's trying to protect her."

Zelda wasn't listening. She swung wide onto Sixth Avenue. "There's a lot I don't understand, but I do understand when someone doesn't respect me. And he doesn't. He doesn't listen to a thing I say. He nods and looks through me, like I was a kid or a dope. Well, I'm not going to be a wuss for anybody."

She was quiet for a block or two, then spoke again. "I've renovated my hair, my body, my wardrobe, myself. I'm so new from the skin out I don't even know who I am anymore. I've done everything I could to get Stokowski's attention. Fat lot of good it's done. I should have saved my money and sagged into middle age in comfort."

"You aren't sagging, Zelda."

She snorted. "The point is, I want Lee to love me for who I am, if I still know who I am. Not only does he not notice me when I'm decked out to kill, he doesn't have time. You put him on a case, and that's all he sees. All he does. And there's never any in-between cases. That's it."

She pulled into her driveway, braked, and turned to me. "You know, that might be enough for me, if he'd just look at me the way Jason looks at you. If he would get upset when he thought I was in trouble the way Jason did when he thought you were hurt."

Her voice was tough and cold, perhaps colder than I'd ever heard it before, but a tear trickled down her cheek. "Stella, I really love Lee Stokowski. I think my heart is breaking."

Zelda did her best to be good company. She made popcorn and cocoa and tried to pretend she was excited about watching me try to feed Fluffy, but she had a bad case of the lovelorns, and it showed in her frequent heavy sighs.

Fluffy's dinner was miraculously still alive, and I put it in with him. He wrapped his tail over his nose and hung upside down from the cage wall and ignored it. His skin was a healthy green, and he didn't have a runny nose, but he was still lethargic. I tried to convince him to drink some water, but he wouldn't open his mouth. A sulky lizard is not good company. Neither is a lovelorn secretary.

Finally, by eight o'clock, desperate for more spirited company, I called Jason, expecting him to rant and rave, but all I got was his answering machine. I couldn't remember when I'd dealt with so many machines and so few people. After that I collapsed on the bed in Zelda's spare room and fell asleep within seconds of my head hitting the pillow.

An hour later I woke, aching with loneliness from a dream that involved Jason's comforting arms. For a few minutes I struggled with the wisps of sleep, then I rose and showered. I toweled off, slipped on a fresh purple-paisley teddy, and pulled back on my navy jumpsuit and sweater. I was beginning to hate them, I'd worn them so long.

Zelda wasn't the only one whose love life was in a tangle. I thought that if last night's lovemaking had had any meaning for Jason, he would at least try to call me, maybe to explain about the nightie for Bipsie. Cleota would have called him back as soon as I left Little Nothings with the nightie. And if she gave him my message, he'd for sure know that I knew he was buying intimate apparel for someone else.

I felt like Jason was doing the same thing DeAngelo had been doing—stringing along multiple women as if we were a series of Boy Scout badges. He had been so loving. Why couldn't it just have worked out right?

In all honesty, I had been wanting him terribly. Too much, perhaps. It sure made me more sympathetic to Meredith's situation. And Zelda's. We all wanted the long-term intimacy of a good relationship. So much, maybe, that we overlooked things, like the fact that they never said, "I love you." Of course, I hadn't said it either, but that was because I wasn't sure I did. Clearly, he wasn't sure, either.

I called my answering machine at home; nothing. Next I tried my office voice mail. There were two messages. The first was from Jason. "Stella, where the hell are you?" It wasn't much, but it was a little satisfaction. The grin fell from my face when I heard the second message. It was from Lizette. At 6:15, almost four hours ago.

Her voice was hurried, almost frantic, begging for help. "Please help—I was just trying to get some money. You don't know how hard it is. It was dumb, I know. I never should have done it. Please help me, Stella, I'm so scared." Her door buzzer sounded, and her voice dropped to a barely discernible whisper. "Please come as soon as you can." Then she disconnected.

I wondered briefly why she had called me, not someone else, but I couldn't ignore her plea. It was that desperate.

Zelda had bravely offered me the use of her car and left her keys on the dinette table. I took them and closed the door quietly, leaving Zelda and Fluffy sound asleep.

# TWENTY

LIZETTE'S APARTMENT BUILDING was a stark cubicle washed by the jaundiced glow of the streetlights, the darkened windows like dead eyes. Her car was still parked on the far side of the building.

On the third floor, Lizette's window was glowing, lit by the living room lamp. While I watched, the curtain billowed out, then in with the breeze. A shadow fell across the window. I hurried down the sidewalk to the entry.

I had pressed her bell for the third time when through the door I saw a slight figure at the far end of the hall. At first I thought it was Lizette, coming down to open the door for me herself. But it wasn't. It was Gerta.

For a fleeting moment she stared back, her eyes wide and terrified; then she turned and disappeared down the back stairs.

I slammed out the front door and raced to the side of the building. Ahead of me fifty yards, Gerta was climbing into her car. "Gerta, wait!" I yelled. She barely hesitated.

Pelting after her, I reached the car just as the engine caught. Her face was white behind the car window, her eyes orbs of fear, as if she'd seen a ghost. She gunned the motor and sped away in a shower of street grit.

Dread folded in like an early-morning fog, chilling me to the bone. I pulled my jacket close to me and rubbed my arms as I ran back to the apartment building.

I was afraid I knew what I'd find, and it made me want to lash out. I took it out on the doorbell. I punched Lizette's bell one more time, then blasted the manager's.

It felt like forever before he appeared, sleepy-eyed, furious, and smelling like a wet ashtray. I drew myself up to look official. "Emergency, sir. There's a medical problem in number eighteen," I said. "We need to get up there immediately. Bring the oxygen."

He was not an empathic man. "Who the hell do you think you are?"

I ignored him and ran up the stairs.

"I don't have oxygen. This ain't a goddamn nursing home here," he panted after me. "Hey, you can't bust in here."

"It's life or death. Where's your passkey?"

"So I'm some kind of nurse, I gotta go see if Liz is sick?"

"She has a heart condition, and if she dies because you wouldn't let me in to check on her, her family will sue the socks off you."

By the second floor, he was behind me and breathing like a walrus. He hadn't moved that fast in years. "Everybody sues. Friggin' mess. Plot...by lawyers...to wring honest dollars...from the innocent."

By the third floor he lagged behind. I ran down the hall and threw myself against her door, twisting the doorknob. It was locked. I fell against it, banging my head noisily on the door.

The manager arrived and started to protest again.

"Where's the key? Hurry!" I urged.

He knocked loudly, then jammed his key into the lock, twisting the knob simultaneously. The door popped open. He gripped the doorjamb with one hand and pretended to examine the living room while he caught his breath, his shoulders heaving from the climb.

I pushed past him. Heat poured over me, blowing from the air vents. The thermostat was set at eighty. I felt immediately nauseated.

A glance showed that the living room was unchanged from my last visit, except the ashtray was gone from the coffee table, and magazines now littered the couch where Lizette had been reading. *Self* magazine was open to an article about toning buttocks. My mouth was dry. My attempt to call her name came out a croak.

He sniffed the air like a wounded basset hound. "She's cooking herself, is what's wrong with her."

"She had the window open and the place cool earlier," I said, my voice almost back to normal. "Lizette!" I called.

I crossed the living room, hesitating by the telephone. I was tempted to dial for police, but that would erase whatever number might be stored in redial. Instead, I turned to the manager. I'm not sure why it feels so good to order others not to do what you really want to do. "Don't touch the phone," I ordered.

He pointed with his head to the bedroom. "You can go ahead there. I don't feel good. You go." He slid down the wall to the floor, green around the jowls and sweating. "You're a woman. You go."

My stomach churned. "You all right?"

He nodded, resting his head back against the wall.

My stomach lurched around again. For once, I was glad it was empty. I moved quickly, scanning the floor for I don't know what—blood spots, weapons. A quick peek in the bathroom revealed an orderly, all-towels-hung-up neatness, but the room was damp, as though she'd recently had a shower. A heavy sickly sweet scent of gardenia bath powder hung in the humid air. I've never liked the smell. If Death had a mother, she wore that scent.

The door to Lizette's bedroom was closed. I pushed it wide. For a moment I was unable to step in. I barely recognized my own voice. "Lizette?"

A numbing chill blanketed me. Inconsequential things stood out: the wadded-up tissue, the tilt of the lampshade, the way the light spilled on the queen-size bed, highlighting the ripples of the bedcovers, thrust back as though she'd just decided to roll out of bed. Another issue of *Self* lay open, facedown on the pillow where she must have thrust it before she got up.

Strangely, it took a moment of staring directly at her to recognize Lizette in the mound of dark green satin on the floor. She had collapsed in a heap, ripples of green satin peignoir covering her. Her left arm, buried in dark green, was flung wide, and her right was draped over her head. She looked like a broken doll, her spiky mahogany hair in stark contrast to the deathly pallor of her face. Her eyes were open, staring at the ceiling.

I felt the room spin. My breath caught in my chest, and my heart skipped a beat. I knelt to search for a pulse in her wrist. Very little warmth lingered in her skin. Her eyes were open, unblinking, and fragile blue. Doll's eyes.

Even when I grasped the lamp and held it close, no responsive constriction showed in her pupils. No breath stirred in her mouth.

Behind me the manager wavered in the doorway. "Is she all right?" His voice quivered. He knew she wasn't.

And I knew it too, but though it was probably too late, I wasn't ready to give up on her. "Quick, call an ambulance and the police—from your place. Fast."

I heard the thud of his feet on the stairway and the bang of his door. Raising her chin to clear the airway for CPR, I saw a thin nylon cord, wrapped around her neck so tight it disappeared into the folds of her skin. I yanked it loose and slapped her palm, but there was no response.

Then I noticed the telephone receiver on the carpet just beyond the reach of her fingertips, near a bundle of letters almost completely hidden by the bed skirt. Meredith's letters! In one swift, impulsive movement I snatched them up, confirmed they were hers, and shoved them deep in my purse.

I couldn't believe I'd really done it. But they were there, inside my purse. I think I stopped breathing.

If I put the letters back, Meredith would be implicated. Of course, if she were still in custody she'd be clear. But I didn't know for sure. If she was out— My stomach cut loose, rolling over and rising. I barely made it to the bathroom.

THE LIVING ROOM that had been so optimistic when I'd visited the first time was suddenly drab. I noticed nail holes in the walls where Lizette had moved pictures and a cloud of fingerprint smudges around the light switch plate. They stood out now, glaring and unnatural, like the eyebrow pencil on her face. Before, I hadn't even noticed them; Lizette's vitality had drawn all the attention to her, away from the flaws. Now every imperfection, every sign of neglect, was apparent and ugly. The place was as dead and empty as she was—and as I felt.

Lizette had been in the perfect spot, at the receptionist's desk, to see people in the salon, to know where they were. With the possible exception of Gerta, who was upstairs all the time. Lizette had to have been murdered because of what she knew. My purse bumped against my hip. I shook my head, trying to banish the unthinkable. Meredith couldn't have done it. She'd have taken the letters with her. She couldn't have done it. She was in jail. She couldn't have done it, because I know her and I know she wouldn't kill anyone. She doesn't even kill the damn spiders in her apartment. She throws them out the window.

Numbly, I inspected the ashtray and glass in Lizette's otherwise spotless sink.

So, if the letters were a plant—by who? Gerta? Had she come back to stash them after she killed Lizette? Could be, depending on how long Lizette was dead. Gerta was crucial. And Gerta was getting away.

Any other time, it has taken the police seeming hours to get there. That night, in nanoseconds official police voices echoed from downstairs. I'd be stuck there, watching the forensic crew dust and squint at everything, reducing Lizette's little life to a collection of fingerprints, pictures, notations. Once they began, it would take hours. And since Lizette lived, and died, in Glendale, that meant the Glendale Police and then Denver Police. Two jurisdictions meant exponential trouble.

Once Stokowski arrived, with his careful attention to detail, his quiet measured words to the officers, his appraising scrutiny of the apartment, and his piercing, truth-seeking stare, I'd be in disaster up to the top of my teddy. If I were honest, I'd probably go to jail. If dishonest and caught, I'd go to jail. If dishonest and successful, I'd be exhausted and have lost precious hours. No win.

Like one pistachio nut or one lie, one impulsive act leads to another. I hesitated on the threshold.

Footsteps on the front stairs. Heavy. Thumping. Like my heartbeat.

I fled. Out the door, down the hallway to the back stairs I sneaked, following the route Gerta must have taken. By peering around corners I managed to get to the first floor without being seen and then out the back door.

My car was a hundred yards away, under the streetlight with a squad car right behind. I stalked to it, head down, shadowed, my jacket tight around my shoulders, using the heaviest, most purposeful tread I could muster, to look as though I was going to work construction. No one challenged me. I slid behind the wheel, exhausted, started the car, and pulled away.

Most important was to locate Meredith. If she was safely in jail, at least she was clear, and that would mitigate my crime in stealing her letters. As I drove, I pulled out my cell phone and then remembered the battery was too low.

At the corner of Colorado Boulevard, headlights appeared behind me. I swung at the last moment across traffic lanes into the King Soopers parking lot, alone. No one followed. I pulled into a shadowed slot, braked, and cut the engine. Now, in the relative safety, I began to react. My hands trembled, my knees shook, and my stomach growled. Not hunger, pure upset.

I hadn't been fond of Lizette or known her well, but she had had a childlike appeal, and so much life left to live. Years in which she could have turned into a loving woman and mother. And she had begged for help. I had done my best to stay in touch with people, through the answering machine and voice mail. I might not have been able to help, but I hated her life being cut short, and especially with Meredith's letters at hand.

I pulled them from my purse, locked them in the glove

compartment, and leaned back against the seat to think for a
minute—something I should have done a long time ago.

However I looked at it, Gerta had motive and opportunity.
The fact that I liked her only got in the way of my judgment.
The pay phone was in front of me. It took only a minute to
reach Stokowski at home. It was only 11:10, but he sounded
as if he'd been asleep. I reminded myself that he didn't know
about Lizette's murder.

"Where are you, Stella?"

"Just tell me if Meredith is in jail, still. I have to talk to
her."

"Maybe she doesn't want to talk to you."

In spite of myself, intensity crept into my voice. "Cut it
out, Lee. This is important. Is she still in jail?"

"Why? What's happening? Stella, if you're up to something, you're going to wish you'd never been born."

"I'm afraid for her. Tell me if she's safe."

He hesitated, then answered slowly. "You're the one who's
in danger, Stella. Someone is out there trying to get you.
That's what that damn bomb was about."

"You're not helping, Lee. Tell me where Meredith is."

"Please come in, Stella."

"Where is she?"

"I don't know. She's probably still at the motel. I never
arrested her."

She could still be a suspect. And the letters would be considered important evidence. "What motel, Lee? At least give
me her number." He did. I'm not sure why.

"Thanks, Lee. You're okay. Lee?"

"Yeah."

"Lizette was murdered tonight—call Glendale PD."

I hung up while he was still swearing.

I called Meredith as soon as I'd hung up on Lee. There was
no answer. I made a quick call home for messages. There were
three, one new, two saved. The new one was eerie, because it

was breathing only, then a hang-up. I saved it. You never know when you're going to want to hear a breather.

I skipped Lizette's; it was too hard to hear. After that, I replayed Jason's "Where the hell are you?" It sounded like a warm, fuzzy blanket. I even tried his number, but there was no answer. It was just as well; I didn't know what I would say to him that wouldn't start an argument. I left him Meredith's number and then replayed the breather several times, because there was a curious background noise that I thought might identify who was calling, or from where. But while this works fine on television, for me the noise turned out to be a noise, nothing more.

Chocolate helps the brain work. God knows I needed help. I dashed into King's for a chocolate-glazed doughnut fix and coffee. The clerk reminded me of Gerta, petite and friendly.

The sky was clear, cold, and dark, with icy stars and the moon already sinking. It was nearly eleven-thirty. It seemed like days had passed since I left Jason that morning.

I drove to Gerta's house as fast as I dared. I figured she wouldn't be there, but I had to check. Her house was dark and empty looking. The papers were still on the porch.

A sharp breeze blew from the northwest, tossing leaves against the skirt of her porch. I pulled out my mini flashlight and stepped gingerly from the car.

I crept along the side of the house, hoping the kids next door were sound sleepers. Their bedroom faced Gerta's house. I knew by the Halloween skeletons pasted on the window, which was raised a couple inches.

On tiptoe I peered in the kitchen window, playing the flashlight beam around. The dishes were untouched in the sink, and the grimy cat bowl was still on the floor.

By the time I reached Dorothy Walleen's house, it was nearly midnight. Her house was shut down; not even a porch light shone. The garage door was shut and locked.

Both her house and the one directly north of hers were dark and slumbering. The neighbor to the south was comparatively lively. The porch light shone, and a bluish television light flickered against the front drapery.

I blocked Dorothy's driveway with my car and cut the engine. As I started up the walk, I saw the drapery in the neighbor's front room move. I was being observed.

I reached her porch, rang the bell, and waited patiently for maybe five minutes. That was longer than ordinary. I pressed the bell again. Again, nothing.

The door of the next house opened, and the voice of an older man called out. "Hold it! Who you lookin' for?"

Colorado has a make-my-day law. I raised my hands in case he held a gun and crossed the lawn to where he stood in the doorway, the porch light shining down on his angular features, making a shadow of his brow so that I couldn't see his eyes. He was stooped and thin, with pink spots on his lined cheeks and linear folds of skin where the neck of his worn flannel shirt was open. When he waved his hand I saw a large red-purple bruise staining the back of his arthritic hand.

"Hello, sorry to bother you. I was supposed to meet with the Walleens tonight, but I was delayed. No one answers the door." It was still Sunday, so I halfway expected the heavens to open and lightning to strike me for the lie, but nothing happened.

The old man's gaze darted from me to my rental car in silent question. His mouth worked like he was shaping questions, but nothing came out. It occurred to me that he was torn between his suspicions and his desire to talk to somebody. Finally he spoke. "They're gone. They was in a hurry, so maybe they forgot to let you know." He opened the door farther. The warm air from his house rolled out, smelling like an old man's closet. "Somethin' musta come up, 'cause they didn't stop for nothin'."

"You sure you saw them leave? All of them? Gerta, too?"

He nodded. "All of them. Piled in that old station wagon of his and drove off. Like the geese in autumn, they just flew. Up and away." His left hand fluttered in the air to illustrate, but what I saw was the narrow band of pale skin at the base of his third finger.

I walked back to my car, aware that he was watching me. I was oh, so tempted to try to get inside, just to make sure they weren't there, but I didn't. Vicky was alive, and she had her mother back. I just hoped that was a good thing.

I was staring at the backs of my hands on the steering wheel and thinking of the old man's hands when I realized the meaning of the pale band of skin on his third finger. He'd recently removed a long-worn ring.

And then I remembered another hand with a similar pale indentation and shuddered. It was all coming together.

# TWENTY-ONE

I WAS AT a dead end, and the newspaper office seemed about the safest place I could go to. It had already been broken into, the police had come and gone, and chances were the killer wouldn't think of it. And I still had my key, if they hadn't changed the locks.

I didn't see anyone following me, but once downtown I drove a circuitous route through Cherry Creek and past the closed salon, then over to check on my rental car, which was still undisturbed. When I was sure I still wasn't being followed, I parked around the corner from the *Daily Orion*.

The dark alley was the entry spot where I had by far the least chance of being seen. It smelled of leaves, garbage, and musty old things. I hesitated, poking with my foot at the wind-blown papers wedged into the straggling bushes, listening for odd out-of-place sounds. None.

No light shone there, nor over the newspaper office back door. I skulked along trying to look normal, whatever that was. At the back door, I slipped my key into the lock and twisted. It didn't budge. I double-checked the key. It was definitely the office key. I flashed my little flashlight over the door. The dingy old lock had been replaced with a shiny new one.

Then I saw the plywood nailed over the shoulder-height windowpanes where the burglar had broken in. I was willing to bet it was the same person who broke into my apartment. I flicked off the light and sneaked around to the front of the building.

Sunday nights in this neighborhood tend to be quiet. This one was more than quiet. The homes across the street were darkened, except for one upstairs bedroom window, dimly lit behind drapes. Both sides of the street were lined with parked cars. The leaves blowing across the pavement provided the only sound and movement. I scrutinized each car, looking for the telltale shape of a head, watching. Not a thing. I double-checked for large police vehicles and a white van. Saw neither.

I eased down the street, keys to the door ready. There were no approaching cars this time. I moved to the front door, opened the screen, slipped the key in, and turned the key and knob together. I slipped inside, shutting and locking the door behind me. There had never been a burglar alarm before, and with any luck there still wasn't.

The smell of the place was familiar, comforting, and there was enough light filtering in through the windows to see my way to the back room and my desk.

It looked to me as if the police had made a very minimal attempt to find fingerprints. Mr. Gerster's office appeared almost untouched, by the burglar or the police. The file cabinets, as well as the back door area, sported orange dust, but otherwise the place was its usual chaotic self, except that files littered the floor. It looked as if most of them had been hastily pushed into stacks, some in corners, some on the desks. My file cabinet was virtually empty.

I called Meredith immediately and finally had to leave a message, telling her about Lizette. Then I called my answering machine at home, hoping to hear from Meredith, and was delighted to find three messages from Jason: the first furious, the next anxious, and finally the last resigned and a little sad sounding. I replayed these several times, listening to his voice. When I realized how much I enjoyed it, I became uncomfortable. I didn't want any dependency—mine or his. No chains of love around my freedom. I banished the thought that I was whistling in the dark.

I called my voice mail at the office. There were only the three saved messages—the breather, the scolding Jason, and Lizette. I replayed Lizette's, listening for any subtle sounds I might have missed.

I shuddered and felt a kind of infuriated sorrow settle on

me. She was dead, and all for a little money. Such a waste. I saved the message, feeling sad and angry and, underneath it all, frightened.

One new message had come in while I was listening to replays of Lizette's. A whisper, which could have been male or female, came over the wire. "I'm waiting, Stella."

Every hair on my body lifted and curled in fright. I dropped the phone and automatically ducked behind the desk, hugging myself. Where was this ghoul? Outside right now?

I listened for footsteps, for breathing, for anything that would indicate a stalker. My first thought was to book a flight to Brazil and lie low for the next seventy-five years.

The reality was, I couldn't outrun this.

It didn't take long to go through the stacks of files on the floor, in the corner, and on the nearby desks. I couldn't tell for sure what was missing—that would take days—but I was only looking for one file, Ami's. And it was gone.

Why would Ami's file be taken, unless something had happened to her and it would incriminate somebody? The only person she had mentioned was her husband. Big Dick. I shuddered. What if Mr. Gerster was right?

There had been no telephone calls from Ami, although she had promised to call in her letter of last Wednesday. Bad feelings were piling up all around. Most likely, I told myself, Ami was too busy enjoying her new freedom. If I hadn't had that spell, I'd believe it.

I stepped carefully around and over file piles to my desk.

I was starving. That's anxiety for you. I dragged out my mini flashlight and started scrounging for food. My mind was working fine, and my appetite was at full steam. I found two Hershey bars and half a bag of corn curls in my desk.

In Jason's desk I found a note in the bottom drawer:

Stella,
     Help yourself. What's mine is yours.
                                        Jason.

It was scary how well he knew me. But it was a perfectly safe offer. All he had was two cans of V-8 juice. That much vegetable juice at once would shut down my system.

I got a diet cola from the pop machine and munched through the chocolate and corn curls, alternating the salt and sugar to keep my taste buds alert. As I ate I decided to be more organized about how I approached this.

I decided two things.

One, Meredith's situation took precedence over all. Ami had to wait. So did the blond van man. And if they were linked, they both still had to wait.

Two, DeAngelo's murder had to do with the salon, and in all this, I had to know something that would clear up the picture. Meredith was not a killer. That left Suzanne, Gerta, David, and Virgil. Lizette, my favorite suspect, was dead. And the killer was working hard to frame Meredith.

I went back over the whole day, looking for seemingly inconsequential things. Lizette's pen from the Hair Spa, and her lie about not having worked for a hairdresser before. DeAngelo having a second, private telephone line in his closet. Suzanne, who had complained too obviously about her injured foot, with water from her footbath spilled everywhere.

I thought about that. Suzanne had an enormous stake in the salon. What did she know about how it was run? What if she knew that, as DeAngelo was managing it, it was a financial disaster coming down the pike? She stood to lose a bundle—unless he died. Especially if he died accidentally for double the price.

Suppose Suzanne rigged the footbath. She was upstairs; she could have seen Meredith going up to the love loft. She was at the salon so often that she would have known all about the Meredith, Lizette, and DeAngelo triangle. Suzanne, who had expensive taste and a house that looked as if it had been stripped of its pretty things.

Suzanne was a beneficiary of the insurance policy. With DeAngelo dead, her money problems would be solved. I wondered if there was a double-indemnity clause, doubling the insurance amount in the case of an accidental death.

Suppose all of this was tied together and carefully planned. Everything centered on the salon. DeAngelo, the passion he incited in people, the love and jealousy, the insecurity that drove people to create the illusion of—what? Being desirable.

Why hadn't Gerta been killed, too? Or Vicky? Then I shivered. There was that spell I'd had yesterday. The suffocating one. Maybe it didn't have one thing to do with Ami; maybe I had tapped into the killer's thoughts coincidentally at the right moment. I didn't always have to touch something to trigger my spells.

I tried to reach Stokowski first at home, then at his office, and ended by leaving him a message detailing my theory on Suzanne, her inheritance, and the computer accounts, and suggesting that he check on her alibi for the time when Lizette was killed, which I timed at about six-thirty, based on the message she'd left. At the very end I hesitated, then told him it was crucial to make sure someone wasn't already at the salon, erasing the computer files.

For a few minutes I tried to convince myself to wait sensibly at the *Orion* office. Then I remembered Lizette. And Gerta and little Vicky. And Meredith. Any one of them could be the next victim, any minute, until the killer was caught. So far I'd stayed ahead of the killer, by a hair, but time was against me. It was find or be found, and I didn't want to be the findee.

But where to start?

It all came back to the salon and Lizette, and what Lizette had seen. Foolish Lizette with all her lies, even down to not knowing the computer.

Lizette could have accessed the computer and figured it all out. And then tried to blackmail Suzanne. The proof of Suzanne's motive, big and bold, would still be there in the computer. It would only take one disk full of data, and I'd have her.

And the client cards. I couldn't figure out where they fit in, but somewhere. I could deal with that later. It was more crucial to get to the computer before someone erased it all.

And who would think of looking for me at the salon? In the dark. On a Sunday night. And it would take what, minutes? I could swing by Suzanne's house and see if she was there. If she was, I was home free.

For several minutes I considered the possibility that I might fail and what that would mean. I decided I couldn't die without telling Mother I loved her. And I had to own up that I loved Jason, too. I wrote two quick letters, left the one for mother on the desktop and stuck the one for Jason under my desk mat. If I died, he'd find it eventually. And if I lived I'd be able to retrieve it—I didn't want to admit I was in love before he did.

It was eleven-thirty, but Suzanne's kitchen lights were on, and I could just make out her head bobbing in the window. It was a little hard to imagine, but it looked as if she was washing dishes. Surely she hadn't hocked her dishwasher, too? That would make a woman mighty testy.

I parked several blocks away from the salon. I'd have given anything for a rope, some crampons, and maybe an elephant gun. As it was I stuck a couple of credit cards in my pocket along with a pen, my trusty mini Swiss pocketknife, and my flashlight, then locked my purse and everything else in the trunk.

Even though I was pretty sure I wasn't followed and Suzanne was safely at home, I eased down the alley as quietly as possible. I tried to keep to the shadows, but the overhead streetlights cast a shadow-piercing orange light everywhere, making secrecy iffy.

No light shone in the garage. Virgil's Yugo was nowhere around. He must be out and about. Just to make sure, I peered in the window, then knocked, but there was no response.

The back door of the salon was locked, of course. And the box to the right of the door had a tiny red light glowing, proving the burglar alarm was armed. That nixed entering through the doors and windows on the first floor. I couldn't remember whether the second-floor windows were wired, but the porch roof was too far from the railings for me to scale. I checked the basement windows; all were barred and wired.

But not the coal chute.

It was my night for sliding into dark holes. The chute cover was heavy cast iron, miraculously not bolted on the inside, merely latched in place. A little leverage, and it came away. Nice and easy. Too easy, maybe, but I didn't have much choice.

I knelt and played the flashlight beam around a narrow, empty room with coal-dust-grimed walls. It looked like a six-foot drop to a packed-earth floor. I started to put my feet in, then hesitated. Once inside, I wouldn't be able to climb back out. The window was too high. I flashed the light around the little room again. The door to the room was ajar.

A car turned into the alley, its tires crunching the leaves, headlights flashing along the garages. It slowed.

I jammed my feet into the chute, scooted forward, and slid in on my spine, balancing momentarily. Then I lurched forward. My head smacked the top of the chute and my fingers clawed the wood frame, holding me for a split second before I crashed to the floor in a heap of pain.

# TWENTY-TWO

MY FEET STUNG from the impact, my backbone from the scraping, and my head from the bump. It took a moment to get myself together. I heard the vehicle in the alley stop, then proceed.

I shivered and crept to the door of the room, playing the beam of the light in front of me.

It was more of a cellar than a basement. One large, dark room, partially paved with bricks, warm and cobwebby and heavy with the odor of curing cement. A lightbulb swung from the overhead beams. I pulled the cord chain, and a feeble twenty-watt electricity-saver shed lukewarm light over a furnace, a large hot water heater, and an odd rectangular shallow hole in the packed earth, the size of an empty grave. Two five-gallon water jugs stood to the right in an old laundry area with a stone washbasin, and several bags of dry cement were stacked neatly in the corner.

Straight ahead of me halfway up the wall was a wooden door, leading to a crawl space, no doubt. I flashed the beam around until I located the new cement, on the floor beside the furnace. I felt it. It was dry, but cold, still curing. The odor hadn't dissipated because the basement wasn't vented.

Stairs on my left led up. It might have been because I'd broken in, or it may have been the oppressive feeling that followed me, but whatever it was I sneaked up the stairs, even though there wasn't another soul there. I tried the doorknob. It was open. This was easier than I'd expected. Too easy. It made me nervous.

The basement opened onto the hall where the back stairs came down and the kitchen opened up. It was a thick, inky

sea that smelled of ammonia and almonds. I discovered that
the blinds in the kitchen had been drawn tight.

My first, most important job was to copy the accounts files
from the computer. I crept up to the third-floor love loft, ghost-
silent. It took only minutes to find a diskette, access and copy
all the files, and close up. I shoved the diskette into my bra
and nearly jumped for joy. Now for the bonus. If I could just
find DeAngelo's special client book and the client cards, I'd
be set.

I went first to Lizette's reception desk. Carefully I searched
each of her drawers, looking for the customer data entry cards
and DeAngelo's special book. I was sure she'd lied about not
knowing where they were kept. Lizette, who saw everyone's
moves, also saw all the clients who came and went.

I searched her desk, inspecting the back, sides, and underneath of each drawer. Nothing. Even the appointment book
was gone. I tipped her chair up. Its wheel screeched. I stopped,
heart pounding. I thought I heard a rustle from the kitchen. I
pressed the flashlight against my thigh, dousing the light. And
listened. Nothing.

I drew a releasing breath.

Lizette had used Gerta's station, ostensibly to do the nails
of Gerta's customer, but it gave her an opportunity to thor-
oughly search the station. Gerta's license had been removed
because it had her address on it, but I wasn't convinced that
Gerta removed it herself. Suzanne could have done it, to hide
Gerta's address as long as possible.

I listened again. It was an old house, and every so often it
creaked as if it were respiring. Even more eerie, the everyday
noises of traffic outside on the street seemed strangely muffled.
I thought of the old fourth-dimension stories and wondered if
DeAngelo's spirit lurked in the corners of the house. If so, I
thought, please help me. I shook myself, trying to slough off
the dread.

My eyes grew accustomed to the oppressive darkness. I
could see vague shapes, enough to get to the stairs and tiptoe

to Gerta's station. There I used the flashlight again. I ran my hands over the sides and bottom of the cabinet and drawers. Nothing.

I scanned the bottoms of the jars, the tissue box, and under the towels. I checked the bottom of the client's chair, and of Gerta's. I was on my knees on the floor when I remembered where my aunt Lil used to hide her diamonds, under the bottom drawer of her bathroom cabinet in the vacant four-inch space. I pulled out the bottom drawer, set it on the floor, and played the flashlight inside the drawer cabinet. Way at the back, on the floor, I saw a scrap of paper.

I pulled it out. It was an old grocery list. Then I reached in again and felt around. There they were. Taped to the inside front of the cabinet. Easy enough when you knew where to look. I yanked them out, glancing down at them. Across the top one was printed, "Ami Johnson." In the upper right corner was a little *D*. Ami...Johnson.

Gerta had hidden two cards, mine and Ami Johnson's. Why? I ran through a series of coincidences. I'd had a letter from an Ami, my apartment had been searched, I'd been sent a bomb meant to kill me, I'd been there when DeAngelo was murdered, and the newspaper office had been broken into and my files ransacked. If Ami of the letter was tied in to De-Angelo's murder, then...

I was pretty certain I knew who DeAngelo's killer was and why I was a target, but it was more complicated than that. There was the insurance.

A floorboard creaked. Someone was behind me.

A nasty cold sweat broke out on my forehead. My fingers shook. I dropped the cards back inside the cabinet. I forced myself to scrabble around inside the cabinet as though finding nothing, then grabbed the grocery list and pulled it out like a big deal. I picked up the drawer as if to replace it.

"Hold it! Put it down." A heavy male voice thundered out behind me, and a brilliant flashlight beam cut across the room.

I swung the drawer backhanded as hard as I could in the direction of the intruder and rose to my feet in one motion.

The drawer caught him by surprise, hitting his hand. He yelped. His flashlight went spinning across the room, smashed against the wall, and went out. I smashed into him, feeling suede and smelling leather.

I shoved him hard out of the way, jumped through the doorway, and raced down the hall to the back stairs. He pounded behind me.

At the top of the stairs I grabbed the newel post and lunged to one side, sticking my foot out. He tripped. Stumbled toward the stairs. His arms flailed, grasping.

His hand, iron-hard, came down on my arm, grabbing it, bruising me. Then his grip loosened, slipped, clutching my sweater. I hugged the newel post, kicking at him. The banister vibrated. He caught himself. Lunged after me.

I scrambled away, yanking my sweater from his fingers. I heard it tear, then felt the sudden release as it came away. I raced down the hallway to the front stairs. If I could get down to the first floor, I could possibly break out the front picture window.

A gunshot, then a second, rang in my ears. A white-hot pain seared the left side of the top of my head. Stars exploded in front of my eyes. I staggered. Thrown by the pain, I stumbled and fell against the wall, a long, rolling fall. I hit the floor hard, woozy and terrified but conscious. My head throbbed. Blood ran warm and sticky down the side of my face. Other than that, I'd only had the breath knocked out of me. I lay deathly still, peeking from under my eyelashes.

He came cautiously down the hallway, gun in hand, looking surprisingly solid and broad-shouldered from where I lay. He pocketed the gun and stalked to the window, raising the blind to let in the streetlight. Briefly in silhouette, I saw he had light, shoulder-length hair, exactly like the driver of the van that almost ran me down at Meredith's a week ago. Could he have been following me all this time?

He turned, his face hidden in shadow, and trudged back toward me. His foot nudged my shin sharply. "The card," he said, waving his hand. "Give it to me."

His voice was low and menacing.

He thought the grocery list I'd pocketed was the card. I feigned unconsciousness. I steeled myself for a kick, clamping my mouth shut to keep from howling. There's something about a woman helpless on the floor that makes a scuzzbucket want to kick her.

He kicked. Thank God, not in the stomach. On the shin. Painful, but not as deadly. Pain shot through my leg, sickening in its intensity. A moan escaped from me, but at least I didn't cry out. I braced myself for a second kick.

It didn't come.

He seemed satisfied that I was unconscious. He leaned over, fumbling for my jeans pocket.

I grabbed his arm, yanked him forward off balance while I pulled myself toward his feet. I was trying to topple him onto his head while I rolled out under his feet. It almost worked. He fell forward and smacked his head. But he fell heavily on me, pinning me under his surprisingly heavy weight.

Fear makes muscles.

I pulled myself away from under him and staggered to my feet. I couldn't move fast enough. My arms and legs were like lead, slow and heavy. A rough hand circled my ankle, painfully tight. I kicked at him, connected with some body part, and scrambled away again.

Back down the hallway away from him, I stumbled to the back stairs. Half falling down them, I ended in the back first-floor hall, dizzy. Shadows from a passing car darted suddenly around the walls. They confused me momentarily. That fraction of a second was fatal.

My foot was on the threshold of the kitchen when his fingers clamped on my shoulder. His fingertips and thumb bit into me. He dragged me to him and drew his other arm across my neck, squeezing. Pinching off my air. Pinpoints of light flashed before my eyes, oxygen deprivation.

He marched me into the first-floor salon. I remembered this room had two doors, one near the back leading to the kitchen, one at the front leading to the reception desk. If I could get to the front of the room I could try jumping through the window. Or at least breaking it to set off the alarm. It had to be soon. I was getting weaker by the second.

I jabbed at him with my elbow. Kicked at his shins, stomped on a toe, which brought a bellow of pain and a terrible tightening of his arm across my windpipe. The world was fading from me. Blood pounding in my ears.

If I could reach the counter...maybe grab the scissors...

He jerked me back farther. I sagged, full weight against his arm. He flung me across the room.

I fell against the counter, scraping my arm, a burst of pain from my back ribs whacking against it. But my hands landed on the countertop. And flew down its length, searching for scissors.

Cold, hard steel beneath the fingers of my right hand. I grabbed all of it. A rat-tailed comb.

I clutched the comb, tail out, dropped my right hand to my side, and turned sideways to him, presenting a narrower target. I couldn't see his gun.

His breath was coming in short, sharp gasps. He wasn't moving very fast. Headlights from the street flashed around the room. His hands were empty, high in a boxer's stance.

I wished I'd kept up my tae kwon do. A high green belt isn't very high or very skillful.

Hands fisted, I roared and lurched sideways to position myself in a bigger space, hopefully closer to the door. I had always excelled in the roar part of tae kwon do. I held my hands close in and cocked my foot, ready to kick.

He was silhouetted in the window against the light from the street. Heavy on his feet, staggering slightly, but dangerous.

"What happened, David? Did you get too jealous of DeAngelo?"

He didn't answer. His movements were surprisingly awkward in the semidark of the room, as though he was unfamiliar with the space. He circled slowly, his hands loose, arms outstretched. He lunged.

I kicked. I was lucky. He was surprised.

He roared and rushed at me.

I feinted to the left and leaped away. I kicked again, a roundhouse kick, whirling on one foot, then a back kick. He got me with a basic football tackle.

I grabbed his hair with my left hand and yanked. It flew off. A wig!

My surprise slowed me down. He got me in a headlock.

The comb was still tight in my sweaty hand.

I whacked him in the leg.

He roared, loosening his grip enough for me to wrench away, although my head nearly came off its little stalk. He was between me and the front window, yowling.

I ran to the kitchen, yanked on a drawer, grabbed for anything inside, and found a fork.

He crossed the hall toward me, snarling.

I hurled the drawer at him.

He knocked it away with a forearm. It crashed to the floor, the rest of the flatware scattering across the linoleum.

I held the fork ready, backed up, and grabbed desperately for the doorknob. Couldn't get it. Got the light switch, though. The kitchen was suddenly flooded with blinding light. I blinked, trying desperately to adjust my eyes.

He advanced, breathing heavily, his mouth open. I think he was laughing. He gripped his belt buckle and gave it a tug.

# TWENTY-THREE

"VIRGIL? IT'S YOU, isn't it?"

"Shit yes, it's me." He edged toward me, his work boots grinding against the floor tiles. The thin crust of cement on the lower edge—the sandy grit I'd felt when I knelt in the solarium.

He tugged at his belt buckle again. I tightened my grip on the fork. But Virgil was merely adjusting his Jockeys and trying to think. He took another step toward me, eyes wary, fingers flexing.

I glared back at him, feeling the blood ooze freely down the side of my face. I wiped a trickle away from the corner of my eye with my left hand and drew a surreptitious breath, gripping the fork tighter in my right hand, tense, coiled, ready for his next move.

If he charged me, I'd put that fork in his throat. With survival on the line, all pretense of civilization is out the window. I planned death in the cruelest form for him.

There was a thumping sound from upstairs. Stokowski?

He heard it, too. He stopped and licked his lips. "Meredith is waitin' for you," he said.

"You lie." But as I said it, I saw in the triumphant expression in his eyes that it was true. I hoped she was unhurt.

"So how'd you find her? Play on her sympathy? Pretend to be hurt?"

He rubbed his forehead with his thumb. "You all think you're so smart! I just left a message on her phone, and she came running. Simple." He frowned and shifted his weight toward me.

"Don't you want to know why I came here, Virgil?"

He frowned deeper, his eyebrows a ridge that hid his mean little eyes from the overhead glare. "Yeah, how come?"

I edged closer to the doorway. "I noticed your hand the day of the murder. Look at your left hand, Virgil. There's a ring mark there. You can't wear a wedding ring for years and not have it leave a mark."

"Yeah, well, you're not so smart. I said I'd get you. And I did." He laughed, a hollow barking sound that was bone-mean. My heart was thudding, and I struggled to keep my breathing even and my glare steady. Showing fear would weaken me and encourage him.

Would Stokowski have checked his messages yet? I could hope that he had, and had figured it out, and was on his way. I needed to play for time. The blinds were drawn in the kitchen; if I could get to the light switch, I could possibly flip it for attention. Maybe someone would see it. I eased back toward the wall.

"Okay, Virgil, you've been really smart," I said, groping for the switch. My fingers curled around the switch and flipped it back and forth. A thin stream of light flashed through the blinds.

He shoved the table aside. Its wooden legs screeched on the tile. "Get away from the wall," he yelled.

I sidestepped, keeping the table between him and me.

"Don't underestimate me. I'm not stupid."

I wanted him to talk, maybe get distracted. "It was an act, an illusion, wasn't it? A masquerade. You played dumb, and it all worked out."

"Nobody notices the homely and dumb. I showed them I knew how to fix a few things and then acted dumb, and they hired me. Just like that. The only thing that counted with these jerks was being pretty."

"Pretty smart, all right. Where'd you learn about bombs?"

He hitched his belt again, but kept his eyes on me. "Army. I was in demolition. Fuckin' cops wouldn't hire me, though. They'll wish they had after I'm through here, though."

"And you were determined to get a job here, weren't you? I'll bet your wife came here, didn't she? You thought De-Angelo was after her, didn't you? What did she do, tell you that he propositioned her?"

He grunted. His gaze dropped to his hands.

It was a chance. I feinted to the left, then darted to the door, rattling and twisting the doorknob. I spun around. He was nearly on top of me. I jabbed his side with the fork. His leather jacket deflected it. The fork slid harmlessly to the side.

He grabbed my arm, twisted it, and pulled it up behind me. "Walk, babe." He twisted my left arm up behind my back and propelled me out of the kitchen and up the stairs. With my arm hurting so much, I forgot about the pain in my ribs.

After the light of the kitchen, the rest of the salon seemed sunk in darkness. I stumbled at the top of the stairs, hoping to throw him off balance. It was a bad idea. He wrenched my arm up. Pain burst over my back, paralyzing my arm.

At the door of the solarium he shoved me through to the back wall, against the chaise longue. It was the same one I'd been cocooned on while my skin was rejuvenating. He pinned me against the side of the chaise, releasing my arm in a rush of agony.

I couldn't move to resist. He gripped my wrists and yanked them behind me in a burst of pain that nearly gagged me. At least I was still standing. He pulled a strip of familiar black plastic from inside his jacket and bound my wrists to the railing of the chaise. I bowed my wrists as much as I could so there'd be some slack when he finished and started to talk, trying to keep him off balance. "Is that the same black plastic I saw you hauling out of the box in the garage Friday? What did you need that for?"

"Shut up."

The sharp scent of eau de armpit filled the air. I wondered if I'd struck a nerve. "Why're you so touchy about plastic, Virgil? What's it about?"

He grabbed a cloth from the shelves and stuffed an end of

it in my mouth. "Say your prayers." He turned on his heel and left. I heard his clomping footsteps echoing down the stairs.

It took only a few minutes to work the cloth out of my mouth. He'd left an end hanging loose. "Meredith?"

"MMMph!"

"Are you hurt?"

"Uh-uh."

"Can you get over here?"

"Uh-uh."

"Damn." I yanked on the plastic binding. I'd always thought of plastic as stretchy, but this stuff was thick and impossible, particularly at that angle. It gave a little, but not enough.

My fingers reached the top of my back jeans pocket. My little pocketknife was way at the bottom of the pocket. It was the only chance I had. I inched my fingers over the edge of my pocket until I could hook it with the end of my finger.

Footsteps sounded on the stairs.

The knife snagged on something and slipped from my fingers, dropping back into the pocket. I thrust my fingers desperately into the pocket, felt the knife, and dragged it out.

I pried with my thumbnail and felt it give, then snap shut. I hadn't opened the knife in months. It was stiff. I switched hands. My left thumbnail held. It came open. It was dull as a butter knife. I started to saw.

Virgil's footsteps were now on the second flight of stairs.

I stopped sawing and considered the chaise. Its wheels were secured with a simple metal pedal brake. If I could unlock the wheels, I could roll it. I stretched out my foot, reaching first one and then the other of the locks to spring them. Then I leaned back against the chaise, concealing my hands, and resumed sawing.

Virgil staggered into the room, carrying the water jugs I'd seen in the basement. He dropped one heavily to the floor, the liquid sloshing on the inside. "You two broads sit tight till I get back." He laughed at his feeble joke all the way upstairs.

We heard a sickening sloshing sound from upstairs, like he was slopping water on the floor. Then a thick, oily stench rolled into the solarium. Gasoline.

I heard him sloshing gasoline in the hall and along the walls; then at the door of the solarium he flung the empty jug across the room with a clatter. I sawed desperately, the binding loosening perceptibly.

He flicked on a flashlight. Meredith was bound hand and foot with the same plastic to the chair DeAngelo had last sat in. Virgil had wound a similar plastic strip around her head, covering her mouth. A little farther, and she'd have suffocated. I flashed her a glance and what I hoped was an encouraging jerk of the head. She bobbed her head. At least she could respond.

"Now, Virgil, when we're all dead, just who do you think the police will blame?"

He laughed again. "Meredith was gonna take the fall, but you screwed that up, so she dies." He hitched his belt buckle again. It was a sickening gesture. He hefted the second jug and unscrewed the cap.

"Actually, Virgil, you screwed it up. With the bomb. That's when the cops stopped thinking Meredith was guilty."

He snarled and threw gasoline on my legs. The fumes made my eyes tear and the skin on my shins burn. "Who will take the fall now, Virgil?"

"Shit if I care. Let David, the little squirrel, eat it." He sloshed gasoline in the corners of the room. The fumes were sickening, and the fluid soaked into the bottoms of my shoes.

"You planned to get Meredith and David here and kill them, and—what? Frame Meredith as a murder-suicide?"

"You got it, babe."

Meredith's eyes leaked tears, wetting the tops of her cheeks in twin streams.

Rage boiled inside me. "So, Virgil, when did you begin to plan this little serial-killing spree?"

He set down the jug and scratched his neck. "Not my fault.

Ami suggested it. She said, 'What're you going to do, kill everyone who looks twice at me?' So I thought to myself, 'Yeah, bitch, I just will.' So here we are.''

"Ami!" I thought so. "Big Dick."

He laughed, a short barking sound that made my heart race and my breath come in ragged gasps.

"And you were looking for Ami's letters when you rifled my place and the newspaper office."

"Yeah. She said she'd sent you a picture."

"But you didn't find them. So where's Ami now?"

"Here. Right here." He jabbed with his right forefinger toward the floor.

Poor Ami. I was nearly choking on the lump in my throat. "Ami's the one... And you knew where to come...because of Ami."

"Oh, yeah. Ami told me all about DeAngelo. She thought she'd get a better deal than me." He rubbed his hands together in a washing movement. "I brought her with me and found him. He and David, the two of them. They were arguing, but I gave them something better to think about. I told DeAngelo what Ami said."

"That he loved her, right?"

"Yeah. And he just stood there looking like a stupid pretty boy. Finally he said he could understand why she'd say that, and why she'd want to leave me. So I took her home. And I told her what would happen to her if she left."

"And she said she didn't care—"

His eyes blazed with fury. "And she said, Just try it."

The spell. The smothering came to mind. "And you smothered her."

"No. Then I hit her—to knock sense into her. I'm the one she married—for better or worse. She was mine. He didn't have the right." He focused his gaze on me and ran his tongue over his lips. "And you. You made it worse, too. So you get to go, too."

"So when you hit Ami, she...?"

"It was her own dumb fault. She was always clumsy."

"And I'll bet she bruised easily, too."

A look of disgust crossed his face. "Well, sure. She was that kind. And mope! And whine—forever whining. God, she made me mad."

I shuddered inwardly, fighting to keep my voice expressionless. I wanted him to talk, perhaps even reach some humane feelings, but I didn't want to provoke him. "And then she died. After she fell."

He looked into the space over my head, as though he was replaying, like a home movie. Maybe for him it was, because his voice lowered a notch and his speech patterns altered into longer sentences. "She was okay for a couple hours, just had a headache, then she went and threw up. On the rug, for God's sake. Then she started to twitch and moan, so I put a pillow over her. And she fuckin' died on me! She hadn't even done the goddamned laundry." He scratched his head, puzzled. "She always did the laundry." His voice dropped to a near whisper. "Real good at the house, you know."

Meredith whimpered, tears on her cheeks.

My blood pressure had to be 320 over 265, my temples throbbed so. I could barely control myself. My fingernails itched to scratch his eyes out. "So, Virgil, you really miss her?"

He missed the sarcasm totally. He glanced at me irritably. "You don't understand. She was mine. She was me. She killed me first when she said she'd leave. She said we were two different people, but we weren't. She said I smothered her, but I didn't. I just loved her."

At first I thought he was being sarcastic, but he wasn't. He was emotionally dead, a zombie, devoid of all feeling, living through his program of revenge. If I ever saw a picture of primitive, profound despair, it was this man. And it was ugly.

If I could humanize him without resurrecting his rage I might get him to spare us. That meant giving him back some sense of himself as a person worth loving. I shuddered. He was not a lovable person. We're talking major emotional hurdles here. But I didn't have to convince him that *I* loved him, only that Ami did. God knows, it was worth trying.

I cleared my throat and tried to pitch my voice so that it was gentle, and tried to reframe their relationship. "Virgil, Ami must have loved you. Maybe she didn't know how to show it."

His eyes were lusterless. "She said she was leaving me."

"She had to love you to do all that laundry. Clean laundry can be a woman's way of showing love."

"She hated laundry."

"See? She only did it for you, because she loved you."

"I punished her if she didn't do it."

"She cooked for you."

"Yeah..."

"That's love. Lots of women don't cook."

Meredith's eyes were round and horrified. I struggled on. "She was with you a long time."

He glared at me. My hopes fell.

His glance fell to the floor. "She was a good cook," he murmured.

He was actually thinking about this. My hopes rose. I continued, "She wouldn't have fixed herself up and made herself pretty if she hadn't wanted you to love her even more. Maybe she thought you didn't love her."

"She said I never paid attention to her, but I loved her." He rose and hulked over me, shaking. I'd finally severed the plastic bindings. My heart thumped wildly, adrenaline hitting my veins. I was afraid he'd see it. I glanced at Meredith.

She coughed behind her gag, then mewed, struggling in her chair as if she were choking. For a minute even I was convinced. "Virgil, Meredith's choking. Help her."

"She's gonna be dead anyway in a few minutes."

"She'll slip away from you...like Ami did. And you didn't mean to kill Ami, did you?"

He frowned, stepped toward her, arm outstretched. The minute he turned away from me, I positioned my hands. He halted.

I gripped the chaise and thrust it ahead of me, shoving it as hard as I could toward the small of his back. He heard the wheels on the floor and turned. It caught him in the side. He stumbled, immobilized by the kidney blow. The wind was knocked out of him.

Thank God he'd tied Meredith carelessly. I cut through the plastic binding her ankles and jerked her to her feet, dragging her with me out of the room. Her legs were stiff. She stumbled, leaned heavily against me. Virgil was slumped against the wall, gasping.

Downstairs a door slammed. Meredith straightened. "We're up here!" she shouted before I could stop her. I glanced over my shoulder at Virgil. A chill ran over my spine. He was laughing. He pulled a gun from his jacket.

# TWENTY-FOUR

WE DODGED AROUND the corner, out of the line of direct fire.
I thrust Meredith ahead, both of us scrambling down the stairs.
Suddenly, she stopped, alert.

"Hurry! He's got a gun," I said, meaning Virgil.

"David!" Meredith gasped.

David stood in the door to the kitchen, his shoulders im-
mensely broad in a dark brown leather bomber jacket over
snug black jeans. A cap covered his brow, hiding the expression in his eyes. "What's going on here?" he said.

I had a sudden, ugly thought. All the insurance and inheritance questions were still unanswered. I had a sinking feeling
David was even bigger trouble. "Let's get out of here. Now!"
I twisted the deadbolt. It didn't budge. "David, unlock this,
will you?"

He moved closer, his chin set stubbornly. "Why were you
here? This place was supposed to be locked up."

Meredith grabbed his jacket lapels, drawing him to the door.
"Virgil did it. He got me here. I thought he needed help, but
he's going to kill us. He's going to burn the place down."

"Wait a minute. What's all this about?" He took her hands
from his jacket, pulling her toward the little table.

I leaped after her. "Meredith, stop. We can talk outside. We
have to get out of here." I grabbed her sweater, pulling her
my way. She was caught between us, David pulling her hands
and me pulling her sweater. It's a wonder she didn't unravel
on the spot.

"David, let go of me," Meredith wailed.

"David, give me the keys," I said. I snatched a paring knife
from the stuff scattered on the floor and whacked off Meredith's wrist bindings. "The cops will be here any minute."

David looked startled. "Virgil, get the hell down here. And explain all this."

I interrupted. "David, what are you doing here?"

"Virgil called me," he answered.

Meredith eased toward me. "David, Virgil killed DeAngelo because he thought Ami was leaving to be with him. He was jealous."

David's eyes narrowed. "Virgil, get down here."

"David, Virgil was going to let you take the blame for all this." Meredith, panting with the stress, started to pace, kicking the flatware on the floor to one side.

Virgil's footsteps thumped on the stairs. He appeared, carrying the gasoline jug.

"David," Meredith yelled, "Virgil has soaked the place in gas. It's going to go up."

Virgil laughed and tossed the gas jug down the basement stairs. It bumped three times, then landed on the bricks below.

"Cut it out, Virg," David said, and glanced at him. "Now, explain what's happening here."

Virgil hitched his belt buckle. "What's happening here is that in five minutes this place is going up. It's set. It's that simple."

I watched David's face. Not a flicker of surprise in his expression; and there should have been, unless he already knew about it, but I was sure he had known, maybe even engineered it to get control of the shop, debt-free. I wondered how much of this Virgil knew. "Virgil, when did you decide that Lizette had to be killed?"

"Huh?" He turned ponderously toward me. "There's nothing wrong with Lizette. I didn't kill her."

"But you did. You were there. I saw your cigarette butts, and the wire you left, just like the one you left here in the corridor under the breaker switch box."

"I didn't kill Lizzie." He rubbed his chin, doubt creeping into his eyes. "I did DeAngelo and I was going to do you, to get you for stealing Ami away. But not Lizzie."

I turned to David. "Lizette tried to blackmail you, didn't she, David? She followed you upstairs, didn't she? She would know that you gave DeAngelo the coke, maybe a little more than usual. So you had to either pay up or kill her. And after you realized that Meredith would eventually be exonerated, you set up Virgil."

David started toward me.

Meredith snatched up the remnants of the cutlery drawer from the floor and threw it through the window in the door. The glass fell in sheets, shattering on the floor. She reached through to twist the knob of the security door. "It won't open."

Virgil laughed, a chilling sound. "You can't go anywhere. He has to unlock the door with the key. It's a security measure."

At the least, the burglar alarm would draw the guys in blue. Then I saw that the red eye of the burglar alarm had been deactivated. We had to stall; Stokowski might still get here.

"David, you hired Virgil, didn't you? You knew he was Ami's jealous husband because you were here when he brought her in to confront DeAngelo. I'll bet he didn't confront DeAngelo, did he? He talked to you. You calmed him down then, but that gave you the idea, didn't it? You could use Virgil, a human engineering project, to get rid of DeAngelo."

David raised his chin, his eyelids lowering disdainfully.

"You hired Virgil as a handyman, and then you inflamed him. Ami wasn't DeAngelo's customer. She was your client. Your cards have a *D* in the upper right corner. DeAngelo's have a *DA*. You took DeAngelo's client file, so no one would discover she wasn't his client, but Gerta figured it out, stole the cards from your file, and hid them—not as blackmail but as insurance."

Virgil scratched his forehead, frowning.

David waved his hand at me. "She's making this up to upset you, Virgil. Have you set the timer?"

"Four minutes to go."

I wanted to work on Virgil. "Virgil, you might get off by pleading temporary insanity over Ami's death. Or even accidental death. But if you kill all of us, you'll go down for the count."

He ignored me. "We gotta get going, David."

All the first-floor windows had bars on them, but the second-and third-floor ones didn't. If they stuck us upstairs, at least we could jump from a window, or crawl out on the porch roof and drop to the ground.

Virgil flexed his hands. "Let's put them in the basement, David."

A sudden swirl of cold air came from the basement door. Incredibly, I saw Jason sneaking up the basement stairs. I thought I would faint. I could barely draw a breath. It was bad enough Meredith and I were in this mess, but to add Jason to it was intolerable.

I raised my hand in a halt sign to keep him from showing himself and shouted to distract Virgil and David, "You've got a firebomb in here, don't you, Virgil? It's going to detonate and set the place on fire. And you've doused the salon so it'll flame fast. So we'll all be killed, right? So do one last nice thing, Virgil. Anything, anything, but not the basement. Oh, my God, not the basement."

"Let's put them in the basement, David."

David squinted at me. "Hold up, there, partner."

Virgil eased over to the basement door, staring intently at me. "Three minutes, David," he said, and glanced into the black well of the basement. He flipped on the light switch. "I think there's somebody down there, David."

David looked at him, seemed to come to a decision, and moved to the door. "Take a quick look, Virg. I'll watch these two."

"I don't think so. I'll get blown up down there."

"Go quick. There's time."

"I dunno." He took a step down, peering into the basement recesses.

David's arm flicked out, shoving Virgil. He stumbled, then pitched headfirst down the stairs. David slammed the door and threw the brass bolt, locking it.

Before he finished, I grabbed Meredith and we pelted through David's salon room to the stairs, up the stairs to the front of the house and the window that overlooked the porch roof. I could hear David's steps on the stairs. I figured we had a minute at best.

I kicked the window out, shoved Meredith onto the roof, and shouted, "Jump and get help." Then I turned and ran down the hall.

David was at the top of the front stairs, waiting for me. He grabbed my arm, pulling me toward the stairs. "I can't let you go," he said, jerking me to the railing.

I grabbed the wooden spindles of the banister with my free hand, kicked out at him, and heard wood splinter. He fell slowly, twisting.

I scrambled back to my feet, grabbed a splintered spindle, and raced down the back stairs to the basement door.

The bolt slid open easily. The light was on, but very dim. I looked for Virgil, didn't see him, and started down the stairs. Halfway down I saw Virgil through the open stairs, lurking, a shovel held like a baseball bat at the ready.

"Stella, get out of here." Jason's voice came from the other side of the cellar by the furnace.

I crept down the stairs, spindle at my side. Virgil was stalking Jason. I wondered why he didn't draw his gun. On the left were the washtubs, over them a box of detergent. Not much, but it might help.

I reached the bottom of the stairs.

Virgil was ahead of me, moving stealthily toward the back side of the furnace, shovel ready.

"Jason, he's coming to the rear—"

Virgil turned, started toward me. I darted to the laundry tubs and grabbed the detergent.

Virgil came closer, trying to get close enough to hit me with the shovel. I made my tae kwon do shout and flung soap at him. It didn't work. He stepped back, and the soap fell to the floor harmlessly.

But behind him across the room, Jason stepped out from behind the furnace, pointed to the wall door, then darted to it and dove in. Then he threw something, angling it to hit the furnace and draw Virgil's attention.

It worked. Virgil turned back to the furnace where he thought Jason was.

I dashed to the wall door and crawled inside, pulling the door shut and wedging the spindle in to lock it in place.

It was ghastly.

The crawl space was home to seven thousand spiders and I don't know how many other creatures. It stank, it was musty, and there was a large plastic roll on one side.

"Over here, away from the door, behind the wall," Jason said, and pulled me close to him. "Cover your head. If we're lucky—"

The explosion blew the door past us, deafened me, and rocked the house on its foundation. The next thing I remembered was the smell of smoke.

# TWENTY-FIVE

THE CRAWL SPACE was under the front porch.

As soon as we could, we combat-crawled to the opening into the basement to survey the damage. Most of the salon had blown up, then collapsed back into the basement.

I started to crawl out into the room, but Jason held me back.

"Stella, there isn't a way in hell you can get through that mess, and even if you do, where are you going to go?"

"We can't stay here, we'll suffocate from smoke and poison gases."

The sound of fire crackling was growing louder. A faint glow from above us sent light into the crawl space. I could see the outline of his face, smudged with dirt. He shook his head. "I'm still sort of deaf from the explosion," he said, shouting. A little current of air caught his hair.

I pointed to the far end of the crawl space. "Jason, there's a draft. That means there's a hole somewhere." I crawled to the far end, feeling overhead. It was about three feet high, with wooden beam construction overhead.

"Stella, if there's fresh air here, the fire is going to follow it."

"Well, if there's fresh air, we may be able to punch a hole in it before the fire gets here."

"We have to block this opening somehow." The flickering of the flames threw a dim glow into the crawl space. We both saw the plastic roll at the same time.

"Help me drag this over," I said, tugging at the end of it. It was deadweight, almost impossible to move. Finally Jason rolled it to the door, then shoved dirt up around it. It still left four inches of space where flames and poison gases could come through.

I was exhausted, panting. "What's in this thing, anyway? Maybe...we can unwrap it—"

"No!" Jason shouted. "Just heap up a little more earth. Don't unwrap it! We don't have time," he added, lamely.

"Let's put the door back, then."

It was wedged against the back wall and the overhead beams. It took both of us pulling to free it.

Jason put a hand on me. "A battering ram—" He rammed it up overhead. No result. The wood was new and held fast.

"Try over here," I said, and pulled it over two feet. We battered there several times, no luck. Finally, we tried another two feet over. My hands were bleeding.

"Keep going!" Jason shouted. "It gave a little."

My head swam, breath was coming hard. "The gas...and the heat..." I could feel the warmth on my back.

"Again!" Jason shouted. I gave it one more heave. The wood splintered. He wedged the door up, pried, and broke through a blessed eight-by-fourteen-inch space. I gulped in fresh air, my head clearing almost immediately.

"I'm going to put the door back now. You stay here." He crawled away, taking the door with him. I heard the plastic rustle as he moved it aside.

I lay on my back and kicked at the wood, too tired to do much good. By turning my head to the side, I could see him put the door back in place. The heat abated as soon as it was up. The light also was gone, but I was stronger from the fresh air.

"What was in the plastic?"

"Nobody—kick!"

My eyes filled with tears. I knew what he didn't want to tell me. Ami was in there. A little more time and she'd have been under the cement floor. I kicked with all the rage I had for the loss of her. Another board came loose. It wasn't much, but enough to squeeze through. Jason started to go through. I clutched him. "Wait—David could be there."

"Nah," he said, but he peeled off his jacket, balled it up,

and stuck it on the end of a scrap of wood, then poked it up through the opening.

It disappeared. Sliced clean away.

Sirens sounded in the distance.

Jason poked another stick up through the hole. It was grabbed too. He jerked it back, pulling David after. His face, glazed and white, came into view.

"I've got a gun. You either come out now, or I start shooting down through the wood. You have to the count of three. One... Two..."

I stood up. "I'm coming out."

"NO!" Jason grabbed me, shoved me down, and stood slowly. "David, it's Jason. I'm coming out. Don't shoot." He held me down and whispered. "If he shoots me, duck and hide in the corner."

"Remember, David," I shouted. "There's two of us, and we're too heavy to carry as deadweight."

Jason stood up, half in and half out of the hole. "Stella, come up slowly, he won't shoot."

I didn't think rising slowly would guarantee a thing, but the gases were coming through the door again. I was dizzy and sick. If I stayed there, I'd die for sure. Jason's legs disappeared upward. I rose after him, my legs shaking and weak. The air helped, although I was very dizzy. Jason grabbed me by the waist, steadying me. David stepped back, motioning with the gun.

Jason helped me out of the hole and kept his arms around me as we walked ahead of David. We were halfway down the block when the first fire truck rounded the corner.

David pressed the gun to my back. "Keep walking. Regular. Don't do a thing to attract attention. We're going down to the end of the block."

The second fire truck wheeled up to the salon. They had no time to pursue us.

"You don't think you're actually going to be able to get away with this, do you, David?"

"Shut up. Keep walking."

Ahead of us at the end of the block stood a white van. One of the at least seventeen thousand in Denver, but this one had a broken headlight and a dented fender. I was willing to bet there was a streak of paint from my Taurus along the side. "Is that your van, David, or Virgil's?" I asked.

"Virgil's. Stop at the back of it." He marched us up to the back door, then with his back to the street, he reached up to the door handle. "I'm going to open it; I want you to get in and sit quiet." He reached up, opened the door, and took a step toward me.

A police car rolled by, followed by the fire chief in his car. David had the gun pointed straight at me, sheltered from their view. I didn't dare to wave or yell.

Out of the corner of my eye, I caught sight of a movement. A fleshy, blood-raw hand and arm, blackened in patches, whipped out, grabbed David's hair, and pulled him backward half into the van.

Jason and I dove behind the hedge.

David's gun dropped to the pavement, and there was a terrible scream. Then the rest of David was hauled inside the van. The grisly hand reached out and slammed the door shut. I was absolutely frozen in my tracks.

The van engine turned over.

We jumped out, raced to the curb, and grabbed for the gun. Jason got it and shot out the tires on the near side of the van before it had gone twenty feet. It bumped to a stop.

Stokowski rolled out of the squad car, stared at the two of us, then drew his gun and ran to the door of the van. He yanked it open, then stood back in the two-handed official stance. Virgil emerged, arms high. He stood for a long moment, glaring at me, then turned and walked with Stokowski to an ambulance.

The shakes came over me, and Jason tried to pry me away, but I had to watch. I couldn't feel safe until they cuffed Virgil to the gurney and left for Denver General.

Jason left me for a few minutes to speak to the officers, then returned and led me to his car. Before we could get in, Meredith rushed up. She had called the police and then hidden herself so that she wouldn't have to deal with them. We all squeezed into the Miata and left.

WE WERE SITTING in Zelda's apartment, having finished her sandwiches. Fluffy was dingy brown, clinging to the side of his travel cage. Meredith was propped in a chair, a cold pack on her swollen ankle. Zelda was sipping a highball, and I was next to Jason on the couch, leaning back and wondering if we were truly clear of it all yet. There were so many unanswered questions—like whether I still had a career as a columnist for the lovelorn. The floor lamp at Jason's shoulder shone on his hair, highlighting the blond, making the roots look dark. Why was he having his hair dyed, and why didn't he want to tell me? And what was with the half-name business? I didn't quite have the strength to challenge Jason yet. He had just saved my life.

Zelda's door buzzer sounded. She returned with Mr. and Mrs. Gerster and Lee Stokowski in tow. Lee had his arm around her waist. She was beaming.

Zelda smiled shyly. Speaking of strangeness, Zelda being shy was strange. "I had to let Mr. and Mrs. G know about this, and they wanted to see you. And of course, Lee was coming to see me. You all just happened to be here."

Stokowski got a beer and settled on a straight-backed chair. Zelda stood next to him, her hand on his shoulder. Her heartbreak appeared to be in abeyance—for now, I guessed.

"Well," said Mrs. Gerster. "I was left out of everything, of course. And I for one want to know, how did you, Jason, figure out to get to the salon?"

"Actually, I didn't know Stella was there. I, uh, thought I might get a story before she did. After Stella called Lee trying to find Meredith, and told him Lizette had been murdered, Lee called at my place, thinking Stella might be there. I had no idea where Stella was, but I remembered Lizette bragging about her computer skills when I was there—for a haircut—and I started thinking that Stella might know that, too, and so I went by the salon on a hunch. I saw a white van nearby, and I saw David go inside and never turn on the lights. So I thought he was in trouble. Then I noticed the open coal chute, and that's it.''

I looked at him, and his gaze dropped to his hands. ''Jason, why were you having your hair lightened?''

He was acutely uncomfortable. ''Would you believe me if I told you I just wanted to look different? I wanted to look different.'' He sighed. ''I think your real question is, who is Bipsie? Isn't that why you told Cleota to tell me the nightie looked better on you?''

''For one.''

''Bipsie is a dear friend who helped me out once, nothing more. She's not the woman I'm in love with.''

Not the most convincing explanation, but we could fix that later.

The tension in the room was heavy, thick. Mr. Gerster couldn't stand it any longer. ''Well, Stella, I think you have to agree that I was right. Big Dick wasn't safe.''

Mrs. Gerster looked at him with annoyance. ''Don't gloat, Henry. It's not becoming. Her column is the most popular item your paper runs, and if you're as smart today as you were yesterday, you'll put it right back in where it belongs.'' She turned to me. ''Now, Stella, you let Jason off the hook. There's been enough trouble. Meredith needs attention now.''

She was right.

The next day Jason and I took Fluffy to Colorado Seed and Pet. They were very understanding and helpful.

It was hard—actually, I cried—but I put Fluffy in the anole cage and let him do his little push-ups, head bobs, and jaw flaps until he found the lizard love of his life.

Jason pulled me into his arms. They were strong and warm

and gentle. "Stella, think of it this way: you aren't losing Fluffy, you're getting a lizard-in-law."

"Jason, why did you change your name and your appearance? What are you hiding from?"

"I really do want to look different. I changed my name because I've been disowned, and I'm not hiding from anything, or anyone."

"Jason, why did you really come to the salon last night?"

He sighed. "The truth? I was crazy to find you. I was afraid you'd be killed. Stella, you just don't seem to have any"—he paused, thinking—"any...fear."

"Jason?"

"Yeah?"

"Use of the word 'fear' instead of 'sense' probably saved our relationship."

"I'm learning." He kissed me. "And do you know why I'm learning?"

"Why?"

"Because I love you."

If you enjoyed the humor and mystery
of this story by

# CHRISTINE T. JORGENSEN

Don't miss the opportunity to receive this previous
title starring your favorite astrologer/amateur sleuth,
STELLA THE STARGAZER.

#26231-0   A LOVE TO DIE FOR           $4.99 U.S.☐ $5.99 CAN.☐

**(limited quantities available)**

"Stella's quirky humor, human frailties, and sudden
trances will endear her to many." —*Library Journal*

| | | |
|---|---|---|
| **TOTAL AMOUNT** | $ | |
| **POSTAGE & HANDLING** | $ | |
| ($1.00 for one book, 50¢ for each additional) | | |
| **APPLICABLE TAXES*** | $ | ___ |
| **TOTAL PAYABLE** | $ | ___ |
| (check or money order—please do not send cash) | | |

To order, complete this form and send it, along with a check or money order for
the total above, payable to Worldwide Mystery, to: **In the U.S.:** 3010 Walden
Avenue, P.O. Box 9077, Buffalo, NY 14269-9077; **In Canada:** P.O. Box 636,
Fort Erie, Ontario, L2A 5X3.

Name: _____

Address: _____ City: _____

State/Prov.: _____ Zip/Postal Code: _____

*New York residents remit applicable sales taxes.
Canadian residents remit applicable GST and provincial taxes.

 **WORLDWIDE LIBRARY** ®

WCJBL1

## Worldwide Mystery™
## is on the case...

We've taken the guesswork out of finding the
very best in mystery entertainment—and
every month there are three* new titles sure to
please!

From spine-tingling suspense to unabashed
hilarity, every Worldwide Mystery™ novel
is a guaranteed page-turner! Criminals
always have something to hide—but the
enjoyment you'll get from reading your next
Worldwide Mystery™ is no secret.

### Worldwide Mystery™—
### stories worth investigating.

\* Not all titles are for sale in Canada.

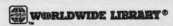

WWMGEN

When little Adam Kingsley was taken from his nursery in the Kingsley mansion, the Memphis family used all their power and prestige to punish the kidnapper. They believed the crime was solved and the villain condemned...though the boy was never returned. But now, new evidence comes to light that may reveal the truth about...

# The Kingsley Baby

Amanda Stevens is at her best for this powerful trilogy of a sensational crime and the three couples whose love lights the way to the truth. Don't miss:

## #453 THE HERO'S SON (February)

## #458 THE BROTHER'S WIFE (March)

## #462 THE LONG-LOST HEIR (April)

**What *really* happened that night in the Kingsley nursery?**

The three McCullar brothers once stood strong against the lawlessness on their ranches. Then the events of one fateful night shattered their bond and sent them far from home. But their hearts remained with the ranch—and the women—they left behind. And now all three are coming

**HOME TO TEXAS**

**Gayle Wilson** has written a romantic, emotional and suspenseful new trilogy and created characters who will touch your heart. Don't miss any of the cowboy McCullar brothers in:

**#461 RANSOM MY HEART**
April

**#466 WHISPER MY LOVE**
May

**#469 REMEMBER MY TOUCH**
June

These are three cowboys' stories you won't want to miss!

Detective Jackie Kaminsky is back—and this time *First Impressions* aren't adding up...

# Second Thoughts

Jackie Kaminsky had seen enough break and enters to know that intruders usually took something. This one left a calling card and a threat to return. The next visit was from a killer. Jackie had a list of suspects, but as they became victims, too, she found herself thinking twice about *everything* she thought she knew—professionally and personally....

**"Detective Jackie Kaminsky leads a cast of finely drawn characters."**
**—*Publishers Weekly***

# MARGOT DALTON

Available in March 1998 wherever books are sold.

**The Brightest Stars in Fiction.™**